Praise for the Base Branch Series

"Megan Mitcham's books are well-paced, well-plotted suspense novels edged with stunning sensual intensity. Her lovers are cold and deadly--except when they are skin-to-skin. I can't wait for the next book in the series!"

- **DELILAH DEVLIN**
New York Times and USA Today bestselling author

"Nail-biter all the way to the end."

- **Michelle**, MsRomanticReads
Adult Romance & Erotic Book Reviews

"This is a fresh and exciting story with lots of great characters."

- **5 Star Amazon Review**, Enemy Mine

"Megan now joins my elite team of must read authors. I fell in love with her work in *Enemy Mine*, and it just gets better the more I read."

- **TNT Reviews**

BOOKS BY MEGAN MITCHAM

BASE BRANCH NOVELS
ENEMY MINE
JUSTICE MINE
STRANGER MINE
WARRIOR MINE
DANGER MINE
PRISONER MINE
SURVIVOR MINE - 2017

BASE BRANCH SUB-SERIES
VERSIONS - updated 2016
VIRTUES - 2016
VARIATIONS - 2016

BUREAU NOVELS
FOR ALL TO SEE
PAINTED WALLS
FORD'S BOOK - 2016

ANTHOLOGIES
ANTICIPATION
CONQUESTS
ROGUES
SEX OBJECTS - 2016
COWBOY HEAT
HIGH OCTANE HEROES
WILD AT HEART VOLUME II
benefiting Turpentine Creek Wildlife Refuge

Justice Mine

Base Branch Novel #2

Megan Mitcham

Copyright Warning

Published By MM Publishing LLC
Edited by Lacey Thacker
Cover Design by Deranged Doctor Design

Justice Mine
All Rights Are Reserved. Copyright 2014 by Megan Mitcham
First electronic publication: October 2014
First print publication: October 2014

Digital ISBN: 978-1-941899-02-1

Print ISBN: 978-1-941899-03-8

To my JM for believing in me and loving me better than fiction.

Chapter One

After two years of servitude under Devereaux Kendrick, the most notorious arms dealer on the African continent, Law thought he might just go crazy from the liberation. Though the bonds were off, the tightness in his chest cinched, strangling like never before. The fact that he had no fucking clue *why* irritated him more than the itch that had settled over his skin a month ago. Law shoved his chest into the long bag, hugging it in the knot of his arms before pounding his knee into the belly of his imaginary opponent. He released it from his deadly embrace and plowed a forearm against its slick leather face, roaring as he did so.

The chain rattled above Law's head. Its shrill protests screamed in rhythmic jerks timed to the impact of his raw fists. With each punch, the leather smacked under his knuckles. The cacophony of sounds accompanied by the *whoosh* of his breaths filled the murky garage, echoing back the rage he could not escape. No matter how hard he hit. No matter how much he drank. No matter how he fancied himself free from his corrupting emotions.

He honed in on the logo which shone vibrantly under the puny workbench bulb in contrast to the black bag and his equally tenebrous mood. The white form mocked with its purity.

Sweat puddled and splashed across the concrete floor as he beat the shit out of what looked to be a winged V or phoenix split in two. His muscles bunched then protracted in rapid succession, the tempo of his hits rising with his ire.

How much longer can you lie to yourself, fuckwad?

As long as it takes to beat back the beast.

Law knew shit was getting bad when he answered himself. In further denial, he looped one arm around the heavy bag. The leather slid in his sweat-soaked grasp, rasping his bare chest and athletic shorts. His fisted hand battered into the logo time and again. Under his punishing weight and ceaseless whaling his abused skin gave way. Stamps of red marred the offending trademark as blood seeped from the top of his fist.

A small measure of satisfaction curved his lips. It lasted all of a second before the overhead lights burst to life in an open *screw you* from the one thing he could admit chapped his arse in two distinct and vastly different ways. The space expanded from Law's dimly lit man-cave, which housed his tools and home gym. Massive fluorescents arced one to another on the ceiling, illuminating each lane of the four-lane shop in a brilliant glow. Law rejected the interruption, shoving the bag away and hammering it with another hail of his hands.

"Fucking pummel me, why don't you? Maybe then we can move on. You've been avoiding me like I've got the clap, and brooding like a lion with a hyena up his arse. Enough already."

Law turned on his best friend. The bastard ate the space of the doorway leading to the kitchen as if it were a snack. Baine's wide shoulders brushed one side of the frame and gave the other only an inch of breathing room. His chin dropped and royal blue eyes gleamed in open challenge. Only his defiance kept his muss of unruly dark hair from brushing the architecture.

"I damn well should knock you to size," Law threw back. His fists clenched and the resentment bubbled to the forefront of his mired brain.

Never one to back down from anything since Law had known him, Baine strode down the steps. He passed his sleek onyx Audi and Law's like-colored Hog, closing the gap between them in short order with his hulking frame and efficient movements. The man he'd pulled from the brink all those years ago, the man who'd returned the favor, though he'd never known it, crowded the air Law panted from his hours on the heavy bag.

Baine blocked some of the glaring light as he burst Law's personal-space bubble, taking the edge of pain from Law's beer-soaked eyeballs.

"Let's have it," Baine said. "All you've got."

Law looked up to the bloke he loved like a brother. Literally, looked up an inch or two, watching his wide jaw flex under the stubble-covered skin. He wore faded jeans and a T-shirt from Sullivan's, a local pub, giving off a laid back appearance. But no one would be fooled into believing Baine McCord was mellow.

Both men were highly trained operatives of the United Nations' Special Operations Force, known to very few as the Base Branch. The agency had bases across the globe with the singular goal of maintaining or fostering peace, though only the highest tier of government and Branch officials knew the intricacies of the network. Indeed, Sloan Harris, a US Base Branch agent and the love of Baine's life, had only recently learned of their kindred employer.

In order to keep peace sometimes death was the great equalizer. It balanced power like nothing else could. The two men maintained the teetering scale with expert potency. In a fair fight either could come away victorious or flat on his duff. But this fight would be anything but clean. At the moment Law had violence-spiked veins and a lifetime of training under his father's expert guidance.

Love and respect be damned. Law would lay Baine flat on his backside for the way he'd blurred the line of good and evil in order to track down every last snake in Devereaux Kendrick's worldwide operation. Not that he wasn't for comeuppance, but the wildness he'd seen in his friend's eyes had unsettled them both. Though Baine seemed to have moved past it since Sloan showed up two weeks ago, Law couldn't downshift that fast. Sod it, he couldn't shift at all. He lived by a strict code. Right. Wrong. Middle ground didn't exist.

"You came too close to the edge, McCord, and I'm going to assure you stay topside, even if I have to kick the shit out of you to do it."

This close, Law could see the worry lines that creased Baine's face only a month ago had faded. But he couldn't understand why. Baine still had something precious that could be taken away in the blink of an eye. Fuck, Law's worry lines would still be there, and Baine's should too.

"Are you two going to quit staring longingly into each other's eyes and get on with it already? Easton and I have money riding on this. I'm ready to collect." Lounging against the doorjamb Sloan prodded them, her leanly muscled caramel arms crossed over her ample chest.

Behind her, Easton Wells, Baine's father figure and house man, scoffed. "Baine's got him on size, but I've never seen anyone take Law. My bet stands. Now, hop to. I need to see the two love birds off before I can go collect my darling Ruth and make it to the airport to retrieve Magdalena."

Sloan, the trained killer, melted at his words. "Aww. I can't wait to meet them both."

The absurdness of their humor siphoned both men's testosterone to a manageable level. Baine's gaze trained dead center on the sultry smile Sloan presented him. The love in each of their gazes kicked Law square in the balls. He looked past them quickly, taking in the old man's shock of white hair before the urge to fall to the ground in the fetal position and gasp for air grew too strong. Easton winked, knowing, seeing way too much for an old English fart. And again, Law swung his gaze away.

The floor suddenly became the only safe place to look. After a moment of scrutinizing a tiny rock on the pristine—aside from his sweat pools—slag floor, Baine clasped his shoulder in a firm grip. The gesture held no fight. Baine's deep blue eyes told him as much. They'd gone mushy, draining of all animosity, replenished with pure adoration for the amber-eyed goddess on the steps. The fight fled Law. His shoulders sagged in defeat, heedless that a battle had neither been fought nor lost.

"Hate to disappoint a captive crowd." Baine's laugh laced his deep baritone. Then the bastard's arm coiled around Law's neck and he pulled him tight into his chest. Law anticipated the next move and didn't fight back. He'd been a total dick over the last few weeks. Baine had looked like death twenty days out of the grave, moping around the estate his grandfather had left him. Law had only added to the bloke's misery, avoiding him or picking a fight in near equal measure.

In all his years he'd never acted so immaturely, except when he was an actual adolescent. Then he'd acted like a total douche as did the entire male population pre- and a few years post puberty. Still, he didn't usually avoid confrontation. He should've just talked to Baine.

His friend had been in the pits of hell. Sloan had been near fatally injured at the hands of Baine's father. Add to that the request she'd saddled him with—complete their mission, take down everyone linked to his father, Devereaux Kendrick's vast web of terrorism—and it was a damn wonder the guy hadn't snapped all together.

Baine had stomped all over the line that governed Law's existence. He'd tortured evil men to obtain the information he'd needed to complete the task. Uncomfortable though he'd been with the scenario, Law stood by his friend's side because the good outweighed the bad. But when Baine had been unable to break one cartel leader through hours of inventive torment, he'd requested the man's young daughter. Law couldn't believe his friend would have hurt the girl, and there was no way in fuck he'd have let that happen anyway. But the simple truth that Baine was desperate, willing to push the boundaries even further to get what he'd wanted, even if it'd been a noble cause, was more than Law could bear.

Fat knuckles serrated his close shaven head. The childish act actually unleashed the steel band of aggravation from his chest. He almost laughed. Only they could go from bar-room brawl to noogie without someone ending up in the hospital. Baine released him and Law stuck a friendly jab in the man's ribs. As apologies and cease-fires went it wasn't much, but it was enough for now.

"Well damn," Easton said, shaking his head. "Next time perhaps. Now, off you go. Shoo. Shoo." He shoved Sloan through the door into the garage with one large suitcase he carried. With the other bag and hand he gestured toward the RS 7.

Sloan chuckled as she quick-footed it toward he and Baine. "Oooh, sounds like somebody's getting lucky tonight."

Baine's nose wrinkled like he smelled something foul, and Law's head shook away the images conjured by such a statement. Disgusting.

The old man's laugh filled the hollow garage. "I'm lucky every minute of every day. I have a magnificent daughter and now I have Ruth. Who I'm off to see. You two be careful. Very careful."

"I'll take good care of him," Sloan said.

Baine pulled her against his side. "I'll take care of her. This time." The added statement garnered him another punch to the gut, only this time from Sloan. "Ow," he winced. "You hit harder than Law."

"I don't doubt it," Law said. The first hint of a chuckle in far too long shook his shoulders. The simple emotion lightened him, cooled the heat that boiled in his gut.

Before Easton hurried through the door Baine called out. "Tell Mags hello for me. I hate I won't get to see her before we leave. With me being gone and her too, it's been forever."

Easton bowed, a smile of parental pride curving his lips. Then he hurried from the door.

Baine's lips brushed the top of Sloan's head. "Wait for me in the car? I'll be right there."

"Sure," Sloan replied. She squeezed Baine's middle before releasing him and stepping toward Law. Her lips pursed. She grabbed his brutalized hand, studying the bloody and skinned tops.

"Enough." The command should have ruffled him, but care radiated from her gorgeously sculpted face and soulful eyes.

He nodded his concession. Sloan tugged his wrist and he bent willingly, suddenly realizing why Baine would do anything for her, give her anything, smudge the black and white to grey. She stretched on tiptoes, brushed her hand across his cheek then planted a chaste kiss on the dried spot.

An ache he thought long-banished tore at his heart. *Clara.* He rubbed at the pain as Sloan turned away and walked to the car. "You two be damn careful, McCord." Law turned toward Baine. "You sure you don't need me to go?"

"I'm sure." A hint of a smile curved Baine's lips; the expression looked foreign on his friend, but good at the same time. "Sloan and I are going to finish this together. Cezar Vilaro. Tracy Walters. Then it's over. Finally over. And I'm sorry I put you in that position, Law."

He didn't have to elaborate. They both knew he referred to the torture. To that small girl he'd used to get information from Miguel Castillos.

Law nodded again. He couldn't forgive Baine, yet. But he no longer fancied parting on bad terms.

Baine's smile fell, his expression growing serious. "Think about what I asked. When Sloan and I get back we're getting married and I want you beside me. You're my family. It would mean a lot." The guy's hands shoved into his pockets. "I know you're in a knot about Mexico, but I never would have hurt Rosanna Castillos."

If the shit fermenting in Law's head only concerned Mexico, he'd be golden. But there was more. "I'll think about it."

"That's all I ask."

Law took the big hand offered him in a firm shake before his friend turned to leave. Moments later he stood alone with his sweat and despair.

Chapter Two

Magdalena shoved a handful of hair out of her face with a huff and spread her handbag open wide. The teal green material yawned, like she longed to, revealing a heap of random crap. She tossed the three packs of plane peanuts and one of pretzels onto the library floor next to her bag, adding to the pile of shit already polluting the granite. Next went the teeny tiny models on the covers of the Elle and Vogue she'd picked up at the confectionary in the Nairobi International Airport. She dropped them unceremoniously on the heap of junk food and cigarettes.

Why the hell'd you even buy that rubbish? Certainly not for a boost of self-esteem.

At least the pile represented three addictions she'd outgrown over the last year. Hell, she deserved the scratchy irritation in the back of her throat. She'd ripped into the cancer sticks with wild abandon while running out of Heathrow, hoping to get one dear sweet drag before her father and Ruth found her in the crush of bodies surrounding the transport hub. She swallowed against the hurt she'd incurred with her haste. Turned out she choked and hacked on the poisoned air like a primary schooler stealing a puff from one of their parents' ciggies.

With a growl, Mags thrust her hand into the thick locks at her forehead and peered into the abyss. The remaining clutter wasn't enough to hide the USB drive she so desperately sought. Still, she abandoned her hair, pulled the straps wide, and sifted through the change, old receipts, and make-up. She scrubbed a hand over her face in irritation and was glad she'd forgone the artful gobs of cosmetics, even though she'd returned to civilization. Yet another thing she'd become accustomed to sacrificing.

Her hair caught one of her lashes and Magdalena cussed, wrapping the ornery hair around her hands and securing it with a tie, something she'd grown intimately acquainted with in the heat of DRC. In aggravation, she grabbed the bag once more and shook its contents, hoping against hope the device would magically appear.

"Blast it to Scotland and back," she complained.

The outburst garnered her two exaggerated *shush*'s from across the expansive Law Library at Cardiff University and had the coeds at the other end of the short table talking behind their hands. One with, "Can you believe the nerve?" The other responded with a haughty shake of her prim blonde hair. "I mean, really. She is so crass."

Magdalena scooped her heap off the floor and tossed it into her carryall with more force than necessary and straightened. She glared at the two, who had nothing more pressing than Lit 101 spread out before them, and stood. A smile curved her lips when the wooden chair screeched as she shoved it with her sandal, making room for her escape. Their hands went up again.

"Christ, just because you put your hands in front of your face doesn't make you any quieter than me."

Before she got thrown out on her bum, Mags turned and headed for the door. Exhaustion and anger took turns rolling through her on the six-block walk back to her apartment. When she grabbed the information she needed at the flat she could change from her white shorts and blue tank, so, when she went back to the sodded house for dusty old books and co-ed bitches, no one would recognize her.

The cool glass of The Corrier's front door soothed the heat from her arm as she sagged against it while digging for her pass card and keys. *Home.* Jet lag, which had worked on her all day, receded to the background for a moment. Joy burst like tiny fireworks through her chest as she breathed deep the scent of exhaust, humid fog, and sausage from the restaurant around the corner. All she fancied was to curl on the sofa, catch up with Willow, watch a movie, drink some wine, sleep. Any order would do.

Her brow knit as she fished the magnetic card out and swiped it across the reader. Unease dampened her excitement of being home, much as it had when she'd rushed through her door this morning. She'd expected wide arms and girly squeals of delight from her longtime friend. What she'd gotten was a meek smile from a Willow look-alike, mild interest, and a request for Mags to vacate the flat for the evening. Her first evening back.

Magdalena wasn't conceited by any stretch, but had it been so wrong of her to expect a warm welcome from the roommate she'd had since freshman year? *Shit, it's not like I'm a sophomore.*

She snorted. They didn't have a neat term for what she was. *Lifer, maybe? No, that's a prison term. Seventh-year senior, maybe.* Who the hell cared? This damn dissertation was the final hurdle to get her life rolling. After so much time wondering what she was going to do with herself, Mags knew. She finally knew.

She breathed a sigh of relief at the accomplishment then groaned when she rounded the last banister and came face to face with her front door. The thing may as well have an unwelcome sign tacked to it for all the warmth its current tenant gave. Willow's cold reception hadn't been the only thing off with her flatmate. Gaunt features hollowed the beauty's usual voluptuous curves. Something the two had in common from the start. In the land of stick figure models they were the buxom babes, sticking out in a crowd, well, like their asses did.

Sure, nothing was wrong with Willow shedding a pound or two. Lord knows Africa had melted a few off Magdalena. But the deep, dark circles under Will's eyes looked like bad horror film make-up. More than anything though, Mags didn't like the way her friend had hugged herself so tightly around the middle, like she'd shatter if she didn't hold the running crack together.

With deliberate care not to disturb the artists' guild meeting, for fear of further alienating Willow, Mags turned the key in the lock and eased the door open without a sound. She slipped inside and closed the door behind her with the same consciousness. Expecting heated debates of Pissarro over Gauguin, when silence greeted her Mags pursed her lips, irritated at having to be so quiet as to not draw attention. She pressed to the side of the corridor, slipped off her sandals then tiptoed toward her bedroom.

She tried not to look into the living room, but it was an exercise in futility for a nosey gal like herself. Surprise double-arched her forehead. Not a single person crowded the small living space. The teal sofa sat vacant. No tushes warmed the rug, a grey vomit of geometric shapes. Only Willow's small sketchpad lay on the coffee table.

Before Magdalena could take a step into the common room, a throaty moan reverberated through the otherwise still apartment. A wave of heat rushed over her body from the tips of her pink toenails to the top of her messy bun. She exhaled hard against the sensations brought to life by that tiny noise and tried to shake the tension coiling in her most intimate zones. *For the love.*

It had been a long time since she'd thought about sex and even longer since she'd had it. *A damn shame.* But getting aroused from Willow's moan made her skin feel a little dirty and the rest of her feel a whole lot horny. She eyed her tits and the fabric covering her erect nipples. *Sorry gals, but now is not the time.*

Willow could have said, "Hey, my boyfriend's coming over and I need to get laid. Could you give us a few hours alone?" Sure, she'd have been jealous her friend had chosen to get laid over welcoming her home, but she'd have understood. Willow had been way overdue for a good lay when Mags left.

Hell, maybe he's married, or her professor. Maybe he's a she. Magdalena smiled. The possibilities were endless, and she didn't have time or brain power for all of them right now. She'd talk to Will tomorrow.

With a shake of her head, Magdalena crept down the hallway, ignoring the sliver of light piercing the darkness from Willow's bedroom, and ducked through the first doorway. Grateful, for once, a streetlight with the same wattage as the sun hung just outside her window, she avoided the two large suitcases she'd dumped in the middle of the wood floor only hours ago and closed in on the third smaller one on her desk chair.

Like it had every other time before, the painting above her tiny lilac desk stole her breath. Strokes of vibrant green livened the background while bold swaths of violet, curls of yellow and brown, and wisps of white formed the most intricate Bee Orchid she'd ever seen. Her hand rubbed away the ache its sight composed in her heart. *Better to have loved and lost. Than to never have loved at all.* The pain eased with those words because they were true. She and her dad had taken them up as their motto the day her mother died.

Willow whimpered and Magdalena automatically turned her head toward the sound. Her twin bed and wall collage of snapshots filled the space between her and the wall from which the passion seeped. *Well piss. Where the hell am I going to move my bed? Can't leave it on the fuck wall.* It just wouldn't do to get shaken out of bed before her alarm went off every morning. She stepped toward the pictures for a quick look at the wall-o-men she'd missed out on while getting her life together. They inhabited a majority of the photos, each a delightful memory of a shagging good time. And if she stayed in this sexed-up place a minute more she'd be tempted to give one or two of them a ring. Old habits and all.

Mags turned away from her past, figuratively and literally. She crouched and reached for the zipper to collect her USB drive. A slap split the air. The unmistakable crack of forceful skin on skin contact crackled her instincts to life. Willow cried out. The shriek held no hint of throaty lust, only stunned pain. Magdalena's guts origamied and a crane threatened to spew from her throat. Her hand fell from the bag and she leaned toward the door, straining to hear more and at the same time hoping like hell she didn't.

No wonder Will hadn't told her why she needed the flat to herself. Her pitiful appearance made sense now. Willow dated some sack of crap who beat not only her self-esteem, but her body too.

Willow May Wren, what the bloody hell have you gotten yourself into?

Magdalena shot to her feet ready to knock this ass-hat for a spin, but stopped as her mind steamed ahead, taking another corner. She was all boobs and bluster. Sure Baine had shown her a few things over the years, things a lawyer shouldn't be able to do. Still, she was only a pie piece past five feet and a pie past one-hundred pounds. How exactly was she going to help?

And leave it to Magdalena's brain to loop again. But...the lady next to her on the plane had a novel with a silver key chain on the front. It had stirred a memory on the forever-long flight. Magdalena placed the book by a conversation she and Willow had at the beginning of her time in Africa. Will had said that bondage novels were all the rage in America and making a splash back home.

Maybe she's into BSDM. No, what the hell was it. Bondage. Dominance. Submission? Sado-something? BDSM. Maybe that's why she wanted me out of the flat.

Not that Magdalena would ever label Will a freak, not about any sexual proclivity. *Except the peeing thing. Golden showers. I'd for sure freak-label that one. Gross.* The tension seeped from her stiff muscles and her shoulders wilted. Suddenly her bed seemed like the best place in the world. The only place she wanted to be, regardless of the damn streetlight or kinky bang going on next door. It'd been more than twenty-four hours since she'd garnered any decent sleep.

Taking even one step seemed impossible. If she gave over to gravity, the majority of her body would make it onto the bed. She slid the tote from the crook of her arm, welcoming the tingle of circulation to her fingers, and settled it and her shoes next to an old pile of fashion magazines. Mags had just given herself permission to dive for the bed when a bitchy male voice screeched its way into her ears.

"You daft bitch. I get it all. Didn't he tell you that? I get your cunt and your mouth. I'll even take your ass, if I fancy."

The blows that followed left Magdalena's hands shaking. Fear and anger churned inside her veins. The world slowed, as did the viscous blood pumping through her body. She wobbled to the closet and gripped the white doorframe for anchor. Her forehead dropped to the backs of her hands while she inhaled past the nausea.

"Open your damn mouth or I'll go and tell them you wouldn't cooperate."

There was a possibility Willow was exploring her sexuality. Lord knew Magdalena had done more than her fair share. But this was nothing like she'd ever experienced. It didn't sound safe. Sane. And how in the hell could Willow consent to the degradation of his mouth and the beating of his... fist?

Fetish or not, this shit had gone too far. Willow's appearance earlier in the day told Mags all she needed to know. The relationship wasn't healthy. She pulled the closet open then dove into the recesses of garment bags, scattered shoes, and old textbooks. When her hand hit a slab of wood she fumbled up its length until she found the dowel-shaped top and wrenched it from the far corner. Thank God her dad had made her learn cricket. She'd scoffed as a young girl playing with all his grey-haired friends, but no more. Her fist gripped the bat like it were a billion pounds and Magdalena stalked toward Willow's room like she had big fat balls.

Unprepared. Magdalena was completely unprepared for the scene before her. She longed to shrink into a ball, cover her eyes, and wish the image away. Willow knelt on the floor beside her bed. No rigidity held her posture. Her naked body caved in on itself, shoulders hunched in retreat. All of her beautiful curves had vanished into the pit of hell she found herself wading through. The blood smearing her precious face took a back seat to the horror Willow's expression unleashed deep in Magdalena's soul. Vacant eyes stared blankly at the man before her, unseeing. Resignation weighted her usual smile into a wretched frown.

"That's right," the man said as he shoved two fingers into her mouth. "Suck em' like you will my cock." Her lips sealed stiffly around the chav's bony index and middle fingers as he pumped them in and out while his other skeletal hand wound tighter into her bronze hair. Willow gagged and the man spat. "Take it, bitch, and beg for more."

When his fingers left her mouth, swinging back high in the air and balling his fist, Magdalena freaked. The truckload of nerves coursing through her veins took an exit ramp. Her convulsing stomach settled to a calm sea. Steady legs carried her forward while strong arms levered the bat like she was on the cut. Before his knuckles moved, Magdalena unleashed the full force of her fury in a hot arch straight at the man's belly.

The impact jarred the handle in her grasp and Mags fought against the instinct to release the bat and retreat from the pain. It hurt a hell of a lot more than hitting a ball. Her bones resonated from the force, but the sight of the abusive ass hitting the ground on all fours stole her attention from the pain. His chest spasmed and his face arched for air. It was the first time she'd gotten a look at it. The sight twisted her stomach back in tightly thatched knots.

He looked like a weasel. She'd thought the things were cute before. But bugger. Near pitch-black eyes matched his slicked back hair. A button sized nose set between those round eyes held not the slightest slant of natural curve. His lips, thinned in outrage, or agony, capped off the rodent-like features that would haunt her dreams for the foreseeable future.

Rats rally quickly, to eat you out of house and home, and this one was no different. Magdalena took a step toward Will to collect her from the floor and make a run for it, but stilled in a battle ready stance when the weasel staggered to his feet.

"You stupid bitch. You have no idea what you're getting yourself into."

Coming from a naked chap holding his stomach when he should have been hiding his pathetic excuse for a dick, the threat shouldn't have cut Mags to the quick like it did. Maybe it wasn't him, but the look of utter panic etched in Willow's expression that frightened her.

"Please," Willow said. Her red cheek shook back and forth as her eyes finally engaged, pinning Mags by the throat. "I'm fine. It's not what it looks like. Please, just go."

Weasel puffed his impotent chest out at that. "Yeah, so fuck off."

Screw him and to hell with Willow's opinion. Her friend needed help. First a doctor then a shrink. Magdalena squared her shoulders and took a step toward the man. To his credit he took one back toward the window.

"You sod off, mate, or I'll knock your balls all the way to Manchester. I'm sure United wouldn't mind lobbing them around, sailing a few in the net. My straight drive'll do the trick," Mags said. To emphasize the point she tightened her grip on the handle.

"Stupid bitch," he tossed, scooping up his clothes from their neatly folded pile on the bed. "You'll get yours."

"You're not man enough to give it to me, asshole."

"I know people who are," he snarled.

Chapter Three

The metal-on-metal *thunk* had never sounded so sweet. Magdalena secured the feeble knob lock in addition to the deadbolt and chain. "Does he have a key?" she hollered through the flat, which still seemed to reverberate with the dramatic aftershocks of a Roman tragedy. When Willow didn't answer she dragged a chair from the kitchen and propped it under the handle. She hadn't the faintest idea if it would work or not, but hell, they did it in films. Now the only problem would be getting out if the place caught on fire.

Magdalena snatched the bat from its prop in the corner and headed back to the kitchen. They'd upgraded to this flat from their closet-sized one after Willow graduated art school. It afforded them more living space, which Will used to create canvas masterpieces. The artful kitchen with gleaming stainless steel appliances had been for Mags' benefit. If she had the time and inclination she could make any kitchen her bitch, but none really compared to Baine's. Though, the exquisite mix of old-world charm and modern technology that existed in her brother's estate really belonged to her father.

When it'd been Desmond McCord's home, her father had made that place sing with aroma and she'd been his eager pupil. Mags ignored the flood of happy memories and appliances. She propped the bat under her arm and reached for a glass of water and a dishtowel. The cool liquid soothed her dry throat as she swallowed several gulps. What the fuck had she walked in on? *Hell of a homecoming.* She took a deep breath, refilled the cup, and headed for the back bedroom, bat in tow.

Willow lay curled in the center of her double bed, a thick quilt pulled high over her shoulder. Tiny sobs shook the huddled ball of patchwork color. All the anger and fear dripped from Magdalena's limbs as her heart broke for her friend. Willow had always been the good girl, the angel on Mags' shoulder, while she'd played the roll of her own forked tailed devil.

"Willow?"

"Just go away, Magdalena."

The bite in her friend's tone had wicked teeth. It gnashed at the neatly wrapped package of insecurities Mags struggled to bind and banish in the recesses of her mind. Its gnarled edges flapped open at her friend's demand. At the banishment. But this was no time to worry about her inadequacies. Willow needed her, whether or not she recognized her own fragility.

Magdalena shoved her own vulnerability and anxiety back into its obscure corner, and walked to the wrought iron head of her friend's bed. "I'm not leaving you, Will. We don't have to talk." She paused for a minute, realizing the lie only after it left her lips. Her head shook. "No, that's not true, sweet. We need to talk."

"You messed it all up," Will heaved through hiccuped weeps. "Everything is ruined."

"It was messed up before I got here, Willow. If you're into kink, you find someone who respects you. Treasures you, even. You don't deserve to be treated like shit."

One more step brought her even with Willow's face. The crusts of dried blood formed a riverbed for the steady stream of tears coursing down her slight cheek. Mascara obscured her lashes and created a near carbon copy of the terrible excuse for make-up artistry she'd seen on the runway two seasons ago.

"Oh, sweetie." The endearment came from her heart as did the need to comfort her friend. Magdalena braced her weapon against the wall and reached out to smooth back the mussed locks from Willow's muddy brown eyes. Will's body lurched beneath the covers. She cringed, every visible muscle constricting like she prepared for an impending blow. Magdalena's body temperature dropped about ten degrees as she froze in place, her hand hanging in the nothingness that gapped between her and her best friend.

The constriction in her throat and the moisture hitting her exposed cleavage clued Magdalena in to her own torrent of emotion. She snatched back her hand and held it to her chest. Willow's wide, wild eyes stared back.

Through force of will, Mags steadied her quavering insides before she spoke. In Swahili she quietly recited the Introit and Kyrie, a prayer in song for the souls of the dead, she learned from Malaika. The nurse she'd met in a large village she frequented had recited the words far too many times. She had no damn clue what it meant and, obviously, wasn't particularly religious, but the things she'd witnessed over the last year prompted her to echo her friend's prayer. Time and again. The familiar words and their foreign meaning stilled her tears and shaking hands. She swallowed past the tightness in her throat.

"Willow. I would never hurt you." Magdalena held her hands out, palms open, in surrender. Pretty hard to do with a glass and rag in tow, but she managed. "I'm sorry. I won't try and touch you again. Not without asking first."

Whoever held Willow's legs eased off their contorting hold and she noodled against the mattress like an unwound violin string. Her breath came in airy gusts across Magdalena's bare shoulders. Dark circles collected themselves under the lee of Willow's bloodshot eyes. At least her tears had ceased their flow.

"I have some water," she offered. For the first time since she'd walked in the bedroom, her friend's eyes focused on her. So many unspoken thoughts danced their way through those troubled depths. Magdalena wished she'd pick any one of them and start talking. Not only to ease her own discomfort, but to take some of the burden from Willow's too-slight shoulders.

Unable to take the quiet, Mags filled it. "You know you can tell me anything and I'd never judge you. I'm no better than you or anyone else in this world. We're all just trying to find our way in this tricky fucker."

The first flicker of a smile creased the tiny lines by Willow's long lashes and curved one side of her mouth. Bolstered by the sign, Mags continued. "I don't know if anyone has figured their way through it unscathed, but it doesn't stop us from trying."

"I love you, Mags."

Willow's words were a whisper, but they rang in her ears like a chorus. Magdalena enjoyed the warmth that thawed the uncertainty in her chest and hated that she needed reassurance from her friend. But like she told Will, they were all damaged goods on one level or another.

"I love you, sweetie. Now, let's sit you up." Willow's fingers whitened at the knuckle as she clutched the quilt to her. Mags could have kicked her own ass for not thinking about her roommate's state of undress. "Hold on a tick. I'll fetch your smalls and a shirt."

Since they used to wear the same size and shared clothes like sisters, it only took Mags a second to locate a bra, panties, and T-shirt. She laid them on the bed and turned to give Will privacy, something she'd never done before. Yet, this situation called for as much personal space as Mags could give without allowing Willow to continue down the destructive path she wandered.

"Does he have a key, Willow?"

After an audible breath, she answered. "No."

As reassurances went it was nice to know that bastard couldn't let himself into their flat on a whim. It also meant Willow let him inside.

"Good. I'd hate to have to kill him, if he came back."

"No, Magdalena." The voice sounded surprisingly sturdy for a girl who'd been in a blubbering heap only minutes before.

Mags turned, uncaring what she caught sight of since she'd seen it all before. She had the same bits anyway. Willow stood, chin up. Her hands fisted at the hem below Mick Jagger's bright red tongue. The paint-splattered mouth insulted Magdalena's help, as did the expression on Will's face. Gone was the sad girl. In her place was the strong-willed friend she'd left a year ago. But something about her narrowed gaze and the stern set of her shoulders said this show of power wouldn't help either of them extricate that piece of shit from their lives.

"I don't understand,"   Mags said. The effort to keep her jaw off the lacquered floor and her hands from shaking sense into Willow just about snapped her in two. Heat flushed her cheeks and her close-cropped fingernails indented the skin of her palm.

"I don't expect you to. I do expect you to respect me and my privacy."

"You're going to pull that shit with me while you're standing there with blood and the beginnings of goddamned bruises on your face?"

Willow's chest rose and fell several times, but the facade of control didn't budge. "You've been gone for a year, Magdalena. You can't walk through the door and start ordering me around like you know what's best. I mean, how many mornings did I shove blokes out the door for you?"

Magdalena's mouth gaped. *What the fuck is wrong with her?* "I'm sorry I wasn't here for you, when you obviously needed someone, but you can't hold that against me when you're in danger. And those guys fucked me. Because I wanted them to. And not one of them hurt me."

A tear rolled down Willow's impassive face. She batted it away with excessive force, clearing a swath of red with the moisture. Her flushed cheek and smooth skin peeked out from beneath. "Didn't they?"

"No," Magdalena bit. "I did that all on my own."

Willow's jaw worked. "I don't need you or anyone else."

"Yes, you do, and I'm here for you. No matter how much you try to push mc away."

The unflappable exterior broke and Willow buried her face in her hands. Sobs wrestled from Willow's chest, saturating the air with desperation. She sank to the floor, a ship taking on water.

Magdalena needed backup. Crouching, she sought Will's gaze. "It'll be okay, Willow. You don't have to be afraid of that ass. Your dad could ruin his life with a few well-placed calls, if he didn't take the bastard out at the kneecaps instead."

At the mention of her father, Will's head reared. Her reddened skin paled despite the blood. "No," she shrieked.

"You don't have to tell him the whole story. He wouldn't ask questions. He'd protect you, Will. He's a powerful man who loves you more than life, more than Parli—"

"I think it's time you found your own place, Magdalena."

The last words Mags ever expected to hear from her friend cut deep. It didn't matter the reason for the extrication had nothing to do with Magdalena, personally, and everything to do with the intimate drama unfolding in Willow's life.

"Hold the fucking ringer! What did you just say?"

That deceptively strong chin shot up again and Willow's eyes cleared slightly with renewed authority. "I'll give you a week to clear out your belongings."

A gleam sparked in Willow's eyes and all the fight left Magdalena in a rush. Her hands wrapped around her middle in an effort to ward off the ocean trying to drown her and force her to create a new life for herself.

"You've gone bloody mad, Willow."

Chapter Four

"No. Thank you," Magdalena said with a stalling shake of her head. "I've got it. Really."

The middle-aged cabbie pinched the brim of his woolen flat cap, closed the trunk, and shuffled toward the Taxi's open driver door. "You take care now. A lass like you has no business being about at this time of night. Mornin', really."

"Thank you," Mags repeated. She tried to keep the huff out of her tone, but she already had a dad who'd be none too happy with her early morning arrival. Especially since she had to turn around and head back to campus in a few hours. Plus, it's not like she would have been out at this time, if she could have helped it.

She'd stewed in her room for an hour without a hint of sleep in her future and knew from the butter-thick tension in the air she'd have better luck heading back to London for the night. Mags waved the paunch driver off as he exited the gravel drive of Baine's estate, and then contemplated sitting on her ass in the pokey rocks and using her luggage as a pillow. That's how damn tired she was.

The main house loomed over her like a sleeping giant. All the windows gleamed onyx from the darkness, inside and out. Hell, the full moon even hid behind the ever-present thicket of clouds that hung in the English sky, despite the present heat of summer. Mags heaved a lung full of soggy air, swept the beads of perspiration off her upper lip, and then hefted her bags.

Her father's house, the one of her fondest and most adverse childhood memories, sat tucked in a nest of hazel trees. The vibrant green leaves, thick trunks, and the side yard garden all helped give the place a magical feel. She headed toward the cottage and the front room lamp always lighting the way home.

Instead of knocking, Mags fished her keys out of the depths of her tote and let herself inside. Maybe she could sneak in like old times and avoid a proper dressing down. She slipped through the door and fastened it behind her. She turned to tiptoe through the warmly decorated living room, but abruptly teetered. Something metal caught the toe of her sandal and upended her world, yet again. Metal clacked and clattered around her body as she landed hard on...she didn't know what the fuck it was, but it hurt. Heavy footfalls thudded down the stairs in a rapid beat. And instantly her heart revved a notch.

Easton Wells, her dad, didn't get in a rush about anything, and he was a slender fellow. Not nearly as big as the thunder rumbling in her direction. Though her pulse ratcheted with each closing step, Mags' brain kicked into gear after the tilt-a-whirl ride of the evening and she sighed in relief. *Baine.* Her brother was that big, but why in the world would he be in her father's house?

Still weary, Mags scrambled to her hands and knees. At least, she tried. Tubular metal polls rolled under her palm, caught the edge of the bag on her arm, and sent her sprawling again.

"What the hell," a deep baritone boomed. *Not Baine.* Baine's voice was similarly bass, but this one held a rough quality that quaked its way down her spine.

"Dad," she screamed with every bit of air she held in her lungs. What had he done to her dad? Who was he? What did he want? That fucking weasel from the apartment...he'd held true to his word and worked too damn fast...

A big hand clamped around her upper arm and pulled. Magdalena let the tote slip from her opposite shoulder as the behemoth hoisted her from the floor, and then balled her fist and rammed. She looked past the wide expanse of his bare chest and aimed for his throat, like Baine had shown her.

Before she could blink, he had her restrained. Thick arms coiled around her chest and arms as he pinned her to his body. Her face burrowed into a valley of muscle while her breasts smashed against the rippled tract of his abdomen. Heat radiated from the man, warming every inch of her exposed skin from brow to ankle. He touched her everywhere. Encompassed her completely.

Panic seized her as stories of sexual violation flooded her memory from the interviews she'd taken from Goma to Bunia. Now she'd have her own story, if she survived. Her arms and legs flailed of their own volition in a primal struggle for freedom. For life.

"Magdalena, calm down." His voice brooked no argument. And damn her body, but it obeyed, going rigid as a board.

"How do you know my name? Where's my father? Who are you? What do you want?" The questions, jumbled from her addled brain, fell out of her mouth in a breathless line of inquiry.

"Baine said you asked lots of questions."

At the mention of her brother's name she sagged into the man, completely spent. He accepted her weight without the slightest sway of his stance. On a pivot he leaned over her. Embarrassed and absolutely confused, Magdalena hid her face in the hard ridge of his chest as he hooked one arm behind her knees and collected her in his hold.

"What are—" Her question was a whisper he cut off with that rugged voice of his.

"No more questions. I'm still processing the last interrogation. You'd think you were a reporter or something."

"Journalist."

"College student," he shot back.

Mags hated the smile that curved one side of her mouth because she didn't understand it at all. Nor could she comprehend why the sweaty musk of his skin made her want to lap it clean with her tongue.

Son of a fuck, add it to the list of things you don't understand about tonight.

"That better?" His question came in time with the soft cushion of couch meeting her butt as he sat her before him like a child.

The scene she would have thought couldn't get any more awkward, did. When he pulled back he found himself pinned by her draped arms, which refused to release his warmth. She'd claim shock or jet lag for her peculiar behavior. At this point it was more like sleep deprivation anyway.

"You're all right," he said in an even voice. His fingers glided up her forearms and slipped between her hands. He separated them and sat back on his heels in front of her.

All thought of the *zing* dancing along her skin where he'd touched vanished at the sight of him. The light cast by the single shaded bulb deepened the shadow of his scruffy, wide set jaw. *Screw five o'clock shadows. That bitch is a ten. Ten o'clock. Ten on a hotness scale of one to five.* The close cropped hairs plunged down his neck then receded midway, making room for meters of smooth skin pulled taut over slabs of corded muscle.

Heading north, her bearings did not improve. Thick lips plumped above his mandible. Hued in red, they called to her like instruments of lust. As his beard rose into sideburns it met again, covering his perfectly shaped skull with the same stubbled hair. The shade seemed dark in the muted room, but when he tilted his head to scrutinize her it caught and reflected gold in the light.

His bronzed skin creased at his brow and Mags was further dumbstruck by the most exotic pair of eyes she'd ever seen. Green brilliant enough to match the leaves of the trees outside lay encircled by a ring of black. The contrast of the light and dark, perhaps, gave a hint of the nature of the man who hosted the unique gaze.

His calm reassurance said *safe*. His body said *danger*.

"No one expected you here." His scowl deepened. "Especially at this time of night."

"Morning," she shot back.

"Semantics." He turned her hands over in his own, examining them closely. "Are you all right?"

Mags pulled her hands from his grasp in an attempt to balance herself and order her thoughts. His touch, his nearness set her gauges on the fritz. "I'm tired. It's been two long days and I need sleep, but first I need answers. You're Lawrence Pierce, right?"

"When questioning, you should never lead. You corrupt the mind of your witness and in turn, your information," he said with a lightened scowl.

"I don't have the time or patience for a lesson."

He smiled and Mags had to staunch the urge to punch him or shag him.

"Yes, I'm the lug Baine has tolerated over the last few years. Sorry about your fall." He gestured toward the door and it was all she could do to rip her gaze from his face to follow. "I'm replacing some of the old pipes in the house."

"At this time of night," she said with a shake of her head.

He chuckled. "Morning. And yeah, I couldn't sleep."

"Me either, but not for lack of trying." Mags sighed.

The smirk vanished from his face. "Are you in some kind of trouble?"

"I am. I need a bed, but you're blocking me from it."

His gaze narrowed. "You're not one for unscheduled visits. What's wrong?"

Law's body caged her. His wide, leanly muscled chest blocked her view of the room. Thick legs, stretching the confines of denim, spread in a squat bracketing her bare legs. Unable to take the closeness any longer, Mags stood on wobbly legs and shoved past his shoulder. "You're just upset you didn't have forewarning to run and hide."

"What on earth are you rattling about?"

"Rattling," she balked. "Ass. Of all the times I've come home over the years, I've never met you. Don't you find that a little odd?"

"You've been away at school and on some internship for the last year, and on the few occasions you graced your father with your presence, I was out of town on business."

"Few times? I only live two and a half hours away. And yes, maybe I enjoy my freedom, but I visit. *And*," she said, foisting her hands to her hips, "lawyers don't travel as often as you and Baine do."

He mimicked her posture. "*And*, that would be where you're wrong. Since we *are* lawyers and we *do* travel often."

Magdalena's hands slipped from her curves. "Why am I fighting with *you*?"

Law winked at her. "Because you were spoiling for a fight and I like to oblige lovely ladies, when I can."

I'll bet you do.

"Where's my father?"

"At Ruth's."

"Ew, he spends the night?"

His ripped chest shook with laughter, the thatching of muscle contracting with each whoop. Magdalena swallowed the saliva pooling in her mouth.

"He's been staying over a lot lately."

"Fine," she said, halting any elaboration with a thrashing hand. "Where's Baine?"

"Away on business."

"Right. I'm going to figure you two out one of these days, but not today. I'll get out of your hair, so you can finish whatever it is you're doing."

Mags went to grab her bag, but Law's thick fingers curled around the strap and hoisted it effortlessly. His chin nodded toward the door. "Sorry, but you'll have to stay in the main house tonight. The water is shut off and I won't be able to finish until tomorrow."

"Fuck."

"Anytime," he said.

Chapter Five

As far as tactics went it wasn't the nicest approach, but it seemed to have the desired effect. Magdalena's body stiffened like she'd been hit with a low voltage Taser. She'd label him an ass in fifty different ways, but that he could handle. What he could not manage was her attention. Her body.

The sweet way her shapely contours had melded into him knocked Law with a blow rivaling his HELO crash in Nanyuki, and another hit he couldn't think about. His reaction to the impact of her gaze and the lusty intent that twinkled in her eyes had been a testament to his wherewithal. He should still be laid out ass-over-elbows from it, but the need to get her the hell away from him broke rank over his raging hard-on.

Thank holy hell.

Magdalena rallied, plucking up a duffel. She rushed for the door. Her sloppy mane brushed over her back and shoulders. It cascaded down her front and the memory of her peek-a-boo cleavage assailed him then combined with his imagination. He pictured Magdalena's sand-blonde locks teasing the ample swell of her breasts, revealing only hints of her tight little nipples underneath. Law swallowed hard against the dryness of his throat and cursed himself for the unnecessary torture.

When they exited the house and the moonlight caught on her perfect apple-round bottom as it swayed from side to side in her effort to outrun him, Law's heart skipped a beat.

"How long are you planning to stay?" The nonchalance of his tone disguised the desperation for her speedy exodus.

Her delicate hands choked at her sides and she swung them like tiny battering rams on her way across the gravel to the main house. She slowed at his question, cocking her chin to the sky. "Judging by the moon, I'd say three or four hours tops."

Law's perception had been correct. She had some kind of trouble on her hands, but he dismissed the urge to help her. No, urge wasn't the right word for the hulking, primal need to protect the woman before him. The sassy sway of curves screwed with his already chaotic state. He banded the hunger in solid restraints to save himself guaranteed heartache.

With two swift strides Law beat her to the rear entrance and opened the door. "After you."

Magdalena skirted him warily, slipping as closely as possible along the frame and as far away from him as she could get.

"I won't bite you, Magdalena."

Her head snapped toward him and her emerald gaze pinned him to the door. Her expression was meant to rebuke, but the soft sea-green drew him. As did the moue of her already pouty lips.

"I might bite *you*," she warned.

And I'd like it way too much.

Law compressed his lips together to keep a smile at bay, and her glower seemed to intensify. She slung the bag in her grasp up her arm and settled it onto a shoulder. With an exaggerated kick of her hip, Magdalena settled a hand at the small of her waist and thrust her other hand at him.

"Give me my bag."

Since it was best for them both to retreat to their separate corners, he kicked the door shut with his boot and complied, handing over the luggage. When Magdalena accepted the weight she swayed slightly, but maintained her lick-my-boot posture.

"Now, where's your room?"

Both of Law's brows stood at attention—along with his dick—while her brows couldn't possibly go any lower without her entire body falling forward.

"I'm not trying to crawl in bed with you," she shot off. "In fact, I want to know so I can stay as far away from you as possible."

Law nodded and fancied a good palm to his forehead. He didn't want her upset. "I didn't mean to offend you. It's late and we're both a bit crabby."

"Crabby?" She yelled the question then turned on her heels and hobbled, lugging the oversized travel bag through the kitchen toward the grand staircase.

"Any one of the rooms on Baine's wing are ready for guests," he called.

She didn't respond, only kept lurching until she disappeared behind the kitchen partition. Law braced his hands against the counter and exhaled roughly.

It's going to be a long damn night.

Chapter Six

Magdalena jerked awake, her entire body tense. Her eyes opened then blinked into uncomfortable clarity the rays of daylight filtering through the windows. The room greeted her with familiar warmth and she slumped back into the fluffy down. Tiny dust motes launched into the air and wafted through the streaks of day in no hurry to see the yet discovered world. She smiled. If her dad knew there was the slightest form of dust in the house he would have a shit fit. *Then again, maybe not.* Ruth seemed to occupy a swell chunk of the old bird's time these days. Her smile widened. *Good for him. He deserves happiness.* And the stupid grin he had on his face when he finally introduced them yesterday showed her how happy the silver haired beauty made him.

The windowpanes rattled in their old, perfectly manicured frames and Mags' heart revved with the growling engine passing outside. She scrubbed a hand over her face at the passing motorist and groaned at the slick of slobber covering her jaw. "Disgusting." When the roaring engine refused to dissipate, Mags shrieked in annoyance. "For the love of all that's holy."

Using the back of her hand she wiped away the evidence of her sleep coma. Well, she rid it from her face anyway. Since it already had slobber spots, she rubbed the moisture from her hand onto the pillow. The bloody racket continued to repel the sacred morning quiet.

By damn, enough already.

Magdalena threw back the covering. The anger she'd not slept off roiled to the surface and mixed with new rage at the audacity of some people. This was a rural neighborhood. Not a drag strip, for the love. She launched from the bed. Her bare feet met an antique Persian rug that should be hung in a museum, not stomped over by indignant feet. She stomped over it all the same, making her way to the closest of two floor-to-ceiling dormer windows in the space.

"I just got to sleep, damn you," she hollered at the offending motorist and no one at all. No one could hear a damn thing above the din of some ridiculous number of horses in a blasted engine.

As she closed in on the window she realized she faced the back of the property. The green grass and blossom covered garden stretched out before her and her mind took a side street to a forbidden destination. Law Pierce's green-god eyes. Enraged at herself now, as well as the noise, Magdalena beat her fist against the window.

"Belt up, would you? It's too bloody early for all that prattle."

Miracle of miracles, the engine died down and she was suddenly the loudest thing in a ten-block radius. Mags gave the glass one more whack, but her clutched hand stalled like the roar of the fat black and silver motorcycle Law squatted beside. Apparently the man had a problem with clothing. He rose from the beastly machine, showcasing the most adulterating display of masculinity she'd ever seen in real life. Magazines and fashion week didn't count. Even if they did, they'd lose to this package of sexy man-ness.

His thick shoulders were wrapped with layer upon bulging layer of corded muscle, and it didn't stop there. They coursed down his arms, laying a beautiful palate of peaks and valleys. As wide as he was up top, his torso tapered in a perfectly sculpted V from his ample pecs, across his abdomen, straight into the faded blues that hung low on the Y of his hips. The—*why am I not tracing that thing with my greedy fingers*—muscles had her flattening her hand against the glass for support.

If he were just a body, he'd be easier to look away from. But his face sucked her in with its mischievous smirk. As he cocked his head, his gaze drank her in, so much so he dropped the blue, oil-stained cloth on the ground and gripped the wrench in his hand so hard Mags swore she could see the veins mapping his muscles bulge. He raised a brow at her, and she didn't understand why he looked at her like she was the only item on a buffet at a deserted island.

Magdalena's hand flew to her throat in surprise, but one much larger caught her attention. "Fuck." She screamed and jumped back from the window. She slapped both hands to her face in total embarrassment, when she should use those hands to cover as much of her naked body as she could. She'd had it all on display, honking breasts with her pepperoni sized areolas and an untamed patch covering her mons.

Would the hits ever stop? At this rate, she didn't think so. Mags shuffled backward until her thighs hit the bed and sat. How in the hell had she forgotten about her lack of clothes? It had been a year since she'd slept in the buff, but it had been the only way she was able to fall asleep what only seemed like ten whole minutes ago—well, getting naked and rubbin' one out.

And now she paid a hefty price for the measly hours of sleep. Public humiliation. "Ahhh," she groaned, uncovering her face and reaching for her phone on the nightstand. Only the sleek black thing wasn't there. Leaning down, she scanned the floor then sat up and scanned the bed. She tossed blankets and sheets about, but came up broke. *Story of your life.*

A knock reverberated through the room and Mags hugged a pillow to her front. "Go away. The show's over."

"Open the door, Magdalena."

She hated the effect his rich, scratchy voice had on her. Ignorant of her disdain, her toes curled at the sound. "You may be hard of hearing from that damned machine of yours, so I'll repeat. Go. Away."

"Do you fancy your phone?"

"What?"

"Open the door," he repeated in the same demanding, yet even, voice as before.

"Mad. Every flipping person in my life has gone mad," she mumbled. Magdalena threw the pillow with such force it hit the bed, bounced, then tumbled to the floor off the opposite side. She eyed her luggage, but didn't bother. Instead she yanked the sheet from the already disheveled bed and wound it around her body.

If one thing in the whole of the last forty-eight hours had worked in her favor, it was the shirt-covered torso staring back at her when she opened the door. Had he been shirtless as he'd been five minutes ago, nothing could have stopped her from dropping the sheet and tossing herself at him like a chit. But even the sweat-dampened fabric did little to calm the rush of awareness plumping her nipples and other girly bits. To offset the thoughts bounding like fucking rabbits in her mind, Mags crossed her arms and tried for pissed, which wasn't a stretch.

Before she could open her mouth to berate him, Law produced a phone from his pocket and foisted it into her hands. "I took your phone because the bloody thing chirped every five minutes for an hour and a half, and you didn't seem inclined to shut it off." Mags inhaled to speak, but he didn't stop. "Before you let me have it, I didn't break into the cursed thing to turn it off. I put it in a drawer in the kitchen, under some towels, so I wouldn't have to listen to it."

He raked one hand over his stubbled head before shoving both hands into his front pockets. The innocent gesture looked all wrong on the innately predatory, sexually scrumptious man. Yet, it added a layer of sweetness to his disposition and a hint of vulnerability. Magdalena's heart dunked into her belly in appreciation.

"Wow," he whispered.

"Wow, what?"

Law's thick lips spread wide over a set of straight bright teeth, and her belly plunged to her big toe.

"Just surprised. You didn't beat me to death with those little fists of yours."

Mags glanced down at her folded arms and white knuckles then loosened her balled hands. Law had seen her sleep. Knowing that wound her up, but she hadn't realized how tightly until he pointed it out. She didn't give two flippin' cents about the phone, but the act of watching someone sleep came with a sense of intimacy. A person was never more exposed than when they slept. And she couldn't bear any more nakedness where he was concerned.

Literal or otherwise.

In defense, she changed tracks. "My alarm went off for more than an hour. Why didn't you wake me?"

"You needed the sleep."

Guy-speak for 'you look like shit.'

"Is my dad's car here or did he take it to Ruth's?"

"Ruth's," he said with a shrug. "But I can drop you."

Yeah, flat on her head. That's where he would drop her, and she didn't have the emotional means to deal. The phone peeped and vibrated her hand, sending another shot of adrenaline through her veins. *I'm awake already.* Mags pressed the snooze and went bug-eyed at the time readout. "Two o'clock in the sodded afternoon?"

"It's certainly not one in the morning. We were just there, remember?"

"Fuck it all," she huffed. With a barring arm she shoved Law from the threshold out into the corridor. "I needed to be at Cardiff six hours ago. Thanks for the offer, but there's no way in hell I'm slinging a leg over that thing in the drive. I'll call a cab."

She slammed the door in his gorgeous face and ran for the loo, snatching her bag as she went.

Chapter Seven

So good. Magdalena closed her lips against a moan. It wouldn't do to draw the cabbie's attention, because she wasn't sharing. She swallowed and warmth slid down her throat. Satisfaction pooled in her belly, but greed and the mouthwatering aroma called her back for more. After licking the crumbs from her mouth, Mags sank her teeth into the last portion of her toasted egg and sausage.

Why did he have to be so hot and so nice...in that gruff, rude kind of way?

The brown bag crackled as she returned the sandwich's plastic wrapper to its depths and peeked inside. Two Glamorgan sausages snuggled in their wrapper. An apple, banana, and another napkin canoodled with them. When she'd come downstairs the classy remise had been waiting, door opened, with her big luggage loaded and this bag of goodies on the seat. She hadn't touched it for a while, thinking the previous tenant had forgotten their lunch. The poor sod. But Ralph, the driver, said, "If you're not going to eat that, you can pass it my way, and if you're not head over heels for your man, I know my daughter could make use of a top bloke like that. The man she's with now isn't worth the air he breathes."

She hadn't seen Law again before she left and it was for the best.

"Most aren't," she agreed.

The black cab jarred, riding over a nice dip in the old highway. Unable to eat another bite, Mags abandoned the bag for the view outside the window. Her sleep deprived face reflected in all its dark circled glory, but she looked beyond it at the passing greenery. Fields edged with leaf-bowed limbs carved the horizon as she bemoaned her unceremonious welcome home. Her stomach shimmied. A nervous energy had her flipping the sandal on her foot in irritating time with the flitting past of each tiny car and occasional delivery truck.

Mags still had a few usable hours in the day and, sitting up straight with both feet on the floorboard, she vowed to make the most of them. First, she needed to get in touch with her thesis advisor, apologize for bungling their meeting this morning, and beg for another chunk of her time. Second, she had to talk to Willow and get a read on her friend's emotional state before she started flat shopping. The incessant clapping of leather to heel started again just before the car pulled to a stop. The driver hopped out, opened her door, and set her belongings on the curb.

By the gods, she didn't want to move out. She also didn't want to think about Law Pierce ever again. After thanking the driver, since Law had already paid the man, she grabbed her bags and trudged to her flat. The letter she found on the middle of her kitchen table and the lingering image of Law's stirring gaze said both were inevitable.

Mags,

I'll treasure our friendship always, but we've outgrown one another. I'm going to stay at my father's for the week. This should give you time and space to move.

- Will

Tears welled in her eyes, blurring her view of the trendy furnishings. They all belonged to Willow. After all, she had a gallery job that paid her well, a budding career as an artist, and a mother and father who lavished her with everything she desired. Mags had student loans, a never-ending college career, and no mother.

Negative Nancy.

Mags blinked away the moisture.

You have a loving father, devoted brother, and finally you have some direction about you. So, don't get in a tizzy about a change of address.

But the tears were about more than that. They seeped from her eyes for the certain death of a friendship. *Strap a toe tag on that shit, 'cause it's only a matter of time before the rigor sets in.* Magdalena slumped onto a kitchen chair and let the grief take hold. Disappointment. Regrets. Uncertainty. They fell like raindrops on the painted surface. Her stomach burned, a deep sear of anguish.

When the drips slowed, Mags raised her head toward the sky and squeezed her eyes shut. *Enough.* She stood with a huff and marched into her room. On the bright side, she didn't have much to move. The few valuables she possessed stayed in her room at her dad's house. In fact, most of her things were in London. She'd moved everything home during their flat transition since she'd already scheduled the internship with the UN. She only brought the essentials and decor stuff to the new place.

Mags grabbed her phone and dialed Mrs. Fry's office, ready to beg for a reschedule. Again plans didn't go her way. The line only *rang* and *rang* in her ear.

"Screw it." She tossed the phone onto the bed and propped her hands on her hips. The warmth of the room taunted her. Its billowy white curtains and soft violet bedding, even the collection of smiling faces above her bed, seemed caustic. Two steps brought her even with the masks of happiness the people wore in the photos. She started by the door, pulling the thickly laminated paper from the wall. Some ripped, the staples refusing to vacate the premises, like she should. But nothing good would come from staying in a place she was no longer wanted.

The stack grew in her hand.

Wide grins and drinks in the air. A string of girls hooked arm-in-arm in front of a stage. Skirts short and tops low. Heels high. A couple in an embrace. Sultry party face in place. He blew a kiss. He held her hand. He dipped her in a kiss. His hands covered her breasts, the playful look of surprise stretching his mouth. He hugged her. He spun her. His arm draped over her.

All the he's were interchangeable. None of them special other than they'd made her feel that way. She hadn't been alone and for that she'd loved them. For a moment.

Mags dislodged another faceless guy and stared at him, struggling to recall one unique thing about him and found none. Except the chap standing behind him. Her hand began to shake.

It was the weasel that beat the shit out of her Willow.

* * *

Click. Click. Click. Magdalena's fingers flew across the keyboard. She searched her Facebook page for the picture matching the one from her wall. And par for the fucking course, she came up empty. She'd tried Twitter because her friends used it more often, but people didn't load as many pictures there. Mags rolled her shoulders and kept typing. Instinct kicked in and she followed it like a starved zombie chasing Doyle in Twenty Eight Weeks Later. *Why the bloody hell'd you even watch that movie?* She hadn't slept well for a week after.

After searching Willow's page and turning up nothing, Mags hunched over the computer, dejected. She only allowed the feeling to hang for a moment before she straightened and typed some more. Next she tried the faceless bloke's Facebook page. Thank goodness they'd split on good terms and she could remember his name. Roy Russell. She didn't expect him to have as many pictures as she and Willow had, but surprise, surprise. The bloke liked photos, especially if he was the subject.

For two hours she searched in a sea of narcissism. Her vision blurred. Dull pain joined forces behind her left eyebrow and turned to an ache.

"Bollocks," she moaned.

Ozzy's eerie voice jerked her from the depth of her tiny personal tragedy. *Was it the end of the beginning or the beginning of the end? Was she losing control? Because she certainly wasn't winning. Was it real life or all pretend?*

"Good questions, chap," she said.

Mags muted the ring tone and peered at the unrecognizable number on the display. The song had always been her favorite. She'd chosen it as her ringer for a shot of perspective throughout the day. Now the lyrics just wrinkled her socks. She scraped a hand over her face before answering.

"Hello?"

"Ms. Wells?" a deep voice asked.

"Yes. Who is this?"

"Mr. Davis. I'm calling on behalf of Mrs. Fry."

The man didn't sound particularly young or old. For some reason Magdalena pictured a middle-aged man of average height with a mediocre face and slightly pudgy middle on the other end of the line. Mrs. F had younger students work as her assistants, but maybe this guy just had a mature voice.

"Please, pass on my regret for missing our meeting this morning. Jet lag and some other unforeseen circumstances tripped me up. I'm awfully sorry for wasting her time. I know she's busy."

"She was confused by your absence, but is willing to reschedule, if you can come around six forty-five."

"Absolutely. Thank you. Please thank her for me. I won't miss it."

They disconnected and she sighed. *Finally a break.*

Mags placed the picture on the stack and reached for her thumb drive. What good was a photo of the man without a name? None at all. If Willow wasn't concerned with her own drama, why should she worry? She shouldn't. She would, still, but she could worry while she prepared for her meeting.

Chapter Eight

Click. Click. Click. Magdalena exchanged the clack of her keyboard for that of her black pumps. Seriously, she should've carried the shoes and worn her sandals on the four-block trek. But she'd wasted the afternoon digging for the weasel's identity. She pushed past the irritation of finding damn nothing and embraced the excitement beating her heart like a drummer. Before she'd changed out of shorts and a tank into the slacks and blouse, Mags printed off the information she'd been after last night. Her thesis proposal.

Whew. Her legs screamed from the beat of her gate, but no way in hell was she slowing down. She had fifteen minutes to get to the media building and then up to the race, representation, and cultural politics group of offices on the fourth floor. The trip took eleven minutes on a good day. Meaning when she wore flats.

At least traffic wouldn't hold progress. Campus cleared out hours before and only a few cars dotted the street side parking. By the time she rounded the corner and caught the building she sought, sweat rolled between her shoulder blades. Once she crossed the threshold, crisp air ferreted away the humidity, cooling her skin. One button later, Mags lounged against the elevator, enjoying the climate-controlled environment. She rallied when the car stopped and she exited left toward Mrs. F's office.

Head down, she smacked into a wall of a fellow.

"Sorry." She winced and grabbed the skin just below her hairline.

"Steady there," the voice, the one who'd called to reschedule the meeting, said. His hands wrapped around her shoulders, steadying her. But after completing the task they didn't move. Each digit compressed, molding into her skin.

Mags looked up into dark eyes. The man's bald head gleamed in the fluorescent light. His thick shoulders resembled boulders stacked largest to smallest down his arm. Definitely not what she pictured from talking to him on the phone. Definitely not who she wanted to meet in a dark alley—or a deserted corridor for that matter.

The hair along her forearms stood at attention and Mags took a step back. Reluctantly, his grasp left her. The guy smiled, but no pleasant fuzzies pacified her wariness. In fact, the expression gained a malevolent quality the longer it stayed frozen on his face.

Run!

Her body screamed the demand, but she shook it off. They were in a public place and her professor was just three doors down on the right. If she took off running in the opposite direction, she'd miss her appointment, again, and look like a lunatic.

"Please excuse me," she begged. The step she took around him pushed her short legs to their span limit. If it seemed rude, she didn't much care. The guy gave her the jeebs.

"Ms. Wells?" He repeated the phrase he'd used on the phone.

Her stomach lurched at the dead tone that hadn't come through on the line. Mags took two more steps before peering over her shoulder. "Yes?"

"Mrs. Fry isn't in right now."

"Oh?" Mags hated the fear laced in her breathless question. Disliked the shiver rolling through her body even more.

He smiled again. "Yeah. She's at home with her family. You have family, don't you, Ms. Wells?"

Magdalena's mouth opened, but no sound escaped. Breaths came fast. In. Out. Her chest rose and fell. Again her mind yelled. *Run!* But her legs seemed crafted of lead.

"Father, Easton Wells. Your poor dad's a widower. It'd be a shame if something bad happened to him. And Baine McCord. I can't quite figure your relation, but give me time. I will."

"Why are you doing this?"

"Doing what?" Fat hands spread wide in a gesture of confusion. "We're just talking, right now."

"And later?" Her backbone revived from its noodle state and it showed in her voice. The strength she'd lost returned with her rage. How dare this bastard threaten her family.

"Depends on what we work out now. Ha," he laughed. "You're spunky. I think I could have some fun with you."

Magdalena didn't possess the skills to fight a man his size, but she could run, stubby legs or not. Anger spurred her enough that she finally listened when her body screamed once more. She turned and bolted down the hallway toward the emergency stairwell. No use in heading for locked offices.

Her arms pistoned at her sides. The damn tote flapped back and forth, creating a drag that seemed to slow her pace to a cartoon-like jog. Unwilling to drop the key to every detail of her life,

Mags gripped the handbag with the crook of her arm and kept moving. She stretched and pulled her legs faster and faster. Her heels slipped on the carpet and fear, pure and terrifying, clawed its way up her throat in a window-rattling scream.

"Help! Somebody help me!"

The noise only reverberated in her ears amidst the roaring of her pulse, ten times louder than Law's damn motorcycle. No caped crusader appeared from the shadows to smite her pursuer, whose heavy footfalls pounded closer. She dared not look back, afraid of what she might see.

Like one of those crash test dummies she'd seen on television, her arms and legs flew out ahead of her while her torso slammed into an invisible barrier. Mags flailed, struggling to collect her legs beneath her, but the floor came hard and fast. A shriek of fabric ripping combined with the thud of her ass and right elbow smacking the ground.

Her blouse sucked around her middle and the fabric cried out again as he hoisted her off the carpet. One hairy arm looped around her waist and pinned her back to his torso.

"No," she screamed. Magdalena's legs kicked wildly, seeking contact anywhere. The floor. His shin. The wall.

He shook her like a rag doll. "Stop fighting. You'll only make things worse."

"No," she belted again. But this time a sob broke the word, making it sound feeble. Weak. Defenseless. Just like she felt.

Hot breath caressed her ear and neck, making her wish she'd skipped the pinned bun and left it down. She fancied a brisk scrub of the skin he touched with a pumice. To rub him from existence. To run away. To be free.

"That a girl," he praised as her struggle waned.

She went limp in his hold. Defeated.

Law's smirk flashed in her mind. She remembered the instantaneous reaction his sudden appearance had coaxed. There had been no build up of fear, only response. Action. Which was exactly what she needed now.

Davis, if that's what his name really was, lowered her feet to the ground. Mags remained loose except for the iron-tight fist she held by her side. Her elbow throbbed from the impact, but she dismissed it.

His arm uncoiled from her middle, sliding too slowly over her stomach. When his fingers splayed wide and climbed the peak of her left breast, her stomach heaved.

"Oh, come on. I can make you like it."

Acid boarded the elevator of her esophagus and pressed the button for the penthouse. Mags swallowed against the onslaught, willing herself to fight. To be strong. But his hand traveled to the juncture of her thighs and she was helpless to stop her body's reaction. Bile burned a path of scorching fire up her airway.

Magdalena did the only thing that came to mind. She turned into the man and vomited.

He screamed like a bitch as her stomach's contents splashed onto his black shirt and cascaded down his pants. "Ah, bloody fuck."

His hands got busy holding the fabric away from his body. He hunched and arched his head toward the sky in an effort to get away from the smell. Mags spat the last of the garbage from her mouth, blinking through the moisture in her eyes. Her balled fist connected with his exposed neck and she powered into the punch as Baine had taught her, shifting all her weight into the target.

It worked.

The beast went down face first like gravity had suddenly tripled. One hand gripped the carpet and the other went to his throat. A soft wheeze escaped his lips.

Magdalena snatched her bag off the floor where it had fallen, but abandoned her shoes as she turned and ran. She slammed both hands against the red emergency bar, shoving through the exit. The siren's trill echoed with magnificent symphony in the metal column of stairs, piercing her inner ear. The volume didn't match the frantic pump of blood roaring in her head.

Her legs became rubbery, not so much running down the stairs as gliding over them in a slip-slop fashion. Her grip slid down the rail. Friction burned the tender skin of her palm, but she refused to slow her pace and couldn't let go. If she released the painted metal under her fingers, at this speed, she'd simply tumble to the bottom. At every landing she took two wide strides then slid more.

On the last flight Magdalena slowed slightly and chanced a look up. Davis didn't give chase. Her lungs ached from heaving breaths and the sting of bile lit her throat on fire. The temptation to walk weighted her limbs, but she didn't stop running. In fact, she steamed through the doorway and into the foyer, where she came face to face with a scrawnier version of the man four stories above.

They didn't look alike. Davis was bald. This chap had black stringy hair down to his chin. But they both had the same malicious scowl and dead eyes. Those eyes ballooned at her appearance.

Mags could have skidded to a stop and landed in his reach. Instead, she pushed harder and lowered her shoulder. Even though the bloke was smaller than Davis, her teeth rattled on impact. His arm came up fast and caught her in the mouth. Stunning dots and diamonds glittered behind her closed lids.

The blow couldn't stop momentum. Mags opened her eyes in time to watch the man land flat on his back several feet from where he'd stood. Her hands shot out to the glass bank of doors and she smashed into one on the hinge side. The wrong side. A *crack* resonated a moment before sharp pain radiated from her finger and cut its way up her arm. It stole the air from her lungs. Air she didn't have to spare.

"Bitch," the guy barked from behind.

Instantly the hurts vanished and her feet started moving. With one side step, Mags pushed through the door. Concrete scuffed her heels as she sprinted toward the streetlights. This time she chanced a look over her shoulder. As she distanced herself from the building, Greasy Hair rose from the floor. A spike of adrenaline carried her to the road.

The utterly desolate campus street provided no safe haven. Rows of lantern lights illuminated the nothingness and brought Mags acute understanding. *You're alone. Alone.* She'd been so afraid of being alone in the past, she crowded her bed with men to ward off loneliness. And finally, after more than a year of self-improvement, she no longer feared it.

Except, now, she did.

Chapter Nine

Magdalena's arms waved as wide as they could reach. The effort cost her and she ground her teeth against the pain in her hand, arm, and shoulder. She'd pay the price as long as the damn Taxi stopped. If the men caught her it would cost more than she was willing to imagine.

Brakes screeched as the black cab stopped a few feet from her bare, bloody toes. The driver opened his door. "Fuckin' Christ, lady. You trying to get killed?"

Mags hurried toward him. "Get in and drive," she demanded.

His youthful face wrinkled in rebuke. "Hey, I ain't on..." Thin lips gaped open. "Are you okay?"

"Please," she begged. Mags passed him and wrenched the door open. "Drive."

"Yeah," he breathed.

She fell into the back and the young man closed the door. He hopped in and shoved the car in gear like he was running from the men too. When he pounded the gas, her shoulder hit the seat and a groan filtered through her teeth.

"Sorry," he said with a shrug.

She watched out the back window, expecting the two to come barreling into the street at any moment, but they didn't. When they turned the corner and she could no longer see the low-lit alley of hell, she faced forward.

"I'm Martin."

"Thank you, Martin. You can call me Mags."

Magdalena let the cumbersome bag *plunk* to the leather seat, and then she reached her good hand into its depths. She chunked the file with her dissertation proposal to the floor and continued searching for her phone.

"So, are you okay? Want me to take you to the campus police or the real deal? The metro bobbies aren't far. Station house is five minutes."

"I'm sorry, Martin. Can you just drive for a minute?"

"Sure."

The phone came to life with a touch of a button, but she only stared at it. Dad wasn't home. He didn't have a cell and she didn't know Ruth's number. Baine wasn't home. She needed to get in touch with them before those guys did something to hurt the people she loved.

"Martin?"

"Yeah?" His gaze found her in the mirror and bounced between her and the road.

"I need to go to London. So, if you'll drop me where I can get another cab, I'd be grateful."

"I have friends, Mags. All it takes is a call and we'll take care of your problem. Free o' charge."

She smiled and blood seeped from her swollen lip. The top one, maybe. Hard to tell in the dark with no mirror. Lord, she probably looked like a mess. *Tough shit.*

"You're a wonderful guy, Martin. But I don't even know who they were or why they attacked me." And that troubled the hell out of her mushy brain.

"They?" His ruffly brows rose high. "Damn. And you got away? You're either really lucky or a badass."

"Lucky," she sighed. *Really unlucky. But really bloody lucky.*

"All right then. Sit back and relax. I'll take you."

"You're the best," she said with a sniffle.

"Ah," he said by way of a dismissal.

Magdalena set the phone in her lap, curled her sore feet on the bench beneath her, and held her hand protectively against her chest. The adrenaline ebbed and the questions revved along with a total body and mind ache. Two men attacked her. They had targeted her.

Why?

Chapter Ten

Law's ears pricked at the sound of crunching gravel. Had his head not been in a cabinet the night —morning—before, he'd have heard the taxi and seen Magdalena before he peeled her off the floor. Not that a stalling walk across the driveway could have prepared him any more for the sight of her. He swallowed, remembering her soft skin pressed against his chest and wrapped securely in his arms.

He stood from his prop on the counter and walked to the door. Through the panes he watched another cab roll to a stop between the two houses. As much as he'd hoped she wouldn't return, a shot of excitement plunged into his veins. When the blonde fluff of her hair rose from the depth of the car nothing could keep the words of praise and agony inside.

"Bloody hell."

She turned toward the house, and the exterior light he'd left on in case she came back caught the unmistakable smear of blood marring her creamy skin. "Bloody hell." The phrase took on a whole new meaning. Law was out the door and half way to Magdalena before she moved. When she took a step, she faltered and seized the open door in her grasp.

The cabbie called out, "Here, let me help."

"I've got her." Law stilled the kid's move to exit the car.

Magdalena's gaze found him and her lower lip quivered. She pressed her mouth into a thin line. A hard feat for such sultry lips. The shake stilled and her little shoulders squared.

"What happened to your face?" Law demanded.

In his periphery, the cabbie threw his hands up. "She was like that when I picked her up." His floppy hair shadowed his eyes as he shook his head. "I offered to go kick the shit out of whoever did it, but she fancied this place."

"Somebody did this to you?" His voice quieted, but held no less demand.

Her slender jaw rose and fell so slightly had he not been expecting it he'd have missed the confirmation. His fists clenched at his sides. "Who?"

"Inside, please?"

She looked dead on her feet. Much like she had the previous night. Only this time she damn well could have been killed, judging by the looks of it. Her left arm was tucked against her chest, and, sod it all, her naked feet were caked with crimson. Dirt ruined one leg of her pants and her shirt looked like he'd properly mussed it. But he hadn't.

With three steps he squared with the cabbie and offered his hand along with three hundred pounds' worth of banknotes. "Thank you for taking care of her."

"Ye...yeah, no problem," the kid stuttered. His dark brown eyes saucered at the number of queens in his hand and shuffled the currency into two stacks. "It's way too much."

"It's not enough," he countered.

The kid nodded.

"Here." Law held out his hand for Magdalena's bag and she released it from the hand that also clamped the car. "Are you hurt anywhere other than your face, hand, and feet?"

"My right shoulder is pretty tender," she whispered.

"Is that it?" he asked.

"My right elbow too," she added.

Law stepped around her and looped his left arm, bag in hand, around her back, careful not to brush her elbow, then curled his other arm behind her knees. "You can let go of the car. I've got you."

He expected a fight, but she didn't give him one. That told him how spent she was and boiled his blood into furious steam. For someone to steal her spunk, the vibrant personality that now haunted his days and nights, even for a minute, stirred something inside him so long dead it'd mummified, ground to dust, and set to the far reaches of the globe on a strong wind.

She released her hold and eased back into his arms, fitting like a missing puzzle piece. Cold fingers wrapped around his nape. Her wild tresses tickled his neck as she relaxed and curled into him.

"You're freezing," he whispered.

She nodded ever so gently.

His jaw clenched. The temperature rose to the high seventies in the afternoon and the air wasn't much cooler now. An ever-present blanket of clouds maintained the sticky heat. Sweat broke along his torso and it had nothing to do with the climate.

Whoever hurt her better hope her injuries were superficial. They better pray to every god ever worshiped by every culture past, present, and future that the muted fire in her green eyes roared to life faster than a pub crawler chuffed a smoke.

Or they'd walk with a permanent limp and only see out of one eye. They could have one. They'd need it to watch for his return, peer around corners, and sweat about the possibility for the rest of their days.

With a bowed head Law acknowledged the cabbie. The young man flicked a wave, started the car, and crunched gravel on his gentle departure.

Law strode through the open door, and then kicked it closed with his foot. At the archway, past the entrance, he turned. The light filtered through and he navigated the steps into the rich wooden den. Rounding the lush leather wing-backs, Law continued across to the matching sofa. He plopped her bag onto the wide coffee table sturdy enough to host a small pub band.

Kneeling, Law guided Magdalena to sit on the edge of the soft hide. He pulled the blanket from the high back and settled it carefully around her shoulders. The fireplace gaped like an empty mouth. A damn shame, since that thing could warm the frost off an eskimo. He reached past her and clicked on an ornate standing lamp.

Blood crusted above her red lips, which weren't adequately described as merely lips. They were soft pillows of silky skin crafted for kissing and spine-bending eroticism. Not hitting. Crimson spotted the alabaster of her chest and white of her blouse. Law's mind reeled at the possibilities of the trauma she'd faced. She didn't mention other injuries. Then again, if she'd been sexually assaulted she wouldn't share that information in front of a cabbie. He breathed past the sudden twist of his heart, and then winced at another realization. She probably didn't feel comfortable enough with him to share that sort of information. With the two-

and-a half-hour drive from Cardiff to London she'd likely spent more time with the carriage kid.

Rage stoked inside his chest. As incomprehensible as it seemed, he wanted her to trust him. Confide in him. He wanted to care for her. Avenge her. Even while another part of himself revolted, petitioning him to toss her into Baine's arms and run as far and as fast as he could.

"You should have told me you were in trouble last night. I'm not your family, but Baine is my adopted family and you're his. So, I'd say that makes us at least...I don't know what." He scraped a hand over his scalp and exhaled. "You can trust me, Magdalena. I'll never hurt you and I'll make damn certain no one else does, ever again."

A puddle of tears pooled beneath her green eyes and he'd swear someone kicked him in the nuts. One crystalline drop spilled over the lower lid, rolled down long lashes then tumbled onto her cheek. The sight laid him out. His hand moved to the freckled path spanning the bridge of her dainty nose and rounds of her cheeks. The sprinkled collection of miniature dots stood out only at close inspection. A shade darker than her porcelain skin, they could easily be missed, but the damn little circles bore holes deep in his heart and settled there. He brushed the wetness away with a knuckle, fearing if he started touching her he might never stop.

Her eyes closed at the brush of his finger and her lips parted. *Dear Lord.* He was in so much trouble. Lust roared to life, disorienting his anger and furthering the confusion in his consummately ordered mind.

"It's not that I don't trust you," she said. Her hand rose to cover the skin he'd grazed. "I don't know you, but I trust Baine completely and he trusts you." She pinned him with a sparkling gaze and he reveled in her restoring moxie. "My confidence is yours."

Her words stirred Law's cock to life and he cursed his body to the lava filled pits of hell. *She gives you her trust and this is how you repay the gift?*

Thankfully oblivious to his internal strife, she continued. "What happened last night was between me and my flatmate. I had no idea it could devolve into this." She gestured with her good hand at her face. "I don't even know if it did."

Her shoulders straightened and her chin shot up. "I need to get in touch with my father and Baine."

They were the better ones to deal with Magdalena. She'd surely be more comfortable with them, but the brush-off riled him. "I can reach your dad, but you're stuck with me until at least tomorrow. He went with Ruth to visit her sister in Aberdeen."

"How long are they gone?" she asked in a rush.

"A week, since Baine's away and I don't make that big of a mess."

She sighed. "Good."

"Excuse me? I thought you wanted them here, with you."

"No, I want them away from here and I really think you and I need to leave too. I mean, not together," she hurried to add.

"I think it's about time you tell me exactly what happened yesterday and today, then I need to take a look at your injuries."

"But I don't even know what's going on." Her jaw tightened as she ground out the last of her sentence.

"You may not understand everything, but you know what's happened to you. So start talking."

Chapter Eleven

Law's typical analytical skills, which made him impeccable at his job, deserted him like a clandestine informant when shit got heavy. Relief jumbled with fury as Magdalena recounted the events of the past two days. Emotions shouldn't come into play. But they flipped him the bird while they fucked with his head.

"Don't worry about Baine," he said. "He can handle himself. And I'll have this squared by the time your dad gets back."

Her thin brows rose. "Oh? I spent an afternoon searching for the guy's identity, if this mess is even tied to him, and didn't find a thing. What makes you so sure you can do better?"

"Determination."

"Oh?" Her voice rose as she dragged the word out several beats. A wrinkle formed between her brows and she sought to cut him with her gaze. "Don't insult me and then give me that deadly smile."

His lips stretched wider, a tiny bit of his ire ebbing. "Deadly, huh?"

"Shut up. I'm tenacious and have more invested in this than you do."

"Do you now?"

Her hair shook as she nodded.

"Well, we're not going anywhere tonight," he said. "And tomorrow, I'm going back to college for a while. Didn't much like it the first time, but this time I think I will."

"What are you going to do? You're a lawyer. Right?" Her head cocked to the side and her eyes widened in challenge. "Are you going to recite ASBO laws or threaten a lawsuit?"

"No lawsuits. I might explain the finer points of law while I beat the ability to harm you from his body. Their bodies," he amended. Her lips thinned and every hint of mocking fled her expression. Finally, it seemed she understood the seriousness of his conviction.

"I don't even know who they are or why they targeted me."

Law held his hand out to Magdalena. "Let's have it."

Her gaze flew to the hand he indicated, tucked loosely behind the knitted blanket. The angles of her face drew tight, but she didn't refuse or whine. She uncovered it and placed her small hand in his. Her palm flattened onto his, cooling his heat with her touch. Like the night before, the contact jolted him enough to lob his ass clear cross the room, and he forced himself to breathe through the charge.

At the knuckle of her ring finger, the delicate digit skewed the uniform lines of the rest. It hooked forty-five degrees left. Law positioned two fingers of his right hand on the underside of hers where a man would—were he lucky enough—place a wedding ring. She drew a breath between her lips. He kept his touch light and caressed his way over her smooth skin to the tip of her close cropped nail.

"It's not broken."

"Sure looks broken to me." Magdalena pursed her lips.

"I am truly astounded at your faith in me, tart."

She smiled at that, and the warmth it generated was strikingly similar to sun beamed on his face. A bit of the dread leaked out of his body and a hint of another smile curved his own lips.

"Tart?"

"Absolutely." *Bitter and sweet.*

When he didn't explain, she nodded. "Okay, if it's not broken why does it look like an L?"

"Dislocated."

"And that's so much better." Her blatant sarcasm stretched his face into a full-blown grin.

He set her hand on her knee and reached for her feet, but she scooted them away.

"They're just dirty. I can take care of them."

Lord save him from women. Especially this one. With practiced speed, he snatched both her heels in his palms. "I don't mind getting dirty."

Her sweet cheeks flushed bright pink and his flagging dick soared to life. *Brought that one on yourself, idiot.* Law bent low, strangling his cock to get a good look at Magdalena's scraped and bruised feet.

"Sit tight." For emphasis, he pinned her with a stern gaze.

When she gave a slight nod Law stood and turned away quickly to retrieve the necessary items to clean her up and hide his tented pants. After riffling through the kitchen he returned to find her still perched on the edge of the couch, her gaze following his every move. Law wasn't modest, but he should put on a damn shirt. Maybe then her intense study wouldn't raise goosebumps across his chest as though her soft fingers stroked his skin.

He'd been ready to fight with his mattress in hopes of eking out a couple decent hours sleep. A mission doomed to fail at the outset.

"You really don't have to—"

"Try all you like, but you won't stop me," he said, baiting her.

Her cheeks hollowed like she chewed the insides to keep from tearing into him. He winked to push her over the edge. Law wanted her attention on him and not the torment to come. Plus, he got hot when she cussed. Many women were so prim and proper they'd rather bite through their tongue than give a sharp piece of their mind. In the little bit he'd known Magdalena, she'd lashed him up one side, down the other, and made him angry he didn't have more sides to offer.

"How can someone be so nice and bloody infuriating at the same time?"

"I thought *you* could tell *me*."

"Humph." When he kneeled before her she clamped her mouth and eyes closed, but they flew open when he lifted her feet. Warm water and dissolved Epsom salt swirled around the roaster he positioned beneath two petite feet. As he lowered them, cute reddish-pink nails elongated, shrank, and then widened, distorting under the surface. When they settled on the bottom of the pan, his gaze migrated to hers. He read every emotion as it played across her beautiful features. Pain. Resolve. Acceptance. Relaxation. Pleasure. Each pummeled his flight instincts until they were in a pathetic heap.

Magdalena's shoulders relaxed, but the spark in her eyes remained bright. "My dad's going to skin you, cut you into bits, and cook you in this broiler for using it on my feet."

"Then it'll be our little secret." He winked.

"I'm not very good at keeping those." The fire in her returned to full fury. It glistened in the green and grey flecks of her eyes as they smiled.

"Well, I hope I taste good for you then."

Her blush did stupid things to his head. Both of them.

Escaping his gaze, she looked down at her feet for a moment before returning it. "What makes you the doctor in residence anyway?"

"I have a good bit of experience treating injuries."

One brow, the same color as the tawny grasses of the African savannah, rose. "All your work with MI6?"

Slick fox. Law reached for her hand with a wide smile. "All my siblings," he said easily. If he left her too much time to think, she'd piece things together like an old quilting maid. Slowly and steadily.

Without allowing her time to brace or himself time to think about hurting her, he held the base of her ring finger in his left hand. His right wrapped just below the skewed knuckle and pulled. He guided the bones in line with practiced efficiency. All the while his gaze remained riveted to Magdalena's.

Her silent tears slew him, and her strength and unflappable grace drew him deeper. "Can you bend it?"

She watched the elegant fingers stretch and retract several times before she smiled at him. "It's sore, but it doesn't hurt like fuc... It doesn't hurt like it did. You're amazing."

Law ignored her compliment, too caught up tracing the slopes and lines of her face. Both his hands rose to accompany his gaze. His palms cupped her chin while he padded his thumbs across her cheekbones and under her eyes. Her tears collected on them and he drew his right hand back. When he sucked the moisture from his thumb, tasting the salty evidence of her sadness, Magdalena's lips parted. Unable to stop himself, Law rubbed his left thumb over her bottom lip, careful not to bump the small cut on her upper one.

Magdalena's tongue nudged his pad and slicked it from base to tip. Thunder roared in his ears. Virile instincts joined in the chorus, demanding he capture her mouth and make it his own. Before the tiny part of himself still hidden in darkness had a chance to war against the notion, Law plunged his fingers into her soft locks, wrapping them around her nape, and coaxed her forward. He gave her every opportunity to bail, silently hoping she would and equally desperate for her surrender.

She gave herself to him, going lax in his hold. Her gaze flickered to his mouth before returning to his eyes in a half-lidded search of his own. He inhaled her sweat. The heady aroma made his body scream for sex. He tamped down the urge to take her. As he drew nearer a hint of flowers melded with her corporeal scent. Law inclined his head, maneuvering around the cutest pixie nose he'd ever seen, and ushered her the last breadth between them.

Her lips whispered on his, warm and heartbreakingly soft. They gave a hint of the pleasure to come, robbing him of the oxygen in his lungs. His chest constricted against the thrill raging through the roller coaster of his nervous system.

A crack of glass ended their contact. Law snapped his body around to confront the enemy.

Chapter Twelve

Magdalena had heard the expression "all hell breaking loose." She'd even used it before. Incorrectly. Because nothing in her past prepared her for the kind of hell that rained down on them. Without a moment to process the kiss—almost kiss —she'd just shared, a garden brick crashed through the den window. The high pitch of shattering glass accompanied the small shower of shards onto the dark wooden floor. Surprisingly, the rest of the massive pane didn't give way and allow the intruder entrance.

Law crouched in front of her like a prowling beast, then sprinted for the window. Every cord of sinewy muscle rippled with the effort, making a false fantasy come to life. But she couldn't really see every muscle, only the ones on the back of his arms, shoulders, and the dimples above his flannel pants. The center of his back, along his spine, stretching outward, was a palate of inked artwork. She caught a glimpse of a woman's hair flowing wildly across his shoulder blade, but he moved too quickly for her to discern anything else.

A tiny pang pricked her heart, knowing he had a woman's image tattooed on his body. *Must have been some love to carry her forever on his back.* Magdalena didn't have time to worry about inky art. A liquor bottle with a flaming tail sailed through the torso-sized hole in the glass while a crash echoed through kitchen. Stunned, unable to move, like she'd been in the corridor in the media building earlier, she watched the flames lick toward the lacquered floor.

Fear exploded in her chest as Law dove for the bottle. He slid amongst the piercing diamonds and caught the vessel in his outstretched arm. Before she could blink, he shot from the floor, leaped around the bulk of the glass, and landed a few feet from the window. He hurled the flaming liquor back through the hole. Outside the window, glass shattered. The night carried a mind-warping shriek through the billowing curtain that chilled her blood.

But she didn't have time to dwell on the damage the burning alcohol inflicted on the instigator outside. Davis, the man who'd attacked her earlier, rounded the archway at the kitchen. Magdalena's scream melded with the other shrill pitch.

"That's right, bitch. Scream. You're gonna scream until you can't scream any more, then when I'm done with you, Mike and Aaron are gonna have their turn," Davis said. Eyes wide, he looked hopped up on something and ready to carry out his mission.

Magdalena clamped down on her own dread as concern for herself morphed at lightning speed into terror for Law. She'd dragged him into this, whatever it was, and now he was going to pay the price.

As her gaze sought him, Law advanced from the window toward the center of the room. A grim scowl set his face as he turned toward the intruder. "Tonight you'll learn your place in this world," he said in a quiet, cold voice. "Mike or Aaron, whoever's on fire in the yard, already learned his. So, why don't you go ahead and call in your man left standing. You're going to need him."

Disbelief clogged Magdalena's throat, making it impossible for her to voice the thoughts in her head. They all jumbled there anyway, running into one another, wrestling for priority.

Davis stepped toward the edge of the stairs and his harsh gaze flew toward the broken window. In the distance, agonizing screams carried on the wind. When he turned back to Law, his fists curled into meaty balls. Law placed himself between her and the madman, giving her his back, but she couldn't be bothered with the chick embedded in his skin. All her attention riveted on the frames of the two men.

As size went, Davis had Law in bulk, with his boulder-like muscles bulging the fabric of his shirt. Yet, the way Law ran his mouth, he didn't seem to care. He stood tall, wide and muscled in his own right, but his hugged closer to his body. The way she'd seen him move, they seemed crafted for work, not show. Still, she didn't want to find out which of the two would come out on top.

She stood and water sloshed around her ankles. The rawness of her larynx stung, but she spoke through the pain. "Please, Davis, we can talk this out. I don't know what I did to wrong you, but I'm willing to make it right."

The bulky man's grimace eased and he nodded. "Talk? Sure we can."

The carved ridges in Law's shoulders grew impossibly deeper, but he didn't move. Didn't say a word. Magdalena hoped he'd stay silent. She could diffuse the situation, if he didn't get all macho on her.

"Thank you," she nodded. "Just don't hurt my friend. He has nothing to do with this."

Davis' forehead crinkled. "Looks pretty invested from where I'm standin'. Just come over here, so he doesn't get hurt."

Before she could raise a foot over the high metal edge, Law's voice scraped its way through the tension-thick air and into her ear. "Magdalena. Do. Not. Move." The simple demand given in such a brutal tone knocked her senses for a loop. Never one for orders, her body and mind bent to his will. Something in that grave timbre told her, of the two men about to bust heads, Law would come away the victor.

Make that three.

A bloke she'd never seen rounded the corner with a nasty growl. As wide as Davis' carriage was, this guy's nearly doubled his, but got cut short in the legs assembly. "She's fuckin' dead," he yelled. "You," he roared. His sausage-like finger stabbed the air between him and Law. "You killed Aaron. Burned my brother bloody alive." The guy's voice cracked with emotion and he screamed. "Both of you are corpses. Standing corpses."

Dread and anxiety grabbed Magdalena's intestines with both hands and played double-dutch. If she could move, she'd fall on the floor in a worthless heap. As luck would have it, she stood paralyzed.

Having digested the news, tears streaked Davis' stern face. He let loose a battle cry and ran for Law, as she'd done to the guy at the media building's entrance earlier. Presumably, that had been the dead guy, Aaron. His back hunched and his battering ram shoulder tucked forward.

Law stayed perfectly still until Davis got nearly atop him then he crouched low. His arms wrapped around Davis' shins and he stood, tossing the giant over his shoulder. Davis landed head first on the floor. The defending sound of cracking bone reverberated in the room. The man's body collapsed like jam onto the wood.

Magdalena's stomach vibrated and rocked. She heaved as the scene replayed itself over and again in her mind. Her hand slapped over her mouth, but there was nothing for her gut to expel. That didn't stop it from trying. She might have stayed there all night in a standing hunch if Mike didn't pull a big-ass blade from his back. Her stomach settled out of necessity, but her hand did not move. Instead it stifled her ghastly moan.

Law stood impassive at all the shit going on around them. His posture appeared as relaxed as if he were going to play a few rounds of tennis with a friend, but his gaze never veered from Mike as the man moved down the steps. Mike's gaze darted from Davis to her and back to Law in a whirly-bird of confusion.

Mike stepped in, raking the serrated metal across the air. Law pivoted, moving just out of reach of the deathblow, and countered with a fist to the bloke's fat face. The bulldog looking man stumbled a couple of steps, but shook off the hit with a roll of his shoulders. He circled Law right then left, but her champion outmaneuvered Mike, not allowing him past mid-point, closer to her.

She watched, the air choking in her lungs, as Mike sliced at Law's middle, missing by a few inches, then arching high to strike at his face. When she expected him to step back he moved in, plastering his body to Mike's. Law's left arm coiled around Mike's knife hand and clinched it under his arm. Mike slashed the knife wildly, catching Law's shoulder. Crimson pearled from his tanned skin and coursed down his tricep. Before the droplet of blood reached his elbow, a familiar crack of bone wrought the air and Mike hit the floor in a heap, the knife preceding his descent by a blink.

Law collapsed on his knees next to the body, his hand searching Mike's neck. "Dammit," he ground. His fists clenched and pressed against the ground on either side of his thighs.

Her broken sob turned his head and he pinned her with a gaze she couldn't interpret. His eyes pleaded. His jaw worked. "Magdalena," he said in a firm whisper.

Hand still over her mouth, she nodded.

"You're okay. Use my phone there on the coffee table and call the Met. Tell them there's been a break-in and that three men are dead."

As he talked, he searched Mike's pockets. She had no idea what he sought and didn't want to know. By the time she dragged her gaze away from him, he'd moved on to Davis' corpse. She'd seen dead bodies before, but she'd never seen someone's life leave their body.

Mags sat on the sofa in a semi-controlled collapse, buckling knees and gravity doing most of the work. When she reached for his phone her hand jittered like a druggie's on their second day of rehab. The device fell into her lap. Shaky as her hands were, she'd expected it to land on the floor. Magdalena balled her hands into fists to steady them before she pressed the screen to life.

Her fingers hung over the numbers, but Law stopped her. "Don't make that call. We have to go, now."

Chapter Thirteen

"What?" Magdalena's gaunt features turned ghostly white. "Why? We have to tell the police what happened. You killed…because of me…three men are dead."

Law stuffed the disturbing papers into his pocket and carried their wallets, keys, and phones over to Magdalena. He dumped the collection into her lap then hoisted her off the couch in the crook of his arms. "I know you don't get any of this. I'm still processing, and I am far more accustomed to this sort of thing than you." His gaze traveled to the corpses littering Baine's estate. "Just not this close to home." She dropped his phone into the pile and wrapped one arm around his neck. With the other she grabbed her big tote. "I need you to trust me. Trust me to keep you and everyone we love safe. And don't ever try and sacrifice yourself for me. Clear?"

"Clear," she rasped.

As he hurried through the house, much like they'd entered it, he asked. "Do you have clothes at your dad's?"

"Yes." Her mousey voice dragged him over hot coals, but he didn't have time to worry about her emotional state. Her physical well-being took precedence at the moment.

Law shoved his feet into his boots without socks and yanked his jacket off the hook. Magdalena's eyes zeroed in on his chest. The pink of her pretty mouth formed an O.

"Your cuts! Am I hurting you?"

"All superficial. Quit worrying about me, Magdalena."

He strode through the back door. Since the frame lay in splintered pieces on the ground he didn't worry about closing it. He carried her into her dad's house, which boasted a matching frame, and up the stairs into the bedroom she'd occupied as a little girl. While completing the plumbing job he'd passed it several times, but refused to enter, hoping if he didn't he'd rid himself of her haunting presence more quickly.

He sat her on the bed and scooped the heap in her lap into the green bag. Then he shrugged on his leather jacket and zipped the front. "I need you to pack a bag with enough clothes to last you a few days, but small enough to carry on your back. Can you walk enough to do that?"

"Yeah, I think so," she whispered. Her eyes saucered, but her pupils weren't dilated.

"Socks?" He turned toward a short bureau.

"Top left."

Law grabbed a pair of socks and eased them onto her feet. "You have three minutes." He turned toward the door.

"Where are you going?" The desperation in her voice kicked him in the solar plexus.

"I have to see about the other body." He kept walking, unwilling to look upon the disgust certainly marring her sweet face.

Following the scent of foul barbecue, Law found the third chump in the bushes by the sitting bench of the side yard. The charred lower half of the body told Law he didn't burn to death, but died of smoke inhalation. The bloke hadn't planned on the firebomb he'd thrown into the house changing direction and coming for him. With exercised caution, he extricated the guy's phone and wallet from his pockets, but found no keys.

When he returned to collect Magdalena, she walked toward the front door on her socked feet, shuffling from side to side in a slow but steady pace. The black slacks she wore scraped the floor and the tattered blouse billowed around her middle. A book-bag strap hung over her right shoulder, further impairing her stability.

"Why didn't you wait for me?"

"Because I couldn't sit and think. I needed to move." She swatted a wayward group of strands from her brow.

"I get it." He closed the gap between them and lifted the bag from her shoulder. "Do you need your green bag?"

"No, I consolidated. The phones and *other* things are in the small outside zipper, and here's your phone."

"Perfect," he breathed. She laid the phone in his hand and her fingertips grazed his callused hand. A lump knotted his throat. She was perfect, for him. And she was everything he'd given a wide berth over the last seven, or was it eight, years now.

Law slung the satchel onto his back and bent to scoop Magdalena into his arms.

"I was making it on my own, you know?"

"A damn fine effort, but the rocks are sharp and we've gotta go."

"What's the big hurry? What did you find that changed your mind so suddenly?"

He ignored the question and walked to the garage entrance, punched in the code, maneuvered them through the door, and locked it. He elbowed the lights and hurried through the open bay to his one and only lady, a black and chrome Harley Davidson Springer Classic.

"I'm not riding that thing," Magdalena said with a vehement shake of her head, her mussed strands wagging at him for emphasis.

"Yes. You are," Law countered. He sharpened his point by setting her lush ass sidesaddle on the small rear seat.

Her hands sank into the leather of his jacket, holding him close. "I've never ridden one of these things."

Prying her fingers from his collar and sleeve he liberated the riding jacket from her grip. "She's not a thing. She's a Hog, and," he added before turning away, "I'm happy to be your first."

That shut her up and rosed her cheeks to a high blush. While she stewed he hurried across to the safe tucked behind an old sheet of plywood and confiscated his holstered Sig Sauers. The cherry wood grips peeked from beneath the leather and blew him a kiss. He stripped the jacket and struggled on the guns. His cuts ran the lines of superficial wounds, but they sure stung like a bitch.

Magdalena's gasp echoed in the hollow concrete and brick interior, but he ignored her for the moment. An achievement deserving of a medal. He slipped into the coat, zipped, pulled out four loaded magazines, and secured the safe.

She studied him with her green gaze as he walked toward the bike. She'd kicked a leg over the side of the bike, and, aside from her missing footwear and shell-shocked expression, she hugged it between her thighs like a natural. He couldn't help but appreciate how the rounds of her bottom kissed the black leather. Good Lord, the things he could do with an ass like that.

"Who are you?"

While he loaded the saddlebags with her belongings and two of the magazines, he tried to ease her mind, as much as he could. "Lawrence Pierce, tart. I know you have a million questions rattling around that head of yours and I'll do my best to answer the ones I can, but not here, not now. Okay?"

Magdalena sucked in a ragged breath and exhaled it slowly on a nod. "Okay, for now." He handed her an extra helmet and she balked like he'd handed her a rat. "I'm not wearing that thing. It'll suffocate me. Look, it doesn't even have breathing holes." She gestured to the blacked-out full face shield.

"There's plenty of ventilation. Plus, it will hide your face from whoever's looking and protect your head, in case."

"In case, what?"

"A life and death situation and you're going to argue over a helmet? Put it on your pretty head, Magdalena. Now."

Law woke his phone's sleeping screen and squinted at the time. It'd run past the five minute allotment he'd given them to get the hell out of there, but he had one more thing to do before they could leave. Indecision never addled his brain before, but as he grew to expect, nothing was normal where Magdalena was involved. Not one damn thing. More reluctant to leave her alone than for hcr to hcar the call he needed to make, he chunked caution into the can, turned his back to Magdalena, and dialed.

"Juliet. Uniform. Sierra. Tango. India. Charlie. Echo. One. Nine. Four. Five."

After a series of beeps an operator answered. "Voice confirmation complete. Agent Pierce, how may I direct your call?"

"K. Slaughter."

"Bored already? I told you I didn't want to see your ugly mug or hear from you for three weeks."

"I'd tell you how much you miss me, but I don't have the time."

"What's wrong?"

"I need clean up at Baine's."

"Christ, have you been compromised?" Her words were all business, but her voice squeaked a little at the end.

Law pictured his boss and dear friend as she likely sat now, behind the desk she'd worked so hard for and often resented for keeping her out of the action. Her fist probably threatened to snap the pen in her hand. Grey eyes clouded, ready to strike a man down with a blink. Few could overlook her damn crazy orange-red painted lips pinched in a grimace sharp enough to make some fellows run for the hills and seductive enough to make others kneel at her feet.

"Negative. It's family trouble." As soon as the words left his mouth he knew he should've said it differently.

"Oh, my God. Lill and Love," Khani gasped.

"No, Baine's family, not mine," he said.

"I hate to sound callous, but thank fuck. I couldn't handle anything happening to them. Now, tell me what in bloody hell is going on," she demanded.

"I'll message you details and some names I need you to run in twenty. Just get the maids pronto," he begged.

Khani growled into the line. "Fine. Anything you need, let me know. It's yours. On or off the books."

"Thanks," he said before ending the call.

Law turned to Magdalena, and, ignoring her hanging jaw, kicked a leg over his Hog. He guided the stand up with his boot then slid the key from the pocket where he'd stowed his phone and shoved it into the ignition. One of Magdalena's hands grabbed the hem of his jacket hesitantly, like the thought of touching him after seeing his dark side revolted her. And though it was all for the best, it raised his hackles.

He reached both his hands behind his back and found her thighs. His hands smoothed down her legs. At the crook of her knee Law tightened his grip and yanked her toward him. Lust punched through his cock as open legs engulfed his butt in supple warmth. He hunted her wrists then pulled her chest against his back, wrapping her arms around him. Careful not to jar her, he let his hands glide over the backs of hers. Desire stirred him this way and that. Wanting to protect her. Wanting to be rid of her. Wanting her.

Magdalena's chest expanded and narrowed against his back in easy succession for a moment before she rested her head on his shoulder blade. Her voice came in a whisper. "I was right."

Law started the engine, raised the garage door, and set them off through the uncertain night.

Chapter Fourteen

Magdalena followed James Bond up a second flight of stairs. She'd insisted on walking, which made the muscles in Law's jaw frantic, but he'd obliged. More importantly, he carried her bag and kept an easy pace as she lugged her dashed body. If he rounded to the next set of stairs she'd need a break before she went farther. Every cell in her body quivered from shock and exhaustion. When he headed for the never-ending succession of steps she focused on conquering one at a time.

Thankfully he turned onto a well-lit corridor and unlocked the first door he came to. Law flipped on a light and a one-room flat spread out before them, its interior nearly vacant except for a mattress on the floor between two windows and stacks of books lining either side of the makeshift bed. To the right, an open kitchen protruded. A small refrigerator, oven range, and counters clung to the wall. Across from it, counters mirrored the others, but where a range would sit, a sink took its place. Beyond the kitchen, in the far opposite corner, a partition wall gave little privacy to the shower, sink, and vanity. It did a good job of hiding the toilet, if the place had one.

Magdalena shoved that thought into the dark corner. With her awkward shuffle she headed straight for the bed. She didn't care whose it was.

So long as mice or cockroaches didn't try to snuggle she'd be fine. Justice-1943, Law, or whoever the hell he was, moved to the windows. He peered out while she collapsed onto the surprisingly soft duvet. Every muscle in her body melted from her bones as finally the last drop of adrenaline leaked from her system. If bad guys stormed the tower, they could take her. Right now she wasn't worth killing.

But then she wouldn't have to move, would she? Law, her self-appointed guardian, crossed the room to a small closet. He hung her bright pink bag on the door hook and rummaged in the outside pocket. At the tile countertop he spread wallets and phones across the space, studying each in turn.

Fingers as deft as a teenage girl's flew across the keyboard of his phone as he, and she guessed here, sent the information he'd promised to K. Slaughter. When she'd heard the term, at first she thought it was more code speak. After eavesdropping on the one-sided conversation, she supposed it was his superior, but she couldn't be sure. Not about anything.

Magdalena's ordered world had shifted a bit during her internship. Her eyes were opened to the wonders and horrors of humanity. The shift gave her a sense of purpose. It quieted the static in her head that had played in the background since her mother's death. The events of the past two days flipped her shit completely upside down. Unwilling to lift her head, she raised her swollen knuckle into view. Purple tinted the fair skin already. But her hands hurt more from holding tight to the fabric of her toppled world than it did from the rude meeting with the glass door.

"Laird."

Magdalena's skin seemed to leap off her body for an instant then snap back into place. *Law's voice. Nothing to worry about.* She reassured herself. *But who's he talking to?* She raised her head and scanned the room. Aside from Law, who spoke into his phone, the room remained empty. Gravity gathered her back to the mattress.

"Yeah, I'm still here," Law said. "There's been a threat. I need you to coral Pops and Poppy for a couple days, Lill and the kids too, and warn the others to be alert."

Suddenly her exhaustion vanished. She bolted upright and her gaze tangled with Law's.

He watched her. Consumed her with his eyes. "I should have it squared in a day or two. I'll let you know." He disconnected the call.

"I've waited, very patiently, but I need to know what's going on. Who were you talking to?" Her plea echoed in the room.

Law walked around the counter. The black leather hugged his body like an expensive glove. He should've looked ridiculous in lounge pants, thick boots, and a riding jacket. But the mixture of textures had her fingers itching to feel them again. His shoes stopped only a foot away from her clasped hands, draped over her knee. She could touch them, if she'd only reach out.

Magdalena craned her neck to maintain eye contact. The usual disparagement in their height brought her gaze to his pecs. Should she look now she'd get a full view of the heavy package he toted at the juncture of his thighs. The inequity in their stratum could have bathed her in feelings of inferiority. But lust flashed over Law's schooled features, sending a heady sense of power coursing in her veins.

One of his hands gripped his phone and the other took the familiar detour over his close-cropped hair. "The bloke you called Davis had this in his back pocket."

She accepted the piece of paper Law retrieved from his own pocket and unfolded the banal white sheet. Her breath caught as she read the list of names and addresses. The first three she knew. Her name and address at Cardiff. Her father's name with Baine's address and a note, indicating he lived in the guesthouse. Baine's name and address and a note, demanding they discern his relationship to her.

Mags placed her hand on her stomach in an effort to settle her rattling nerves. Of the last five on the list she only recognized one thing they all had in common. The last name. Pierce.

"Oh no," she gasped. Her hand shot up to her mouth as her stomach threatened another revolt.

Law plucked her from the bed and hurried to the water closet. As they turned the corner, the white toilet gleamed in the bulb light like the greatest gift she'd ever received. Her feet met the ground, but Law braced her back with one arm and collected her hair with the other. The lid and seat leaned against the high tank attached to the wall. Mags gripped the open lid and waited for the retched churning in her gut to expel itself from her body. Maybe then she could breathe without the weight of a Red Bus parked on her ribs.

She waited, but the release never came. Neither did relief. The water in the bowl rippled once, twice, three and four times as tears fell from her eyes. A sob broke through her lips and there was nothing she could do except hold on until her body finished with her. Law turned her into him, tucking her face in the lee of his chin and encircling her quaking body in his arms.

He slid down the wall, settling them on the floor. His torso rocked slowly side to side as he held her close, comforting her like one would a child. After a while Magdalena's sobs receded to hiccupped breaths then finally quieted. The thump of his heartbeat resonated in her ear, lulling the last of her pent anxiety.

She swallowed and cleared her throat to speak. "I don't want anyone else hurt because of me. Not your family. Not mine. I don't know how I'd —"

The pad of Law's thumb pressed onto her lips, but fell away too soon. "Enough of that. You're not responsible for the actions of crazy people. You've done nothing wrong and even if you did, you wouldn't deserve what those three had in mind."

Mags snuggled closer to the rumble of his chest as he continued. "Your father and Ruth are guarded. Baine is in no danger. And my family can take care of themselves."

When he spoke of his family, pride deepened his voice, and it brought the first hint of a smile to her lips in far too long. "Your brother, Laird? Is he... does he do what you do?"

He huffed, but it held no anger. Only a little irritation. "Laird is in the Royal Marines. Larkin the Royal Army. Lovella is a detective. But even Luca and Lilliana, our not-so-starving artists, can hold their own against any of us."

"Does your dad run a military training academy or something?"

Law's chest shook with laughter. "Or something."

When he didn't expound she poked him in the ribs. "That's it? That's all you're gonna say?"

"You really want to know?"

"Yes," she answered emphatically. Law intrigued her, as did his massive family, but more than that, if he talked about this she wouldn't think about all the other stuff.

He nodded. "Okay. My grandfather was a diplomat and Pop grew up in the states. He trained with Royce Gracie. Learned Brazilian Jiu Jitsu. And he started teaching all of us before we could hardly walk."

"Who's Royce Gracie?"

"You're killing me, Magdalena," he said with an exaggerated shake of his head. "Only one of the best martial artists *of all time.*"

She actually giggled at his mock exacerbation. "You have a big family."

"Yeah, big and loud, and growing by the years. Lilliana, my older sister, married four years ago and has two kids with another on the way. Then there's Khani and Zeke Slaughter who my mom practically adopted when we were all kids."

Law tilted his head to meet her gaze and again his virile beauty struck her silly. His eyes still glimmered from laughter and a relaxed smile curved his lips. "You know a little about me. Now it's time for you to share a little more about you."

His tone implied, *Why don't you tell me how you got yourself into this mess in the first place?*

She shrugged, not knowing the correct response.

"Not going to cut it. Start at the beginning again. We need to see if we missed anything."

Mags opened her mouth to protest, but a vibration against her hip stopped the words on her lips. She levered back, allowing him to retrieve the device, and awed at their closeness. It seemed so comfortable only seconds ago. But his hand grazed her hip and suddenly the currents shifted. The strength of its pull, his pull, flushed her body with heat that gathered in a pit of molten desire between her legs and frightened her to the edge of his lap.

When she teetered, his thick forearm steadied her. Some of the impact of his affect ebbed as his gaze left her to check the screen of his phone. A tiny fraction of the overwhelming urge to wrap her legs around his hips and never let go fell away, allowing her breaths to flow more evenly and her brain to shift out of *fuck him* gear.

"Hey, Poppy, I can't really talk right now," he answered.

She wondered if Poppy was another in his long list of siblings, or a cousin perhaps. Law's furrowed brow told her he didn't like what he heard from the other side of the phone.

"He'll take care of it. He's not a kid anymore. Trust him to do what's right. I have to go." After a pause he said, "I love you too, Mum."

Law set the cell on the floor beside his leg and met Magdalena's gaze. Her anger must have shown on her face loud and clear because he recoiled. A shrug came next. "What?" he asked incredulously. "I'm a little busy."

"Not too busy to talk for five minutes," she retorted.

His lower lip tucked into his mouth then he dragged it through his teeth, considering her. "You're just trying to avoid my questions."

"No," she said in a whisper. "I'd give anything to talk to my mother just once more. You have yours. Don't waste the time."

"That's a balls-hard blow, if I've ever taken one." Law shook his head, but grabbed his phone.

Mags seized the opportunity for some space. "While you talk to your mum, I'd like to get cleaned up. If that's all right?"

The point of his knuckle smoothed the skin just above her cut lip. "Sure. Towels are under the sink."

When she stood and headed for the main room, his hand curled over her shoulder, and it took every bit of strength she had not to arch into his touch.

"I'll fetch your bag," he said.

His fingers remained, soaking through the thin fabric of her blouse for a moment longer then his sturdy boots thudded across the floor. Magdalena's cheeks puffed as she billowed a huff. This was no time to fall into bed with a man. But old habits apparently lived long and died hard.

Law returned with the phone to his ear, nodding as he listened. His left lid closed over his wicked green eye in the signature wink that acted like a welder's torch to her resolve. He turned away and Magdalena's gaze zeroed in on his nape. She never found the area erotic. Until now. The curve of his skull sloped down and tapered slightly. Tan skin shown through the base of his prickly hair and four distinct grooves grew from his hairline. They defined two cords of grainy muscles that disappeared behind his short collar, connecting with the framework of brawn she'd seen earlier.

Damn.

Mags stepped up to the mirror and immediately regretted the action. Her hair could house a family of raccoons with all its knots and fly-aways. Judging by the black smears around her eyes, she could join them. A red nose and flushed cheeks from crying, or embarrassment at her appearance, accentuated the blood red of her crusty upper lip. A lip that had nearly, or just barely, touched Law's.

She started pulling pins from her fallen hair and set out to shower and make something presentable of herself. It took some scrubbing, some huddling in the corner to keep from flashing her generous ass, and some careful combing to straighten her hair without hurting her arm. But she rounded the partition about an hour later with a slow, confident gait. As assured as she could strive for in an unfamiliar place, wearing a cotton tank and shorts, wondering who in the world was after her, why, and who in the world her brother's housemate actually worked for and if Baine was part of it too.

Magdalena's head pounded from ramming into too many dead ends. Law didn't look like he fared any better. His playful demeanor from earlier had vanished. In its place his expression bordered on harsh. The set of his jaw froze in flex. His gaze followed her, but never softened as she neared the bed. She sat her bag on the wooden floor at the end of the mattress and took another step, bringing her even with Law where he stood rigidly on the other side of the pallet.

"How's your mum? Scared, I'm sure."

"Nah, she's pissed. Laird won't let her go on her girls' weekend to Hugh Town."

"I'd boil too. It's beautiful there. The ocean outside your window and the sand only a stroll away. I hate she can't go because of me."

"They'll reschedule," he said flatly. His gaze dropped to the bed then rose to her. "I'd offer to sleep on the floor, but I'm not that chivalrous. I need some sleep or I won't be good for anything tomorrow."

Her fingers knotted behind her back, but she bobbed her head. "It's fine by me."

"Yeah," he growled. "Just stay on your side."

Magdalena threw her hands up. "I'm not some perv who's going to try and cop a feel while you're dozing."

"It's not you I'm worried about," he said.

The wide and wild range of her emotions over the past few hours looped her in a fair ground ride of uncertainty. Her right toe pivoted on the scuffed wood planks like it was trying to tunnel her way out of this awkward situation. "You no longer fancy an interrogation?"

"That's not what I fancy at the moment," he ground between closed teeth. He breathed and his mouth loosened slightly. "Just go to sleep. So I can."

Magdalena flung herself onto the mattress like a cranky child, yanked at the covering, and curled into a ball beneath them, facing the wall. After a minute of struggling to convince her tears to evaporate, Law's zipper moaned open. The sound of metal against metal perked her ears as he did something with those bloody guns that made her palms sweat. The room plunged into darkness. When the mattress sagged under his weight, her upper lip joined in the sweat fest.

How in the hell am I supposed to sleep?

Before long the tension seeped from her muscles and she stretched into her sleep pose. One arm straightened beneath the pillow. The other balled and tucked in the valley of her breasts. One leg elongated as long as the stubby thing would go toward the end of the bed while the other flamingoed out, snuggling the bed with her hips. Her eyes roved the stacks of books visible in the moonlight. And sleep came.

Chapter Fifteen

Law one-armed the paper bag of groceries he'd amassed at the corner shop on the end of the street and opened the white door to his building. Showered and in real clothes after the best sleep he'd gotten in years, his outlook on life should've been rockets and race cars, but guilt shadowboxed his heart. And that pissed him off. He had no cause for angst. His hands had stayed folded over his chest like a good boy.

The keys jangled as he slipped them from his jeans and inserted the correct one into the lock. Millimeter by millimeter he turned the mechanism to keep the *smack* out of the retracting bolt quiet. When he'd left, Magdalena had been sleeping like a dead bird stuck to the front of someone's windshield. Her arms and legs spread out to all corners of the mattress. Just thinking about it brought the smile back to his lips.

He eased the door open and stopped dead in the entrance. Magdalena curled on the floor in an inside out ball. Her belly button winked at the ceiling while her legs and arms tucked beneath her back, touching each other in a straining angle. This left her full breasts pointing toward the closet and threatening to fall out of her skimpy tank onto her neck. His lips both tucked into his mouth and he bit down to keep from laughing or running over to suckle the two erect nipples poking the fabric of her shirt.

"What are you doing?" he asked after collecting his wits.

Her head snapped to the door and he feared it might fall over at that angle. She wiggled her feet from where they rested under her long blonde hair. Her arms moved from compressed V's to L's and she kicked off the ground, raising her ass and legs into the air. Magdalena held the pose while he picked his jaw off the floor, closed the door, and set the groceries on the counter. Then she folded over onto her toes and stood.

Sweat beaded on her forehead. Her face and bountiful chest flushed from exertion, but her breath came slow and steady. Palms together and fingers toward the sky, she bowed her head. Her loose hair framed her face as she turned and flashed him a radiant smile.

"Trying to keep fit," she said in answer.

"I know a better way," he blurted. *Dumb ass.*

Magdalena's brow quirked and she investigated him. Her eyes searched his face then traveled down his body, which responded to her attention. A wave of heat rolled over his skin and it had nothing to do with the rising temperatures on the London sidewalks. It had everything to do with the pursed lips and scorching stare across the room.

She winked at him, thieving his signature move. "All right." She walked to him, her gate even and the swing of her hips determined.

Every nerve in his body screamed for him to take her. To grab two handfuls of her full ass and hoist her onto his erect penis. To coil a hand in her hair, holding her just where he needed her, while he pumped into her slick pussy. To drive her over the top until she screamed his name and moaned her pleasure. Until his own climax dragged him to the ground with sweet repletion.

Law shoved his fists into his pockets as she stopped a mere foot away. Her scent crowded his air, spurring his hard-on to unseen heights. The damn thing nearly peeked out the waist of his jeans, challenging her to a winking contest. When was he going to learn to keep his trap shut around Magdalena Wells. She didn't frighten like he'd expected her to. Sure, last night she'd been scared when things got buggered up, but that was understandable. Unlike with other women, his full-on cocky self-preservation techniques had the opposite of their intended effect.

On bare feet she kicked a hip to the side and sized him up. "All bluster, that one," she said with a pointed finger and an incline of her head. She made a little sound with her mouth and turned away.

He caught her by the arm like he'd done in the loo the night before, only this time his hold had teeth. She stopped with a jerk, but she didn't turn.

"I'm sorry. I...I can't." His words sounded hollow. Because they were a lie. He could. He was just the biggest kind of coward. One who judged other people, his best friend, when he couldn't turn the light on himself out of fear. Fear of what he might see. Of what he might lose, if he started living again.

"Just stop sending me mixed signals," she breathed. "You're making me dizzy."

Magdalena took a step, but his grip held, not ready to let her go. She executed a nice finger bend, except it hurt like a bitch, and walked out of his hold. He rubbed his hyper-extended knuckle, pissed at his inability to let go of her and his past. Law rubbed the ache in his empty chest and watched Magdalena's hourglass figure disappear around the partition.

She called out, "Do you have bread in that bag?"

His brows rose, surprised at her quick rebound. *She must not be that hard-up for you, old man.* As real age went, he was only a few years older than her, but as life experiences played into the equation, he was eons older. He couldn't drag her into his shit.

"Yeah," he answered.

"Good. I'm starving. I might save you some, if you're lucky."

"Oh, I thought you were trying to stay fit."

"You know," she yelled above the spray of the shower. "Someone really needs to kick your ass. I'm gonna start training. So look out, buster."

He laughed despite himself and started unloading the goods from the corner. Bacon sizzled in the pan and he rinsed the knife he'd sliced tomato with when Magdalena came around the corner in a blasted towel. Water droplets peppered her shoulders. Her hair sat high atop her head in a messy knot with the errant strand stuck to her wet skin. Law dropped the knife into the sink so he wouldn't chop a finger off.

The minx smiled brightly, sauntering across the room toward the pallet. "Smells like a proper fry-up to me. Don't start without me." She plucked her bag up from the ground and headed back the way she'd come.

The hand-sized swath of black against her pearly skin drew his attention then tossed it for a good loop. "Come here, Magdalena."

Her arms stopped swinging and she turned a scowl on him. "I thought we just smoothed this bumpy road. So, don't go fuckin' it up again. A girl can only take so much."

"This isn't about that," he said, gripping the counter for patience.

"Oh." The scowl melted away and something akin to a frown took its place. "What is it then?"

"Just. Come. Here." When she checked a brow he added, "Please."

She came hesitantly this time. Gun-shy from their last encounter.

"Turn around," he ordered with a jerk of his head.

"Look," she said, smacking both hands to her hips. "I know you saved me, and you're Baine's friend, and you made me lunch yesterday and breakfast now, but if you don't quit ordering me around—"

"I need to see your tattoo," he hollered. Law's mouth fell open in surprise. He'd never yelled at a woman. Ever. But blast it all to Scotland and back, she rankled his last nerve. Law sought his voice to apologize when she put a hand up.

Magdalena's hands levered across the bar from him. Her voice came in a growled whisper. "Say please."

Law exhaled a faint, "Please."

She nodded her approval. "Thank you. I think we need to work on our basic manners before we kill one another."

His head bowed in agreement.

Magdalena turned and suddenly everything, well a whole crap load, came into focus. Africa, in all her rigid beauty, stained the milky skin, starting five inches below her sandy hairline and spreading his palm's width centering her spine. It ran down to the middle of her shoulder blades. The continent wasn't a defined line. Art imitating life for certain.

Instead, rows of words filled its body, stopping where the edge of the land would on a map. He spoke French and Arabic and had spent enough time in Africa that he could read some Swahili, Shona, and Igbo. The words he recognized reinforced his thought that they'd jumped to the wrong conclusion about the threat.

Develop. Accountable. Government. People raise your voice. Peace. Be still. Clarity. Transparency. Let the world hear and know your pain.

"When did you get it?"

"Nearly seven months ago."

"Where?"

"Nairobi."

"What the hell were you doing in Africa?"

Magdalena wheeled on him. Her arms folded across her middle and her eyes narrowed to slits. Somehow she made a terry cloth look haughty and too damn sexy for either of their benefit.

"Bloody hell. If you keep speaking to me like I'm an incompetent twit, you're going to find an early grave. Ugh!" She smacked at an errant hair tickling her nose then continued. "Yes, I'm still in school, but it's to finish my *doctorate*. I'm a journalist and a fucking good one at that."

Why couldn't they have a blasted exchange without somebody yelling or snapping their teeth like rabid dogs? Irritation pricked his nape. His blood pressure knocked on the top of his skull. To keep from losing his mind in the impending explosion, Law went palms-up in surrender.

"I didn't imply you were incapable, you jumped to that on your own." He continued speaking before the breath she'd sucked formed another lecture. "All I meant is Africa is no place for an Englishwoman." He waved his hands to stave off her attack. "I've had too much experience there. Witnessed corruption at its worst. Seen more death than anyone should. And things worse than death."

Law stepped around the counter and grabbed Magdalena's hand. "I've seen the fallout of teenage boys with assault rifles and free reign. When I think of you there, my mind does crazy things."

Her lips thinned. Light brown eyelashes fluttered over her cheek as she thought or remembered. He didn't know which. Then she caught him in the sea of her gaze. "I've seen some of the same, but I've also seen hope and happiness that shouldn't exist in the horror. And I can't overlook the miracle of humanity. Yes, it's dark. It's also light and love.

"I went as a journalist for the UN with the MONUSCO mission to the Democratic Republic of the Congo."

"Jesus, Magdalena. And your father let you go? *Baine* let you go?"

She smiled. "You don't know me very well, but I do what I want. And I needed this trip to get myself in order."

"Yeah, at what cost? Your life?"

Her softly sloping shoulders raised then slowly fell. The solemnity in her eyes twisted his middle. "I wasn't living before Africa. Just slowly killing myself. So, for me it was worth the danger."

Law stepped away, dropping her hand. He turned into the room, pacing, as he processed the unsettling information. Not the least of which was knowing she'd been hurting and needed a brush with death to help her put things in perspective. He rubbed the knot at his pec, damn near his heart.

"You said you got the ink in Kenya. But I thought you were stationed in the DRC?"

"We were pulled out of Goma when things got tense. They talked about sending nonessential personnel out for good, but the Congolese revolutionaries announced a ceasefire and resumed peace talks with the government."

As she spoke his fists clenched. She hadn't just been in DRC. She'd been at the epicenter of the United Nation and Congolese Armies' efforts to hold out the M23 militia.

"Tell me more about your responsibilities," he said, still pacing.

"What does Africa have to do with any of this?"

"That is what I'm trying to figure out. The chavs last night were knuckle-dragging gym rats, but the information they had was more sophisticated. More seasoned than common domestic issues."

"It didn't seem common to me," she said. "The threats that weasel made before he knew I was there seemed more involved than a relationship gone bad."

Law planted his face in his hand. "Please, just humor me."

Refusing to deny her gut instinct, she pressed. "But that bastard threatened me. He told me he knew people who would give me mine for sticking my nose where it didn't belong."

"Stubborn woman," he huffed.

"How about you get breakfast before it burns, and I go put on some clothes and tell you what you want to know over food?"

Law's gaze shot to the narrow cook top and pan of ultra crisp pork. "Damn." He lunged for a fork to rescue the strips from oblivion. "Fine, but don't take an hour changing. Everything is ready."

She laughed. "Yeah. Well-done."

Chapter Sixteen

Breakfast had never tasted so good. Even with Law's narrowed glare her enthusiasm refused to curb. She pinched a slice of bacon between her thumb and forefinger, swirled it in the yellow soup of her fried egg then shoved half the length into her mouth. When she bit down, the salty meat, oil, and yolk blended on her tongue. Her head arched to the ceiling as she inhaled deeply, savoring the rich taste.

She swallowed on a moan and grabbed the last triangle of toast. Breakfast in the Congo had been a scrimp meal of fufu, rice, or the occasional MRE. None of which satisfied the glut of a full British fry-up. Magdalena scooted a slice of tomato and piece of mushroom onto the bread and carried it to her mouth. After two more massive bites she could fit no more into her stuffed tummy.

The stool back squeaked as she leaned into it and stretched. A yawn sang from her gaping mouth. When it was over, bone deep satisfaction snuggled her close. She'd done her best to ignore Law throughout the meal, answering his questions, but avoiding his pissy expression.

But the daft urge to peruse his gorgeous features won out and she scowled back at him, cataloging his sharp nose, wide jaw, and ample lips. "What?"

He sat like a tightly screwed bottle of shaken champagne, waiting to rupture. His head shook side to side and his lips remained clamped in a thin line.

Magdalena huffed. "I don't know what more you want me to say. Two of us traveled with the convoy from Goma to Rutshuru and back, interviewing people as we were allowed, taking photos. Then they left us at the office, with guards and other aid workers, to craft our stories. We were never without protection."

Law's biceps bulged from the sleeves of his blue T-shirt, made tighter by the way he crossed his arms over his chest. Veins meandered over the muscles, touring his fine physique. Sunny blond hairs sprinkled his forearm of tanned skin, making her wonder where he'd gotten all the sunshine, since London only now embraced her summer temperatures.

"The stories and pictures, where are they?"

"I have copies of all the things I submitted in boxes at my dad's. Plus, notes, journals, and my personal pictures. We couldn't keep any of the original documents or press pictures."

He stood with amazing economy, stacking their plates and carrying them to the counter. "Get dressed. We're going to your father's."

She looked down at the billowy floral top, teal blue shorts, and sandals she wore. "I am dressed."

He puffed the air with his sweet mouth and a thrill skated up her spine. Law cleared the dishes and set them in the sink before scooping his keys and phone off the counter. After a few taps of his thumb, he placed the device to his ear and repeated the code he had the previous night.

"Any news?" he asked. There was a short pause.

"Thanks, Khani. Let me know when you do. I'm going back to Baine's to grab some things. Tell your guy. I'd hate to have to take out the rookie."

When Magdalena saw his smile from this angle she noticed a small dimple form among his scruff. The ensuing throaty laugh curled her toes and pebbled her nipples. *What a bloody shame he wants naught to do with you.*

"I probably would," he said into the phone. Then turned toward her. "I could use the stress reliever."

She flipped him the bird.

Law stowed his phone and walked to the door. "Don't open the door for anyone. Not an old lady. Or a kid. Or a delivery man."

Magdalena flew from the chair, crossing the room in four strides. "No, you said *we* were going. You're not leaving me here."

His chest rose and fell as he looked down at her. "Yes. I am. You'll be safer here."

One more step brought her in licking and punching distance. "I thought you were rather smart, but you're not picking up on things very quickly. Do you take vitamins? Maybe your B-12 is low." She reached around him and grabbed the knob, placing her breasts inches from his abdomen. Knowing it would rankle him, she winked. "Unless you want a titty fuck I suggest you step aside."

And wouldn't you know, he'd be the first to decline the offer.

Law moved away so fast she'd swear she'd accidentally offered to chop his dick off instead. But she walked through the doorway with a triumphant grin on her face. He trailed behind several yards, and when they climbed onto the bike, he didn't wrap her arms around him like he'd done before. He did hand her the blasted helmet though.

The bike rumbled to a stop at a petrol station half way between his flat and her father's house. He slid off and she followed, uncomfortable on the bike without his steady frame to clutch. She'd stayed on the tiny seat where he'd plopped her the night before out of fear. Things were still crazy, but hopefully they'd work through it soon and she could get far away from Lawrence Pierce. In an attempt for momentary breathing room, Magdalena wrestled out of the helmet and started for the glassed entrance of the station.

"Where are you going?" Law asked, a twinge of irritation lacing his deep voice.

"Inside," she snapped. "Pub crawlers and footballers, it's not the Congo."

His right hand slicked over his head. It was a wonder he had hair left. "Tart, you're pushing the limits of my sanity. And control," he added, his gaze raking her from head to toe.

She felt it as sure as his touch gliding down her neck, over the swell of her breasts and curve of her hip, against her legs to the tips of her pink toes. "Well, the feeling is extremely mutual." When she turned away his hand wrapped around her wrist then eased down her palm. He interlaced their fingers and with the other began unscrewing the gas cap.

Mags shoved her left hand into her back pocket, struggling to disregard their palm kiss. It proved impossible as his fingers encased her hand. A heady sense of security and girly infatuation snookered her brain. She shifted her legs in antsy steps forward then back again, restless to move and also unwilling to lose the contact.

Law positioned the nozzle in the tank, depressed the lever then squinted at her sideways over his shoulder. "Don't you have any pants?"

His gaze aimed at her fidgety legs. When she didn't answer he faced her. "I thought journalists presented themselves with a little class?"

"Screw you," she shot with little indignation, unwilling to fall prey to his bait. "These gams haven't seen the light of day in a year. They were buttoned up in Africa for fear of enticing the wrong man. So," she said, propping her free hand on her hip, "I'll let them breath."

Magdalena swooshed her legs, provoking his intense grimace. "Why, am I enticing you?"

"We need to keep a low profile and you're drawing unwanted attention." He replaced the tap to the stand, screwed on the cap, and then released her hand.

The withdrawal stung, but she took comfort in the brief view of his tented pants. Someone in his past hurt him deeply and the urge to track them down and beat them to death with her cricket bat kicked her already racing heart into overdrive.

Law swung a leg over the bike and eyed her. His lips parted to speak, but his phone beeped. "Hey, Khani," he answered. The white of his knuckles shone brightly around the black device. "Your guy was supposed to be there so this shit wouldn't happen." He listened for a minute, his eyes roving the horizon. "Hot-headed amateur." His eyes rolled heavenward. "I'm five minutes out. I'll try not to leave him with permanent damage.

"Hop on, tart. We've got to go."

Chapter Seventeen

Worn leather spines lay like swept dominoes on several shelves while others littered the oriental rug and old hardwood, appearing as though someone used her mother's antique book collection like confetti at a celebration. They must have been lauding the destruction of her family's sanctuary. Like a London alley hooker, the sofa lay on its back, skirts flapped open, ready to be taken.

Magdalena followed Law through the living area. He leaned into the kitchen, but she didn't need to see the shattered china more closely. She'd seen enough of it in the dining room. Her father's house mimicked her life. An upended disaster for which she could neither atone or understand.

He turned, but her blank stare into nothingness wouldn't focus. Law's hands cupped her shoulders, but his warmth lost the battle with her woe. His touch migrated to the base of her skull. Her scalp tingled as his fingers dove into her hair and when he tugged, pain pricked her senses. Their gazes collided only a second before his lips brushed over hers.

The haze of anguish receded, shoved aside by a thunderhead of passion. His fingers held her, a willing prisoner as his mouth cuddled hers, their lips fit together like interlocking puzzle pieces. For a moment only the air they shared and rumbling heart beats stirred. Then, as if he were tasting a dessert for the first time after years of non-indulgence, his lips tugged hers.

Magdalena's body conformed to Law's rigid front. Heat engulfed her lower lip as he sucked it into his mouth then laved it with the silk of his tongue. The exquisite torture device curled up the side of her upper lip and, following his touch, her mouth opened. He tilted her head and sealed their lips together. His tongue aggravated hers, much like he did when they weren't touching. It pushed in hard then backed off to a maddening distance. When her tongue chased after his they wrestled, his always ending on top.

Law groaned and pulled her chest and belly against the firm ridge of his penis. Magdalena's hands shoved into his back pockets, yanking him harder into her. She rocked into him. Her body undulated, assaulting him with her soft curves. The air around them heated until sweat broke out over her exposed skin. Images of their sweat-slicked bodies tangled and writhing together melted her brain. Her hand reached under his shirt, but before she could touch his skin he wrenched away from her.

His gaze shot above her head and he thrust her behind his back. Magdalena clung to his black belt, reeling from the intimacy of their contact and the abruptness of its end. Why in the bloody blue balls did he think he could yank her around like that? A yo-yo didn't see this much back and forth. *For the love—*

"Pierce." A new voice boomed from the doorway.

Law centered the weight he'd shifted to the balls of his feet. "Rookie."

"They baited me like professional anglers, mate," the bloke explained.

"I don't need a friend. I need a *man* who can do his job," Law bit out.

The fellow laughed and Magdalena leaned around Law's waist. Her grip doubled on the supple leather. A bloke the size of a Shire horse drank the entrance to her father's home in one gulp. His neck and the traps bulging out of his black tee rivaled the draft horse's in bulk. She pictured him right at home on a rugby pitch, mowing men as big as he like spring weeds.

Shire shook his square, stubble-covered jaw. His laugh waltzed into the mire and he squeezed a tuft of paper-bag brown hair at his forehead before pushing through it. "Go 'ed. Act like you never messed up." Before Law could rebuff him, Shire tilted his head and tightened his gaze on her. "Ms. Wells." He folded his hands to pray between his mountainous chest. "Please, forgive me for allowing those as...men to disrespect your home."

Magdalena's hands fell from Law's waistband and she tried to side-step him, but he shot her an expression that glued her sandals to the floor. She snarled her nose at him then turned her attention to Shire. Since she didn't want to continue referring to him as an equine, she inquired. "Who are you?"

He flashed her a fine set of pearly whites and two grooved dimples. "You can call me Street, Miss."

Heat flushed her cheeks. Dimples did it every time and Street had two. Not that they were any more devastating than Law's. But they were definitely more friendly. "Call me Magdalena, or Mags will do. And this isn't your fault."

"Sure as hell is," Law barked.

Mags poked him in the ribs. "It's not his fault any more than your family being in trouble is mine. Right?"

"It's his job," Law said.

"Does he work with you?" Mags asked with a quirked brow.

Law's lips thinned on his lacking rejoinder.

"Bird's got you by the balls," Street chuckled.

Magdalena narrowed her gaze at Street. "Not helpful."

"Sorry." Street's olive gaze scanned the room. "I got back before they hit the main house, and, I hope, before they did do too much damage here." His soulful eyes found her again. "They take anything that you can tell?"

"It looks like they just tossed everything into the air and let it land where it would," she answered.

"Where are your files, Magdalena?" Law demanded.

"My room," she said.

Law hurried her up the steps while Street followed. Mags chased after their boots down the skinny corridor and recoiled at her bedroom door. Swaths of lace curtains and bedding lay like carpet on the floor. Her closet looked as though it had a night on the town and puked its contents all over her room. Her desk had been its drinking buddy. Irresponsible assholes.

"Son of an ugly whoring fat bitch," she seethed.

"Creative expletive," Street praised. "Guess I don't have to worry about one slipping in front of you. Hell, I'll probably learn a thing or two."

"Stuff it," Law growled. "Or I will."

The banter helped ease her irritation. Nothing appeared broken, just as untidy as her room looked after a week of finals and a weekend of partying. She dug a path to the closet and her shoulders sagged. Two of the four boxes were missing while the other two lay slashed from end to end, exposing their paltry cargo.

"They're gone?" Law asked in a whisper.

Magdalena nodded, unable to speak past the lump in her throat. She sank to the floor, propping her back on the open closet door, and regarded the two big-ass men taking up the available air in her room. Both their jaws worked at grinding the enamel off their teeth.

Street reached out for her. "We'll figure it—"

Law grabbed Street's hand and twisted. "Don't."

With damp palms braced on the floor, Mags held her breath, awaiting the brutal flesh-on-flesh smacks she'd heard the last time Law clashed with a man. When Street gave his attacker a cockeyed grin, air filled her lungs anew.

From profile, without his deep, seasoned eyes on her, Mags finally figured out why Law had called Street Rookie. Vibrant skin smoothed over his baby face while Law's and even hers hosted the beginning signs of age. The fine lines which would eventually excavate to wrinkles. Lord, he looked fresh out of the frat house.

"You don't comfort her soon, somebody else will," Street said. He disengaged Law's suddenly feeble grasp, nodded toward her, and left. Funny, but she didn't hear his boat-sized boots treading their way down the stairs. Perhaps because she was too busy trying to find her way through Law's confounding gaze.

Without the energy to sort through all the things she saw there—tenderness, concern, distress, lust—Magdalena concentrated on the problem that led them here. They, whoever the bloody hell *they* were, took her files. She'd stored every hard copy in meticulous subject and date order. Pictures. Notes. Drafts. Final submissions. They were all gone.

But she still had the blasted flash drive in her backpack at Law's apartment. It held her thesis statement and some of the data she'd collected in Africa to support her claim. Thanks to Owen, her friend and fellow journalist on the trip, she had scanned the first few months of notes and submissions while waiting to leave Goma. She could email him for copies of the pictures and view some of her submissions on the United Nation's website.

Bolstered by the possibility of answers, even by the impending drudge to find them, she stood, giving Law a wide bearing. "Let's go. I have work to do."

Chapter Eighteen

Magdalena clung to Law's waist the entire way to the flat, but it didn't bridge the chasm as steep and jagged as Avon Gorge that gaped between them. The actual changes in his behavior were small. Still, she couldn't help the idiotic twinge in her heart every time they rounded a bend and his arm didn't brace hers. Each time they stopped for traffic or a light, Law's head remained forward, never checking to see if she needed a break to reposition or if she wanted to stop someplace and buy a real pair of shoes so her feet wouldn't continue their intermittent slips off the pegs. Both of which he'd done with irritating frequency on their other rides.

Well, that's what you get for complaining about the attention.

But honestly, Magdalena, whether instinctually or from training and fieldwork as a journalist, knew nothing she'd done had caused his withdrawal. Her lips didn't have that much influence over the man whether talking or smooching. Something extreme and barbed haunted the fierce warrior. It crippled him from the inside. And Law, in all his fierce masculinity, hurting, churned a well of emotions in her overwrought system.

She blinked back the useless tears and vowed to figure him out, if it was the most difficult thing she'd ever done or would ever do in her lifetime.

Add it to the list of impossible feats for the day.

Lord, she really had to do something about this overachieving side of herself. It was far more exhausting than the laissez faire attitude she'd fostered since her mother's death. Wise enough, now, to admit it had been an easy and sometimes self destructive buffer, she didn't have the will to return to those lifeless days. Though the stinging pain of reality often made her wish she could forget it all in a mindless oblivion of drink and man, she'd seen how minimal her problems were in the grand scheme, and more importantly, how she could help.

Magdalena saw the need every third-world country had for media produced by the people, for the people. They would have a voice with which to tell their story. Educate the world. Bring light to the darkness. She determined to defend her dissertation to the committee at Cardiff, and then she had to persuade those with purse strings and media empires to back the idea that a world with honest global communication would benefit all parties involved.

Soon the rumbling beast came to rest on the street outside Law's flat. True to form, as of the last twenty minutes, he climbed from the bike without a sideways glance to help her and headed for the building. With too much other drama to focus on, Mags hurried after the brooding man.

As soon as they hit the front door she growled. "Shit."

Law pivoted in a slight crouch, ready to battle the world, instead of his own demons. At least, that was her take on his extreme willingness to bash

fists with anyone dumb enough to meet the
challenge. His narrowed gaze scanned the area then
his bunched shoulders relaxed. "What is it?"

"I need a computer and printer. I didn't think
a damn thing about it until now. And there's one I
could use at Baine's."

Abruptly, Mags met the width of Law's back
as he headed up the stairs. "I have both."

She hurried to catch him and did so at the
base of the second flight of stairs. Sucking wind,
she asked the obvious. "Where? Under your
mattress?" The flat was nearly vacant, bearing only
the necessities. And not meeting them by her pre-
Africa standards. Lucky for him, she'd evolved past
frivolous things like conditioner and body lotion.

He didn't acknowledge her inquiry, only kept
trudging the stairs. No, *she* trudged. He powered up
the never-ending metal mountain. Inside he waited
for her to drag her wimpy self through the door
before turning the bolt without a wink, a blink, or
even a snarl. After becoming accustomed to his
snappy remarks and flirty manner, his abject mood
rankled her. Made her itch to fight, but it wouldn't
do either of them any good right now. So, she
hurried to the bag at the foot of the mattress and
found the drive she needed.

Law walked to the closet and opened both
doors wide. He parted a sparse collection of clothing
from the middle and shoved them aside. From the
right he removed a large panel of the wall then slid
it to the right, revealing a silver-faced safe large
enough to be her coffin.

Way to think positive, ole girl.

He punched in a code, turned a lever, and
swung the lid open. Several large guns about the
size of her leg gleamed in the interior light. The
bottom of her stomach threatened to drop straight

onto the ground and both hands shot to her middle as Law reached inside the cave of doom. She didn't fear him, but the guns were a different book altogether. Law knew how to use them. She'd seen him handle the small ones the other night with skill and grace, if the word could be applied where cold metal was involved.

The UN troops had carried weapons. It had taken nearly the full year abroad for her to walk past one without a hiccup of apprehension jarring her system. But until then the only guns she'd ever seen had been on television, and even then she changed the station. These guns were on her turf. Too close for her own sensibilities.

But Law continued ignoring her as he pulled a laptop from a high shelf of the vault and set it on the mattress. A thin device came next and she guessed it was a printer of sorts. He righted the closet and Mags' stomach settled with the secure hunk of metal between her and the arsenal. The wall, clothes, and closet doors helped too.

Law hauled both devices to the counter, booted them, pounded out several long beats on the keys then stepped back. "All yours."

"Thank you." She stepped up to the makeshift work terminal and plugged in the jump drive. The computer laughed at her, flashing an unauthorized device warning in steady rhythm.

Mags sought Law for another code, but didn't find him over her shoulder as she'd expected. He stood at the window, arms crossed, looking out at the view. Or nothing at all, since the scenery didn't inspire awe. He didn't look over the lapping waves of the North Sea nor the rolling green shires. Earlier that morning she'd seen only a similar row of buildings stuffed full of flats, the dark pavement of the street, cars, a few pedestrians, and a hint of morning sky.

Tired of his moping, she decided to jab him a bit and see if she could insight a flicker of emotion. Any would do. "Hey, Pierce. I need your magical hands, over here."

When he turned, a scowl wrinkling his brow, smug satisfaction curled her toes, until the brevity of his expression changed. Law rocked on his heels, resting a shoulder on the window frame. His hips extended in the posture and molded the front of his pants to the solid length of his erect penis. Magdalena's lips parted on words that never formed. Because more enthralling than his powerful legs, worship-worthy cock, V'd waist, and corded arms, was the white-hot gaze he settled her with. The nuances of deep pain and uncertainty in the brilliant green rammed headlong into her sternum.

For the second time in her life, Magdalena realized she treaded in a sea wider than her ability to cross. She'd found help the first time, in the expedition to Africa. This time, no one could save her.

Fear of being alone made Magdalena desperate for companionship. She guessed it all tied to her mother's untimely death, but, though she'd taken several psych classes, she was no psychologist. Regardless of the reason, she had always been a fool for love. She also figured out long ago she'd never find it. Not in the droves of men she'd sought it with. Not in the hollow relationships she fostered because she'd been damaged. She'd had nothing to give them, though she'd tried time and again to fill the void, fooling herself into believing sex was intimacy and physical closeness could sustain a relationship.

She'd stopped giving herself away and stopped looking for love.

But she'd found it in the one place she never wanted to find it. In the damaged man across the room.

"Nava. N-A-V-A. Zegen. Z-E-G-E-N. Justice. 1943," he said from his prop across the room. When she didn't move, he straightened and let his arms fall to his sides. "Do you need me to repeat it?"

Magdalena shook her head, unable to speak for the ache in her heart. She'd fancied herself in love twenty times over the years. Each time she could have compared the high to a shopping spree on her father's credit card, followed by a spa package, dinner, and dancing. This love hurt like a bitch. The only thing she could compare it to was being dragged from her plush seat on an airplane and shoved out the door without even an umbrella to break her fall. There was no hope of survival.

Why him? Why now? Magdalena refused to revert to old habits. She had a plan for the first time in her life and it didn't include a man. Not anyone. Finally, being alone did not mean being lonely. Didn't mean being afraid. She only needed Lawrence Pierce to keep her alive. Not for anything else.

But why did his soulful, tormented eyes draw her in? The more she fought the compunction to ease his pain, the farther into the quicksand she sank. *And you can't breathe in sand, Magdalena.*

Thank bloody hell, he turned around as her cardboard fingers struck the keys, relaying the password. And a funny one at that. But she didn't waste time thinking about him, the fact he'd trusted her with the code, or how interesting it was. For the next few hours she dug through pictures, submissions, field notes, and her journals. Anytime anything flagged her attention she'd call Law over to look at it. She held her breath and averted her gaze each time he came near, unwilling to pander to her wild notion one little bit. He never stayed long, just dismissed it or typed it into his text screen, then moved back to his safe haven.

Intermittently, he talked to his boss, Khani, on the phone about what each time became another non-lead. Law had said his mum practically raised Khani and her brother, Zeke. From listening in on the conversations, she concluded their relationship was closer than that of most siblings. It held an air of long memory, if not intimacy. Working with raised hackles over that fact made things difficult. Several times, she read to the bottom of the screen, realized she couldn't remember one thing on it, and had to start over again.

It also didn't help that when he talked to Khani was the only time his mouth opened and sound came out. Law talked about Street and his screw up. "Well, it solves your problem. Fire him then screw him." A hint of a smile creased his cheek. "Oh, I know you didn't say you wanted to, but your body language screamed it from the tallest mountain." He chuckled. "Never. What kind of brother would I be? Thanks for the help. And if I find anything else interesting, I'll let you know."

Magdalena's stomach growled. No, more like roared.

"Do you have any leftovers? I'm pretty hungry," she said, eyes never leaving an article she'd written about food distribution in the eastern region of DRC.

"I was beginning to think you'd switched to robot mode and didn't need food, water, or a bathroom." Perhaps the smile on his lips was residual, but she'd take the sloppy seconds of his brightened face any day.

"Why?"

"'Cause you passed lunch time three and a half hours ago," he said.

"What?"

"Yeah. Seven hours non-stop. Pretty good for a civilian."

Magdalena hated how the compliment lifted her feet off the floor, but she smiled in spite of herself. "So, food?"

"I have the stuff to cook a soup, but it takes a while and I didn't want to break your concentration. There's a great place a few blocks away, if you like sushi?"

The words *I love you* nearly flew right out of her mouth. "Yes." Having forgone her favorite food group for far too long, she squealed.

Law's grin deepened and his dimple came out to play. "I guess it's sushi, then. I'll call it in and grab it, so you can keep working. Just make a note of anything interesting and I'll look at it when I get back." He pocketed his phone. "What do you want?"

You raw. Instead, she went with the next best answer, "Anything and a lot of it. I'm not a one or two roll kind of girl."

The rich peals of his laugh infused Magdalena with a high that lasted until the door closed then locked behind him. Loneliness didn't register. She'd worked past the weakness. However, the weight of her precarious position crowded in, using most of the oxygen in the room. Moving from behind the computer, Mags stretched her arms over her head and concentrated on deep, even breaths.

Just because they hadn't figured anything out, yet, didn't mean the answers weren't sitting at the end of the next article or in the background of the next picture. But the thought of scrolling over another backlit screen sent off a throbbing behind her eyes. She ambled about the room, kicking out her legs and stretching her sore body. Her lip had healed up nicely over the night. The base of her knuckle and elbow maintained a dull ache though.

Magdalena wandered to Law's safe spot and peered down at the street. A group of schoolboys kicked a football back and forth on the sidewalk. She watched them for several minutes before turning back into the room and roving the stacks of books against the wall. Volume upon volume of legal journals, dockets of local and private acts, practitioner texts, and legal reports spread out before her.

More curious than their presence was their well-worn state. Nearly each book hosted cracked leather spines with scuffed bottom edges, like they'd been propped open on Law's chest and read many times. Mags pulled the navy and gold bound edition from the pile nearest the bed. Its crackled filigree title read Norfolk County Law Reports 1960 - 1980. She opened the cover and leafed through several pages. Absolutely nothing spectacular stood out on the printed pages. Hundreds of terms foreign to her melded together on the yellowed sheets, forming a right and proper snooze fest.

When Mags yawned she closed the book with a *thud* and set it back atop its pile. But as she pulled away something stuck between its pages grazed her fingers. She turned the book and cocked her head to see the edge of a picture hanging just beyond the border of the old pages. Her eyes narrowed as she levered the hunk of reports and revealed a photograph of a truly breathtaking beauty.

Inky corkscrews of hair hung to her bikini-covered breasts, which stood pert on a supermodel frame. One arm hung comfortably at her side near a high, tight ass while the other hugged around her middle. The small gesture revealed a hint of insecurity and Magdalena clung to that tiny assurance like a man overboard held tight to a lifebuoy. Because the seas she'd known would kill her just kicked up a squall of epic proportions.

Is this Nava Zegen?

The woman, whoever she was, held a deep and significant place in Law's heart. Magdalena imagined him staring at the beauty for hours on end before finally relenting to sleep's call. She rubbed a hand over her heart to ease the intense burn that settled around it. Jealousy never entered her world. If a guy had hang-ups about someone else, she moved on to the next. Sure, guys had cheated on her, but the indiscretions were more irritating than anything.

Where Lawrence Pierce was concerned, Mags had no reason to feel the bite of jealousy or the sting of betrayal. He owed her nothing, and, yet, he owned her every emotion. When Law stepped into the room she still stood, gawking at the photograph.

Chapter Nineteen

It was a damn good thing Law stayed fit since this woman shocked his system more than the bastard in Columbia who'd strapped him to the parrilla and prodded him with two hundred volts for three days while the bullet hole in his leg festered. Maybe she wouldn't leave a nasty scar. Lord knew he had enough already. But the sadness in her eyes didn't give him any hope of escaping without injury.

The scarce London sunshine backlit her wild hair. The tresses maintained a disordered appearance, even in the pictures he'd seen of her at Baine's house. But the thick mane hung straight here, frizzed there, and lumped with intermittent hints of curl for the fidgety work-over she'd given it while her eyes had been glued to the computer screen. He tried not to look then, just as he did now, failing time and again. Her arms hung loosely at her sides, her chin up, hiding nothing. Not even the picture pinched in her delicate fingers.

"Who is Nava Zegen?" she asked.

Law swallowed, not expecting that particular question. Of course, the little Nick Davies wanna-be would put two and two together like an investigative reporter should. He just hadn't given her time to do research. So, she guessed. Not a bad assumption, but off the mark.

"My grandmother."

She chewed on her bottom lip for a moment while he stood in the doorway. Her gaze roved his face then shot to the bag hanging from his index and middle fingers. The minute stretched into another and still she said not a word, only ground the gears in her head.

Law fell in love with Magdalena probably the instant he'd scraped her off the floor of her father's house. All Baine's stories about his little sister's ability to wow the pants off a priest with her quick wit and good nature, combined with the drop-him-dead gorgeous pictures littering the old estate, had him primed to topple. Which is exactly why he avoided her like the devil. If only he could continue dodging the woman who rankled him like no other.

He stepped out of the doorway and placed their three boxes of sashimi, nigiri, and assorted rolls on the counter. The fact that he hadn't closed the door didn't pass her notice. Her gaze bounced from it to him several times, but again she held her tongue. He leapt first and hoped he didn't need to use his escape hatch. "You want to ask me about the picture?"

Magdalena walked toward him, her gate leisurely, but bold. Her gaze never left his face and the uncertain chew of her lip vanished. Two lines wrinkled her forehead. The rose rounds of her cheek distended in an almost smile and those soft and terribly decadent pink lips ruffled.

"Yes." She exhaled. "And no."

Law waited, hoping she'd choose the latter.

She laid the picture on the white tiles then studied it. Law didn't need to look. For the past decade, every time he'd closed his eyes, he'd seen Clara staring back at him. Only now, when he let the darkness come, Magdalena flipped him the bird, sashayed her legs, blew him a kiss. The killer was he didn't know which hurt worse, losing Clara or the fear of losing Magdalena. Not that he had her in any real way. And not that he wanted her. Because he couldn't handle another explosion in his world. It already resembled so many of the warzones he'd traipsed through over the years. One more artillery blast and everything would crumble.

Sweat gathered across his back and dripped between his shoulder blades. His palms slicked. Magdalena didn't appear to be in much better shape. Her hands rung in overlapping succession. Street, though too cavalier for anyone's own good, was right about Magdalena. She needed comfort, not just protection, and he could only give her one.

"You don't owe me anything," she began. "Are you still...in love with her?" Her hair swooshed about as her head shook. "I mean...obviously you are. I'm just curious, I guess." Magdalena's floral-covered chest heaved. "What happened? Youthful idealism didn't prevail? She cheat on you? Break your heart?"

Three slightly shaking fingers fastened over her mouth like she had to stem the flow of words before she drowned in them. And he was glad because he sank in them too. The pressure of inquiry and the memories they wrought restrained his airflow.

Clara lay in his arms. Her gaunt form only a shadow of the vibrant young woman she'd been. The chill of her lifeless body seeped into his bones and refused to leave. Hot tears stung his cheek and he jarred back to the present, which hurt only a fraction less.

Law wiped the moisture dripping off his nose with the back of his hands. "She broke me...when she died."

Magdalena's tears fell in earnest and suddenly it was all too much. He lurched toward the door. She called out behind him, "I'm sorry."

The words barely registered over the thuds of his running feet. He grabbed the rail with one hand and leaped, clearing each flight of stairs in a desperate effort to get away. Law's boots pounded the pavement as he made his way across the street and down the sidewalk. He aimed for his old running route, maintaining a frantic pace, which matched his mental state perfectly.

Was Magdalena right? Was he still in love with Clara? No. He loved her dearly, but he'd released her long ago for his own sanity. But the wounds she left remained. Festered and obscene like the scar on his leg. He'd wished that either of the two would kill him, but, fuck it all, they hadn't.

A block from his flat he bounded off the sidewalk and into the beaten path at the back of the wooded park. The heat clung to his body, coaxing sweat from his pores. His shirt suctioned to his body as it gathered perspiration.

Law had known he was quick to fall. He met Clara the first day of his second semester junior year. By the third day not another woman in the world existed. So, after she died, he created a false front. The flirting jokester everyone knew and loved. Only they didn't know a thing about him. Baine knew torment when he saw it, but he was a good enough friend never to question it.

Women had become non-entities like waiting room magazines and vending machine candy. He didn't acknowledge their existence. Which cast him into a slim demographic of heterosexual men practicing celibacy. It had been a choice made in desperation for the good of his stability. But the moment he saw Magdalena he knew he should have been banging every bird that looked his way. Maybe then, he wouldn't have screwed himself so royally by reacting to her on such a visceral level.

Law stopped at the apex of the small footbridge marking five miles and braced his forearms on the wooden banister. He spit the mix of snot and tears into the slender stream below and let his lungs rock his body in an easy rhythm. He welcomed the burn of physical exertion. His head hung between his shoulders, and he watched a bug skip across the water's surface onto the tufts of grass at the bank.

He wondered how Baine could love Sloan after nearly losing her in a pool of blood, knowing the pain of it, that it could happen at any moment. How could he bring himself to care about someone else with the same possibility looming over his head?

Chapter Twenty

The doorknob twisted and so did the hold on Magdalena's heart. She hadn't meant to cause him pain, but sometimes talking about things helped. In the Congo she'd had nothing but time, in between stories, and Owen had been an objective third party. He'd listened for hours on end and only gave advice when asked. The process had been cleansing and gave her perspective on healthy relationships. Even if Owen's was one of the same sex. It was rock solid, had overcome familial rancor, college debt, and distance.

When the knob jiggled again, Mags stood from her perch on the mattress and headed for the door. Though her hands shook, she refused to hide from Law and the drama she'd created. About the time she came even with the bar, her brain caught up, slowing her steps.

Law had keys to his own flat. She'd seen him stuff them into his pants while he hovered in the doorway earlier. The hairs stood razor sharp on her arm and she froze, gaze riveted on the door's small silver handle. Fear vibrated through her body.

She couldn't climb out of the window. The building didn't have a fire escape that she'd noticed. Mags eyed the closet, but that was the first place the bad guys looked in the movies, followed by underneath the bed. Not that the second location was even a possibility. The bathroom didn't even provide enough privacy for a poop, much less a hideaway from villains.

Magdalena grabbed the drive from the computer and winced as the thing honked at her for improper device removal. Everything went dead silent for a beat then the knob shook with greater vehemence. She shoved the drive between her breasts and grabbed the computer and stack of papers lying next to it. Running as quietly as she could manage, she slipped into the closet then closed herself in darkness. Her fingers felt along the back wall until she felt the raise of the vault seam. Working from memory and touch, she levered the panel back and shoved the computer, papers, and drive in the tiny gap between the carved plaster wall and metal safe. Her prayers to become paper thin, so she could slide into the crevice, worked about as well as the ones when she'd wished her mother back to life.

She righted the wall and hanging clothes, held her breath, closed her eyes, and listened. The skin of her palms stung as fists clenched so tightly her nails cut her skin. A loud crack reverberated through the flat, followed by a crack as the door smacked against the wall. Only a tiny click sounded as he, or they, closed the door.

Magdalena could practically feel the intruder's amusement as he sauntered with deliberate and even footfalls straight toward the closet. Again she prayed herself invisible, but it helped none.

"Come on out, Ms. Wells," a smooth, even British accent commanded. "No need to make this any harder than it has to be."

The cool affect of his voice chilled her to the bone, even more so than Davis and his thugs. They had been brash and brutish. This guy seemed professional. Cold. Detached. Like he'd put a bullet in her head and go grab a frothy mug at O'Henry's around the corner.

She opened her eyes and found her assessment spot on. Hollowness settled in her gut, placed there by the dark dead stare before her. His ghostly-white skin cracked into a smile that missed his eyes altogether.

"That's it," he crooned, opening the door wider. "I'll make it painless, if you'll allow me." The artifice fell away in a blink. "And I'll make it more horrible than your worst nightmares, if you fight. Which I've heard you're quite adept at. I must say, I'm a bit torn about how I want this to play out."

Magdalena breathed deeply through her nose then out through her mouth, willing away the quiver in her nerves. This was no time to fall victim to mind games. She stepped out from the closet and, though she tried to train her gaze on the menace, her line of sight shifted to the door.

"Don't worry. We won't be interrupted."

Oh my God. What did he do to Law?

He nodded. "Yes, he'll be dispatched momentarily."

Relief she had no right to feel at the moment showered over her. Law wasn't dead. And no matter how confident this guy was that he or anyone else could eliminate Law Pierce, she was certain they would fail. Miserably. Not that it did her well-being any good. But just like she wouldn't give up on Law, neither would she discount herself. No matter what Mr. Doom wanted.

What worked once might work again. And even if it didn't, it was damn worth a try. Mags focused on his throat, even as he pulled a gun from

the small of his back and held it by his side. The
long barrel tapped against the leg of his slacks.

Deliberately, she moved her gaze to the gun,
held her body slack, and hoped, instead of prayed,
that her memory would serve her well. She drew a
shaky breath and punched at his throat as quickly
as her body could move.

He pivoted and her fist glanced the clammy
skin of his neck. The *umph* of impact didn't have
time to translate into triumph as something
knocked her against the head, snapping it back.
The sound rattled in her ears. Another blow landed
in her middle, expelling the air from her lungs. She
met the ground and the room tilted and twirled.

Black suffocated her, moving in and blotting
out every bit of light in the room. Magdalena heaved
for breath, but none came. Weight pushed against
her chest. Her hands flailed, trying to shove at the
burden. Her fingers found cotton and solid muscle
underneath it. She struggled to shift it, but the
casing remained tight about her face, constricting
on her chest.

Tiny shooting stars whizzed past her as
everything tunneled. Desperate for air, she did the
thing that always moved Baine when they wrestled
as kids. Magdalena followed the line of his back to
his pit, rammed her fingers into the bowled flesh
and pinched with every last drop of muster she
possessed.

"You cunt!" he screamed.

He grabbed her attacking arm, and air
flooded her starved lungs in a gasp. If she'd had
enough air, she would have cried out as he twisted
it, slammed it to the ground, and pinned it with a
knee. All too soon, his arm clamped down on her
throat and his weight doubled on her sternum.

Mags held tight to the air she'd stored and focused lower. Her legs wheeled around, but found no body part to decimate. She sought purchase against the floor to bar her hips and tumble him off, but her shoes slipped with each effort. Again her lungs ached for air. They tried to pull in breath after breath, but none came.

A mighty roar echoed in her ears and she thought it her own cry for freedom. For justice.

The man rolled off her, and she choked and gagged on the air she so seriously needed. She watched in helpless horror as the man landed on his feet in a crouch and raised his gun. From across the room her justice barreled like a ferocious beast. Law's mouth opened wide on a thunderous cry. Sweat dripped from his chin. His teeth bared for attack.

He didn't acknowledge the gun as he ran headlong toward its lifting barrel. The long tube spat and chunks of the floor flew into the air in tiny explosions. He didn't seem to notice the gash in his shirt by his ribs or the blood that stained the area around it. As the bullets neared Law's charge, Magdalena stilled, forgoing air for the outcome of the clash.

Law tackled the man with his shoulders. The gun fell to the floor, but Law didn't stop powering his legs. He wrapped his arms around the black shirt, which would have been her final view of her life, and hoisted it and the man inside into the air.

Law's battle cry continued as he accelerated to the window and crashed into the large pane. The crack of shattering glass fractured the overwrought air. Her heart stopped as Law and Mr. Doom careened through the fissures. Law's hands released the man in mid-air and his white knuckles

banded the window frame, halting his momentum.
The man's scream picked up where Law's fell away.

Magdalena collapsed, utterly spent. She
stared at Law's back. The wet shirt clung to the
topography of his sculpted muscles. His torso
heaved air, much like hers. A sickening *whack*
punctuated the intruder's death. Law turned away,
plunged his hand between the wall and mattress,
and recovered the holster and pistols she hadn't
seen since the previous day. He shrugged on the
weapons then scrambled toward her.

His hot palm cupped her face and lifted her
head from the floor. "Are you okay? Where do you
hurt?" The pads of his fingers skimmed the column
of her neck then ran the length of each arm in a
frantic search.

Finally able to breathe without hacking,
Magdalena encircled his hand in her own. "I'm
fine," she rasped. "Are you okay? Your side, did he
shoot you?"

"It's just a scratch from his buddy I met in
the park. Now, tell me, where are you hurt?"

"Really, I'm fine. Just let me lie here for a few
hours."

The muscles in Law's jaw bunched. "Sorry,
tart. We have to go." Before the words were out of
his mouth he looped an arm under her back and
pulled her to stand. For the briefest of seconds, she
nested against his wet chest, happy for the melt of
her fear-frozen core. Too soon, he stepped back and
motioned just behind her with his chin. "Grab your
bag."

Law opened the closet and pulled on his
jacket, despite the heat of the day. While she
grabbed the satchel and swung it gingerly over one
arm, careful not to jar her sore ribs, he snagged

one from the closet and stuffed it with his own clothes.

"Where's the computer," he asked without slowing.

"Behind the panel, between the safe and wall."

He regarded her with a balled shirt hanging from his fist. "You are bloody amazing."

A silly smile stretched her mouth. Law shook his head and turned away. Sirens blared in the distance, stealing her respite from the emotional turmoil. Law maintained a steady pace as he secured the files, computer, and drive from their hiding spot. When he finished, he slung the bag over his shoulders and reached for her hand.

"Can you run?"

His calm assurance and tender touch gave her a sudden spike in adrenaline. "Yes."

"Good, don't stop until I tell you."

They ran from the wrecked room. In the corridor, Law surprised her, taking the stairs up, instead of down. Her legs wobbled like noodles, but somehow she managed to keep them beneath her body. Five stories later they exited onto the gravel topped roof. Law continued to pound one foot before the other. Sucking breath after breath and still not getting all the air she desired, Magdalena pushed herself as hard as she ever had.

When they reached the edge, Mags tempered her speed, but Law urged her on with an unrelenting tug. She ground to a halt and her insides turned to mush as he jumped onto the ledge then stepped into nothingness.

In that second, Magdalena knew exactly what people meant when they said, "Mind fucked." Because two and two didn't make four and gravity didn't plummet the man gripping her hand to the pavement below.

"It's all right," Law said. "It's a metal plank about two feet wide."

"Why the fuck can't I see it?"

"I painted it so no one would know it was here."

"Oh my God. Really? Who do you work for?"

Law's lips thinned and in a flash he hopped down from the ledge then banded his arms around her legs. His shoulder pushed in at her waist and her world flipped. The backpack slung over her arm slammed into the base of her skull. All thirty-two of her teeth slapped together. The coppery hint of blood tickled her tongue. She would have complained about his manhandling, but the pack continued tumbling down her arm.

Magdalena caught the strap just as Law's jean-covered boots stepped onto the ledge. "Don't scream." Then he walked out into thin-fucking-air. Her breast smashed into the bag strapped to his back. She accepted the discomfort, loathe to move the slightest muscle that she might throw him off balance.

Her gaze riveted on the alley below. From this height the trashcans looked like thimbles. The row of cars on the streets seemed to belong in a child's toy collection and the lines on the street appeared to be his wandering doodles on a page. God, she hoped he didn't use red, in the form of their splattered corpses. This vantage point didn't allow her the view from the front of the building or the one already represented.

I'm going to be sick.

After several terrifying strides Law leaped onto the tar top of the next building. She grabbed his belt with her free hand, bracing for impact. Her shoulders relaxed, only to tighten again as his quick gate continued across the roof and onto another blasted plank. By the time he set her to right, they were four buildings away from his flat.

She shoved at his middle. "You scared five years off my life."

"Well, you scared ten off mine. So, we're not even, yet."

"How did *I* scare *you*?"

He grabbed her hand and she glared at his back as he guided them through the building's stairwell and out onto a narrow side street. They walked north five blocks, away from the scene. All the while his gaze scanned their surroundings. When they came to a main street, Law's grip tightened. He pulled her into the alcove of a storefront and thrust himself against her.

A wide thigh parted her legs, nuzzling her suddenly aching femininity. His free hand tilted her chin. On instinct Magdalena's lips parted for him, but his mouth hovered near her lobe. His whiskers rasped like sandpaper on her cheek.

"Take it," he growled.

The words, "Anytime. Anywhere," hovered in her mind, but were scared away by the cold metal he thrust into her palm. "What!" She tried to retract her hand and found she had nowhere to go.

"I need to get the information off the body I left in the park."

"Body?"

"Well, I wasn't going to let him kill me. And I didn't take the time to search him after." His hot breath fanned on her neck. "I barely got to you in time as it was. If anything happens to me, I want you to be able to defend yourself."

Magdalena rested her cheek against Law's, soaking in his heat. She wished so many things were different. How they met. When they'd met. Who they were. "I don't even know how to use the thing. I'll probably shot myself in the bloody foot."

His hand guided hers over the handle. The contrast between its chill and his warmth perfectly encapsulated her warring desires.

"Feel that." His thumb shepherded hers across a small bar with a textured edge.

"Yes."

"It's the safety. If you want to shoot, flip it down, aim, and pull the trigger."

She levered back, trying to see his eyes, but his gaze locked on the street. "You make killing sound so easy."

"It's never easy. No matter how many times you do it. But it's not about what's easy. It's about what's right." He stepped back and pinned her with his gaze. She'd hoped to find reassurance in his brilliant eyes. She found only intensity and calculation. "Walk to the end of the block. Take the tube at West Kensington. Get in the third car and take it to Hammersmith. I'll meet you there." Law scooted her toward the street.

"What about you?" Her voice pitched higher with each word.

"I'm going to get the information and arrange a drop."

Magdalena clung to Law's hand, afraid if she let go, one of them would vanish like a mirage. "What does that even mean?"

"It means this shit just got real, Magdalena. They found you at my flat, registered to a person that doesn't exist. It's not impossible to track, but it takes a load of money and some fancy machinery, or high-level clearance, to accomplish. It means I need help tracking them, so I can properly look after you."

"Why can't I go with you? I'll try my best to keep up."

Law's eyes livened and the tiniest wrinkles formed at the edges. "You've been amazing, but I can't chance bringing you when more of them could show."

"What if you're not at the station?"

"I'll be there." Law's fingers caressed her cheek then over her lips. "I'll never abandon you again."

Magdalena's throat constricted.

He pushed her to the sidewalk. "Now, trust me."

Chapter Twenty-one

"I'm headed into the station," Law said.

Khani groaned into the line. "Street confirmed the pick-up. Law, the blokes from Baine's were dead-ends, literally. Low-level knuckle draggers. You said these two were professionals. They'll be in the system. We'll intercept the second one at the morgue. One way or the other, we'll get you some information."

"Thanks, Khani."

"Watch your back, Justice. I don't like this shit. Not one little bit."

Law stuffed the phone into his pocket and ducked into the brick front building. "Me either."

The sunlight shining through the vaulted rows of skylights did little to brighten Law's grim mood. He'd done a thousand difficult things in life, but sending Magdalena away ranked at the top of the shitty list. The fact that he didn't come up against any opposition to the drop only added to his rancor. They could have at least provided him a suspect to interrogate. When he noticed the homeless man while running in the park, sporting a shiny Glock 38, questioning was the last thing on his mind.

The set-up screamed professional hit. Homeless had obviously watched the building and had seen him leave without Magdalena. His gut formed the rows of knit stitches his mother used to practice for hours on end. He found they helped him about as much as they'd helped his mum make a sweater. The distraction had cost him flesh and blood and nearly cost him everything else.

It had nearly cost him the life that rat bastard tried to choke out of Magdalena. Law crossed his arms, pinning his shaking hands, and leaned against the platform I-beam at the end of the stairs. He held his breath, waiting for the District train to bring her back to him.

In this harsh light, Baine's actions in Mexico no longer looked brutal. A little teeth pulling and finger pruning appeared downright mellow compared to the plans he had for the people who made Magdalena a target. His chest rattled with angst as the seconds ticked by and the tube had yet to shoot down the rails. Two minutes later, when the blunt red-faced machine rounded the corner, Law straightened from his post.

He banked the urge to push his way to the door and scoop her into his arms. Instead, he scanned the area for the twentieth time, watching for any signs of an ambush. People moved off the train and created a light crowd on the concrete platform. A sleek woman in a charcoal business suit hung toward the rear of the group. As she slowed and riffled through her handbag, Law wrapped his hands around the grip of his gun.

The brunette produced a tube of lipstick and smoothed the color over her lips. He relaxed his grip, but everything else in him tightened as he focused on the breathtaking blonde standing outside the electric doors of the third car, just like he'd told her. She looked toward the woman then back at him.

Magdalena mouthed, "Were you going to shoot her?"

"If I needed to."

Again she limped across the distance. "She's a woman." Both her brows shot up and her Irish eyes widened.

Only she could make him laugh at a time like this. He crooked his finger at her and she took four measured steps toward him, still clutching her bag as she'd done walking away.

"You sorely underestimate the power of your sex, Magdalena."

She smiled, but the tentative curve fell from her mouth quickly. Magdalena blinked at him several times. The force of her flapping lashes was enough to blow him onto his backside.

"You're here."

Law closed the gap between them and cupped her soft cheeks in his hands. The silk of her hair danced across his fingers as he turned her chin. Their gazes collided so hard it hurt in the center of his chest. He lowered his head a fraction at a time, until their mouths hovered a whisper from each other. No matter how his mind struggled to convince his body and heart that this closeness was a disaster waiting to unfold, he ignored intellect and went with instinct.

"I promised I'd never leave you again. And I meant it."

A small tear rolled down her cheek and he wiped it away with his thumb. Her gaze sparkled in the moisture and rays of the sun. He found a piece of sea glass one time on a mission in Australia. The translucent green so precisely captured the color of Magdalena's eyes, but her gaze awed him so much more than that ocean tumbled bauble. Law touched his lips to hers in a delicate kiss. The tension in her neck vanished as she relaxed in his embrace while he collected all her discarded rigidity in order to rein in his desire.

He slid his mouth over hers, sparking electricity that had nothing to do with static. The tingle spread through his lips to his heart. The prickle headed south, but was railroaded by the passing lipstick lady.

"Get a bloody room," she scoffed.

Though he had no inclination to stop tasting Magdalena's sweet mouth, the eagerness to usher her to safety won out. He placed a chaste kiss on the tip of her nose.

"She's right."

"Oh?" Magdalena's pupils dilated and she leaned into his palms.

"I need to get you out of the city. It's not safe."

Her slightly drunken expression lifted and she straightened. "Oh. Right."

Law grabbed her hand and pulled her against him as they headed for the exit. When she hauled back he surrendered his hands. "I wasn't trying to invade your space."

Magdalena's lips quirked. "So, that was a non-invasive kiss?"

His mouth fell open then closed.

"Law, I'm not worried about you violating my territory." She flashed him a crooked smile. "I don't want to hurt you."

Would he ever find even footing again? He guessed, no. Not with Magdalena around. And he could maybe live with that. "Huh?"

"Your side. You're hurt," she whispered.

"Come on." He tucked her back against him and led them through the terminal. Their casual pace and embrace belied his acute awareness of everyone around them. Men. Women. Children. No matter their age, race, or perceived disability, they all gained his attention. When they walked out onto the street, his wariness only multiplied. Magdalena slowed and it seemed her unease grew as well, but for a totally unrelated reason.

"I'm not riding on that thing again." Her sharp finger pointed at his Hog as if it were a dragon or some other equally terrifying mythical beast. Tugging her along, he continued to the bike and set about stowing her gear. "You must not have heard me," she added. Both her hands jumped to her hips. "So, I'll say it again."

"What do you have against my best girl?" He slung a leg over and inserted the key.

Magdalena's little mouth wrinkled and she shot him with those laser eyes. "I don't like the way it makes me feel."

"And what way is that, exactly?"

"Reckless. Wild. Completely out of control. It makes me a little queasy. It makes my hands shake and my insides quiver. Like I may have a heart attack at any moment."

"Well, tart, get used to it. Lord knows I've had to."

Her upper lip did an Elvis curl. "Why would you ride the thing, if it makes you feel that way?"

He winked at her and reached for her hand. Magdalena set her palm against his. When he tugged she climbed onto the back of the motorcycle. Her thighs snuggled his ass and her arms wrapped around the leather jacket he sweated to death inside of and held on loosely, careful not to aggravate the raw knife wound.

Law shifted in the seat, offering her the helmet she hated so dearly. "I wasn't talking about the bike, tart. I was referring to you."

Magdalena blocked him out with the helmet and they rode peaceably until they reached the outskirts of the city. When he passed Heathrow International she fidgeted. Law turned onto the M3 and the houses waned in number, overtaken by lush greenery. Rolling hills carpeted in flowing grasses soon turned into tall trees bright with emerald leaves. Magdalena tapped Morse code on his shoulder. Of course, she had no idea what she was saying. But he understood the message: *Where the hell are we going?*

He spoke through the helmet's Bluetooth intercom system. "I don't know exactly where we're going."

"Ha, you've had this capability the entire time we've been riding this thing—"

"This Hog. Or motorcycle. Or Harley," he interjected.

"Whatever, you're just now using it?"

They banked into an easy curve. Intuitively, her arms cinched around his middle and her weight shifted with him. An image of their weight shifting together in an entirely different manner capitulated his thoughts down a path littered with potholes, roadblocks, and mudslides.

"Why?" she asked. "And where?"

"I didn't turn it on because it didn't occur to me. I've never had anyone on here with me."

"You're kidding, right?"

"No."

"Is the...Hog new?"

"Had her for nearly eight years."

"And you've never had anyone on here with you? Not even a random?"

"No. As to your other question, we need to lay low for a couple of days. So, I'm just driving until something looks good."

"Okay," she whispered. "When we get to wherever we're going, can we eat?"

Oh God, he was a total goner. Keister over heels in love with this woman. His shoulders shook with laughter. "Anything you want, tart."

Chapter Twenty-two

Showered and full-bellied, Magdalena and Law sat at the tiny round table in the room they checked at a quaint old-world hotel in the equally nostalgic town of Amesbury. Neither spoke more than the words necessary to orchestrate their respective cleanliness and in-room dining service. And both avoided the bed like the mattress played host to a bevy of bedbugs.

The awkwardness began when they entered the room and Law stilled like he found a gunman lying in wait or a bomb ready to explode. For the barest of seconds, Magdalena's mind haunted her with all the possibilities, but she stepped into the room ready to face the horror. Only she hadn't been ready at all.

Beyond Law, thick tapestries, a low-slung ceiling, and smoke-stained fireplace suffocated the room in a boudoir feel. If she thought the kiss at the station threw her for a loop, the king-sized canopy bed Law's gaze riveted to knocked her smooth out. Four scrolled wooden posters scraped the ceiling and connected beams carved with intricate rosettes. The rich mahogany of the head and foot boards hosted masterfully sculpted flares and flowers. But the yards and yards of gauzy white fabric made it a bed fit for fucking.

Magdalena's nipples tightened beneath the simple tank she wore, just thinking about the sex sled. Awareness of the rough breaths flowing in and out of Law's flared nostrils followed suit. She clamped her eyes shut and willed away the stir of hormones inside her body. The emotions of the past two days were quite enough to handle, without adding sex to the mix. Not that her body didn't scream for his. It had since the first moment they touched in obstinate fashion, attuned to his every move. His every glance. But she couldn't throw every newfound moral in the dumpster because she thought she loved another chap. Okay, she knew she did, but it still didn't give her carte blanche to wrap her legs around him and ride him harder and longer than they'd ridden the bike.

She tried to lighten the heaviness in the room. "Don't tell my father we were this close to Stonehenge and didn't go see it. He'd be pissed. Maybe even more so than he'll be about the house. He used to drag me out here once a year until I left for school."

Law's gaze jumped from his folded hands to her face, then flashed to her breasts before rising again. The muscles in his neck strained and he cleared his throat. "Don't worry about the house. It's been taken care of."

"What do you mean?"

"It's returned to normal, minus a few broken things which I've commissioned someone to replace."

Her hands stilled from worrying the fray of her usually very comfortable boxer shorts. A leave-behind from some bloke along the way. Now they only left her wishing for a thick terry robe to hide behind. "Thank you," she whispered. She worked up the nerve to meet his brilliant gaze. "Really, it means so much to me. You helped my dad. I hate that I couldn't do it myself, but thank you."

"Don't thank me," he rebuffed. His hand scraped across the stubble littering his face. "It's my fault... God, I can't believe I left you... I—"

"Stop, please." She smiled wide to stave off the tears threatening mutiny against her. "Not right now. I can't talk about that yet."

His gaze fell to his lap and he found an interesting stitch in the jeans covering his wide legs. "Clara and I met junior year in a two day pre-law course at UCL. She beat me in a mock trial preceding and I was in love."

Magdalena's heart seared like the chef decided to serve her tattered organ for breakfast and fried it up inside her chest. Jealousy, the ugliest emotion, hurt so intensely she surprised herself by holding back the shriek.

Law pinched his lips between his teeth then released them and met her gaze. "So hard and fast it caught my breath. Everything fell into place like I'd been told it would my whole life." He swallowed. "I have sisters, remember. That plus my over-the-moon-in-love parents, I never had a chance. Clara and I had our lives perfectly planned by the second month."

Mags was lucky to have an outfit planned the night before she needed it. No way in hell could she plan a life in two months. It had taken her years of agonizing to decide on her own goals, without having to take anyone else into consideration. Hearing this made her question her own maturity, and maybe feel a bit incompetent about achieving the lofty expectations she'd placed on herself. But no. Twenty-five years had led her to this place. She wouldn't degrade herself by judging it against others. Different people. Different lives.

"I asked her to marry me a few weeks later." A tear rolled down Law's strong jaw and fell to his shirt, turning the grey fabric it touched into a dark dot. The ominous mark grew as another dropped. He looked off into nowhere, and Mags knew he was reliving his time with Clara.

Her jealously faded away at the presence of his pain. Magdalena would give almost anything to return Clara to him. To ease the hurt that obviously changed the course of his life. Even if it meant she'd never know him or love him in any real way.

"She said yes, and my family immediately went to work planning an engagement party for the next weekend. All of us and some close friends. Stews. Bread. Cakes. It was a great time. The last really great time." Law wiped at the moisture on his face and sniffed, trying to compose himself.

"That night, after the party, I found a lump in her left breast."

"No," Mags whispered.

"We were optimistic. Then denial came. Cancer ate her from the inside out. So. Fast." He leaned forward, steepled his hands, and rested his mouth on the first two fingers, still a million minutes away from the present. "We dropped our course loads a month after the celebration. She couldn't even get out of bed the next week. And then she stayed in that in-between for so long. Not alive. Not dead. A skeleton of the woman I'd first met, but still so strong."

Magdalena closed her eyes and struggled to block out her own memories of the heinous sickness. When she opened them, tears cascaded down her face, but she clamped her mouth together. This was his purge. His chance to free a bit of the memories that preyed on him. He would never forget, but sharing them lessened their piercing edge. Even if only a little. Willow had been her restoration and Africa had been her rejuvenation. She would try to be one of them for Law.

"Then she was gone and so was I. All the plans we'd made for a law firm and future together went with her. The wind kicked me around for a year before I even thought about going back to school and finishing law. When I met Baine, we were both looking for something to help us forget the numbness." He exhaled. "And that's how we ended up living the life of James Bond. Well, parts of it anyway."

Law returned to the present with a vengeance. His left hand cupped her face while the other chased away her tears. "Why are you crying?"

Magdalena's lower lip quivered and his thumb arrested it. "I know her sickness. It's the most dehumanizing condition. When I was a girl I lost my mother to cancer. Clara was lucky to have you. Just like my mother was lucky to have my father."

She covered his hand with hers. "It takes a strong person to ease a loved one into death. But it's what they need. A hand to cling to. Loving eyes to tell them it's okay to go. That everything will be all right."

"Even if it is a lie."

He nodded, seemingly unable to speak for a moment. "What about you?"

"What about me?"

"Who took care of you while your dad took care of your mom?"

"Dad did the best he could. I was old enough to help out around the house."

"But not old enough to understand what was going on," he whispered.

"Who really understands premature death, or death at all?"

"I'm sorry I left you."

"I'm sorry I pushed."

"Don't. I needed a good shove and it seems you're the lass to give it to me. You asked me earlier, if I was still in love with her." Mags threw her hand up to stop him, but he grabbed it and intertwined their fingers. "I haven't been in love with Clara for a while now, but I haven't been living either. I've been caught in a deadened haze.

"When I saw you, you burned the clouds away and I'm just adjusting to the light. Slowly. And not very gracefully."

Law dropped his hand from her face and tugged her from the table. He led her to the far side of the bed, away from the guns on the nightstand, and pulled back the thick comforter. Even though she knew the gesture wasn't sexual, and that he would not kiss her tonight with all the rawness of their discussion in the foreground, her heart skipped at his closeness and care. She slipped between the sheets and watched him walk to the other side and do the same.

He settled the sheet around her shoulders and rested his head on the downy pillow. Their gazes locked in a near unblinking trance, connecting them more absolutely than sex had ever linked her with another human being. Three feet of bed yawned between them, but physical contact was inconsequential at the moment. Desire. Fear. Hope. Excitement. Love. The emotions swirled between them then slowly faded, as did her consciousness.

Chapter Twenty-three

"Look through it again," Law barked.

Magdalena's bleary eyes blinked the massive V of Law's tattooed back into view. *Good morning.* Judging by his tone, Law didn't share the sentiment, but she wouldn't let it ruin her spirit. She hadn't ever slept so well or woken to such a striking view. The Roman goddess Justitia stared at Magdalena, unseeing for the blindfold over her eyes. She stood with her chin high and arms outstretched. In her left hand she thrust a sword in the air, ready to strike. In the other the scales hung in balance. Cuffs of material clasped her upper arms, draped across her chest, and gathered about her legs. The prominent position covering much of his sinuous back and the artful excellence with which it sculpted against his smooth skin spoke to the importance its message had in his life.

Propping on an arm, she angled for a better look. A terry cloth towel, exposing the upper half of two muscle-arched dimples at the small of his back, rewarded her efforts. Her lips curved into a smile thinking about the other half of those dimples, hiding beneath the covering.

One of his arms held a phone to his ear while the other hung loose by his side. "No. I'm not," he growled. The free hand scraped over his head once and then again. When she sat and slid her feet over the side of the bed he twisted his torso toward her. He covered the mouthpiece. "I didn't mean to wake you."

"It's okay," she mouthed.

His chest expanded on a breath and she caught a glimpse of his tight abs as he returned to the vanity and his conversation. Small cuts littered his pecs and there were two punctuated gashes on his side and arm, but they didn't bother his economical movements. Magdalena walked to the image scrawled across his back as though drawn to it. Close, the detail enthralled her greedy gaze. And then her hand.

Law's breath hitched at the touch, but he made no move to stop her exploration. She started at the scales, noticing the barest raise of the inked skin beneath her fingers. Magdalena traced the blindfold, the length of the sword.

"I won't believe it until you check it yourself, or you can send the computer and drive back and we'll look through it ourselves." After a pause, he added, "None of your business. Goodbye, Khani."

Magdalena added two and two together and figured they hadn't found anything in her work files. Her heart sank, but the disappointment didn't have quite the effect it should have had because her hands, both of them, roved the deep groove of Law's spine, the inside curve of his lats and mounded traps. Mags focused on the tat to keep from soaking her panties, but the task became impossible as Law's breaths labored.

"Why Justitia? From the law books in your flat and your profession I know you like the law. Even your name rings true. But there's more to the story." She was sure of it.

"Nava Zegen was my great-grandmother. In 1943 she escaped the Warsaw Ghetto during the uprising after losing everything during the extermination. Her mother. Father. Four brothers and two sisters. And her son, who was ripped from her arms and shot before her eyes because she begged for a piece of bread for her starving child. They took everything from her, except her will to live."

Once again Magdalena's tears fell in earnest at the unimaginable injustice. Her throat tightened and her hands stopped and flattened on his back.

"After Clara died, I went to Europe, visited the mass graves where my relatives may or may not have been buried. I walked the path she took to freedom. I arrived in Finland a month later and got the ink as a constant symbol of what I fight for and of what I have to live for."

Magdalena lifted a hand to stem the flow of emotion, but only soaked her fingers. Her palm fell from Law's back as he turned and she considered every angle of his face. In turn, he stared at the bruise on her neck, which had turned vibrant green and yellow by dinner last night. Like a whisper, his fingers glided over the battered skin. She froze as his head lowered and his lips caressed the same spot.

The gulp that cleared the lump in her throat sounded loud enough to rock the windowpanes, but he didn't seem to care. Law collected her unruly hair in one hand and guided it over her shoulder while his other hand smoothed over her spine, nuzzling the dip of her ass and pulling her closer.

She exhaled in a rush as his mouth worked over her jaw. He licked tears from her cheeks. When his slick lips finally settled on her mouth, her pulse thrummed between her legs. He yanked her belly flush with the solid ridge of his cock. His six feet two inches to her five feet three placed the swell of his head awfully close to the curve of her breasts. Magdalena's nipples brushed his chest and abraded the thin cotton tank separating their skin, and she moaned into his mouth.

Before she could get her bearings, both his hands cupped her ass and lifted. He guided her core over his sex and wrapped her legs around his waist. She clung to him like he were the only source of oxygen in the world, interlocking her feet and sucking his tongue into her mouth at the same time. He groaned as she worked him to the tip then released him. Law turned and the backs of her legs hit the cool countertop as he settled her in front of him.

"You taste like sex, Magdalena. And I'm a starved man."

His words excited her and ignited a yearning she'd denied for too long. But apparently not as long as he had. She arched, rubbing her swollen, and irritatingly boxer covered, pussy lips up the length of his dick. "Eat your fill."

He entwined a hand in her hair and eased her back farther. Her full breasts and erect nipples pointed toward the ceiling. She whimpered as he licked his lips then dropped them to her right, and consequently, most sensitive peak. Wet heat enveloped the tip of her breast and she keened on contact, which spurred him to tug more firmly. He pulled her through his lips then returned with teeth, nipping and dragging the tender, cotton-covered flesh over the rigid texture. Liquid desire coated her lower lips, readying her to receive the thrusts of his manhood. Plumping her left breast with his big hand, he continued tormenting her already aching nipple. Magdalena moaned as his mouth grew bolder, suckling deep pulls she felt all the way to her vagina. She panted and bucked from the overwhelming sensation.

Law rested his head in the valley of her breasts and pulled several ragged breaths. "Christ, I'm like a virgin about to shoot at second base."

"You can, if you want. I won't mind," she gasped.

Teeth caught her collarbone and she giggled. "You ticklish?"

"Never knew I was ticklish there."

"Hmmm," his lips vibrated against her neck. "So, there are other places."

Magdalena's fingers explored Law's back from the new and much improved vantage point and enjoyed the dichotomy of his hard, smooth body. "Maybe," she evaded.

His grip slid to her ass cheeks and he molded the generous curves in his palm.   "God, your body is dangerous enough to kill a man."

"Oh yeah?"

"Fuck. Yes. Pure pleasure overdose. Call the police. I think I'm addicted."

Law straightened and the hands at her bottom smoothed up the slope of her hips. The pads of his fingers stirred her craving as they touched the bare skin of her torso and coasted up her waist.

"Raise your hands, Magdalena."

Her breath hitched in a mixture of excitement and surprise. Surprise she had no compunction about getting naked with Lawrence Pierce, the man who held her heart in his hands. Surprise he had overcome his misgivings and hurt so quickly. Startled and excited, Magdalena responded with complete obedience and willing anticipation.

He was one of *those* people. The ones at Christmas who opened their presents with such patience and care that others mauled their package like a rabid dog just to irritate the gentle package opener. Law took beautiful care lifting the hem of her shirt centimeter by precious centimeter. His gaze left her face and fell to the heated flesh he exposed. That decisive stare delighted her hypersensitive skin as though it actually caressed and coaxed the dewy surface.

An animalistic grunt rattled Law's chest as he finally lifted the thin shirt from her breasts. He disappeared from view for a moment while he pulled the fabric over her face and up the tips of her fingers. Her hair plummeted to her shoulders and Law discarded the shirt over his.

Standing back as he was, Magdalena studied the angles of his chiseled torso with salivating thoroughness. The groove down the center of his back was nearly recreated over his front as abutted ridges of muscle bisected his centerline. Two slabs of pectoral brawn ate up a good portion of the real estate. Flat disk nipples set wide and aimed at the ground. Below, eight. Yes, she counted correctly. Eight bricks of fibrous tissue formed the most glorious abdomen she'd ever seen. Where it disappeared behind the terry cloth intrigued her even more. Magdalena's tongue furled inside her mouth, longing to explore all the light and shadows of his body.

She dragged her gaze from his physique to his equally inspiring face which studied her form as she'd just appraised his, only with more fortitude and endurance. Magdalena couldn't endure much more waiting. Her core clenched, yearning for the thick cock that tented his towel.

Her hunger took the back burner as Law's hand raised toward her breast, but stalled inches away. The pinch of his brow said he wasn't exercising extreme self-control, but struggling with painful memories, or more aptly, their effect on the present. Magdalena grabbed his hand and brought his palm to her mouth. Her lips kissed and grazed the salty skin. Then she lowered his hand to her heavy bosom. The simple coaxing evened his brow.

His callused hands and rough fingers fondled her breasts tentatively. After a few easy strokes, he molded and tugged them with avid appreciation. Magdalena's hips rocked against his cock. She braced her hands on the chilled tile for leverage and worked her clit along the thick column as he teased her distended nipples. Breath rushed through her lips and foreign electricity sparked deep in her core. Its current pulsed with each roll of her hips and flick of his finger, expanding and consuming her restraint.

"Oh, Law," she moaned. Her head fell back. One of his hands coaxed up the span of her neck while the other wrapped around her back, anchoring her to his cloth-covered penis. Law drove his hips forward and the energy boomed, reverberating through her pussy walls. "Fuck. Yes."

"Magdalena." His hot groan coursed over her neck. "I want to fuck you so damn hard."

"Aaaaah." Her broken moan was the closest she could come to consent this close to release.

"I want to make love to you. And never stop."

She didn't know how, but she formed one complete word in answer. "Yes." Then the current of her orgasm obliterated coherent thought. It strangled every muscle and nerve ending in her entire body until she died. The sweetest death. It allowed her breaths to rush in and out of her chest in gasps and his touch to remain ever potent to her flesh.

"Exquisite," he whispered at her ear. His grip tightened as she sagged in repletion. "I've got you."

Law's mouth burned a trail of steaming kisses along her neck to her breasts. He blew humid air across the sensitive flesh then licked a slow spiraling circle to the point, regenerating the electricity that already fried her once. Magdalena swallowed a moan as he sucked her nipple into his wet mouth and flicked the live tip with his tongue.

She levered her head from its backward loll and watched his mouth adore her. His gaze traveled over her heaping breast, locking with her own. He released the engorged flesh then tormented both buds with his tongue. The veins in his neck bulged as he studied her reaction to his loving, which fed her excitement all the more.

"Law, you have to stop. I'm going to come again."

His lips sealed over her mouth and drank her deep, pulling her tongue and fucking her mouth. When he broke the kiss they both gulped air. Firm, confident hands glided over her shoulders and across her breasts. The corner of his mouth quirked as he moved over the soft flesh of her belly. "Magdalena, you're going to come a lot." Law charmed her bellybutton with his index finger and Mags sucked in her stomach. "Found another one. God you're going to kill me." He ground his penis against her core.

Magdalena clutched his hot lats, rolling along his ridge and angling for the perfect contact. She moaned as his thumbs plunged beneath the waistband on her boxers. Her entire body prepared for his touch, but it didn't come. And neither did she.

Chapter Twenty-four

Three raised bumps on Magdalena's hip that would hide easily behind the smallest bikini bottoms stopped Law cold. His entire body seized like an old machine prone to malfunction. Her lusty half-lidded gaze popped wide. And probably looked about as confused as his.

Law stepped back enough to relieve the pressure from his swollen cock and flipped back the band of her shorts. As he had suspected, three horizontal scars marred her skin. The puffed tissue contrasted with the creamy background in hues of pink. The top line stretched only an inch of her flesh while the other two lashed beneath it in decreasing length. The final one looked more like a small circle than a line.

"Where did they come from?"

Magdalena stared at him for a moment longer then her gaze sank to the spot in question. "A family I stayed with for a couple of months in DRC honored me with a tribal mark."

"This was burned, not cut."

"All a part of the ritual." Her gaze narrowed as she deliberated. "It hurt, but not terribly, and it was the greatest praise I'd ever received. They don't include many outsiders in their traditions."

"What do the markings mean?"

Her swollen lips thinned and she gave him a lopsided smile that made him want to bar the doors and windows and never leave this place. She cleared her throat. "They're for fertility."

The words hit him like a dead body dropped from way the fuck above his head. But his response shocked him all the more. Every muscle in his body tensed as it always did right before he came. The blood flowing through his carnal tool doubled, as damn near did its size, along with the need rushing through his veins. An urge, desperate and primal, demanded he spread Magdalena's legs before him and give her his seed. His child. Their child.

Starbursts flashed behind his lids as the earth shattered apart beneath his feet. He'd never thought about kids with Clara. They'd been career driven. And after, the possibility never occurred to him. But Magdalena. The woman corrupted his mind so completely that he wanted to have a child with her and never let either of them go. But sometimes, the decision to stay or go was not his to make. Life hung in the balance every day. And that rocked him to the core.

"Do you want children, Magdalena?"

Her smile evened and brightened, if it were possible for the sun to burn brighter. "Only about five or six."

"What about your career? Baine told me you have big plans for a world-wide media empire."

She winked at him. "I like to have dessert. And I like to eat it too."

Lord save him from those long lashes and open eyes. "What about all the horrors in the world? All the things you saw first hand in the Congo? I saw your pictures. And that's not even the worst of it."

Magdalena straightened, unabashed in her nudity. She placed a hand over his heart and her fingers caressed him. "Children are the light in the darkness. The purity of humanity. Hope for the future. I absolutely want them, *because* of what I've seen. Their smiles wash away all the hurt and heartache."

"What if something happens to them?" he whispered.

"Life gives you no guarantees. So, you love with all you have. And enjoy the time you're given. If not, what's it all for anyway?"

The world shrank in on his shoulders and though he struggled to pull a breath, no air came. He stumbled back. Magdalena's hand fell away. Law watched, unable to move, as he dashed the heat and hope from her face. He turned away from everything in the world he wanted and ran to the door. His hand flew to the knob. Uncaring about his state of undress, he turned the lock.

His own words played over in his head. *I'll never abandon you again.*

Law rested his head on the door with a *thunk* and gripped the handle so forcefully he thought he might leave indentions of each of his fingers. His teeth ground together and he wondered what the fuck was wrong with him. Why couldn't he breathe? Why could he stare his own death in the face time and again without blinking, but ran like a sissy in pink panties when the life of someone he loved was on the metaphorical line?

He hated the weakness crippling him. Hated himself for hurting Magdalena. By the time he could actually inhale a decent lungful of air, she had disappeared behind the bathroom door. He couldn't blame her for running. She'd do well to continue in the same direction for a thousand miles. She deserved someone who could give her all the things she wanted, which was no less than she deserved.

Chapter Twenty-five

Well, fuck it all, she couldn't hide in the bathroom all day. She'd already managed nearly two hours with a shower and cry, shaving, tweezing, make-up, hair drying, a re-apply of the make-up she cried off while blow-drying, and finally, some nail filing. God, she twitched for a cigarette and thanked the lucky stars there were none readily available. On the bright side, there were two bad habits she couldn't fall back into.

Her stomach roared for the fifth time in a minute and she caved. The room had been silent for a long while, and she wondered if perhaps he did break his word and leave. Not that he owed her anything at all. They were nothing to each other. Just victims of circumstance.

If only you could convince your stupid heart, ole girl.

Magdalena reached for the knob, dragged a fortifying breath, and exited her closet sized sanctuary. Law sat in the same chair he had for dinner the previous night, but the similarities to that magical time ended there. The connection they'd experienced only hours before seemed a dream her subconscious weaved. His locked jaw and vacant eyes acted as a force field, discounting everything without the decency of acknowledging it ever existed.

"Are you hungry?"

His voice held none of the playfulness or blatant irritation she'd come to expect. The pain radiated so loudly through her body she couldn't think to speak. Her nod answered his question. Law snagged the menu from the nightstand, and suddenly being stuck in a room with him was more than she could bear.

"I need to go out. I can't be locked in here with you, if you're not going to fuck me." Well, that certainly got a reaction.

Law launched to his feet and scrubbed his hands over the lengthening stubble on his head like he wanted to rub it bald. He laughed an empty bark. "So, you're one of those girls. Just want to get some, huh?"

"Screw you. I'm a woman who knows what she wants and isn't afraid to go after it."

"You want sex. That's fine. I'm certain a million guys would happily give it to you."

Magdalena bit her tongue to stave off her tears. "After my mother died, I was alone. Yeah, I had my dad, but a girl needs her mum. As soon as I came of age, I figured out a way to keep my fear at bay. Not with guns or explosions, but with men."

Law's jaw tightened and the tiny movement gave her hope that he cared. "You ran away from people, afraid you would care for them. I ran headlong *toward* people, afraid to feel alone in the world. For a long time, I mistook sex for intimacy. A really good friend helped me see how I was hurting myself. I chose to leave behind every security escape I knew. I chose to be alone with myself. I chose to face my fear.

"I don't want sex, Law. I want you."

His chin lifted. "I'm not for sale."

Magdalena had never hit anything in her life. Not even her pillow in a fit of rage. But the *slap* of her palm meeting his face echoed in the room before she realized what she'd done. "I'm not buying."

Chapter Twenty-six

Magdalena drank heavily from the glass then returned it to the patio table. She scrawled an F and U in the dew droplets and lifted her face to the sun, wishing it could radiate the past week from her memory. Africa had been so great. Maybe her mistake was coming back. If she hadn't come back, she wouldn't have seen Willow getting the shit beat out of her and none of this would have happened.

She jumped up from her slouch and cut her gaze at Law, who'd been stubbornly quiet since their spat. "I'll be back. I need to make a phone call."

Before she shoved her chair back, Law laid his phone on the wood next to her plate. "You may want to be rid of me, but you're not leaving my sight. Unless you want to lock yourself in the bathroom again."

Nope. She wasn't one bit sorry she slapped him. "Fine." She added the eye roll for effect. Childish, yes, but so what.

The screen lit as she typed in Willow's cell number. After the second try and subsequent voicemail she gave up and slid Law his phone.

"Tell me about the phone call earlier." As an afterthought she added, "Please."

"I'm sorry."

"Tell me about your—"

"I heard what you said," he interrupted.

"Oh," she said before everything clicked into place. He'd apologized. What exactly for, she wondered. Calling her a whore? Fleeing the best sexual experience of her life? Withdrawing from their non-relationship more times than a porn star did a vagina? Unequipped to hear the answer, she ignored the question, for now. "Please, just tell me about the call."

"No links were found between you and any faction in Africa. They went through every picture you had access to and every story you worked on, as well as those of your colleague, Owen Vos."

"How'd they get his stories?"

When he didn't answer she moved on to more important things. "Okay, I think we've been looking in the wrong direction. All this started after I saw Willow getting knocked around by the mystery man. I've tried to call her, twice, without any response, and she lives with her phone attached to her hand."

Law went palms-up in surrender. "Is it possible she doesn't want to talk to you?"

"Obviously, I've thought about it. And, so have you, since it's something you can relate to. But Willow saw me through my bad times. I won't sit by and let her destroy her life just because she doesn't want to let me in. The same goes for you.

"I gave you Africa because, as crazy as it sounded, it fit better than a domestic disturbance blown out of proportion. But now, I'm not so sure. I'm going to pack my tiny bag of mostly dirty clothes then I'm going to my flat, or at least, what *was* my flat, to try and get some answers."

"Magdalena, the guys who attacked us yesterday were professional hit men."

Mags sank into her chair at that heavy dose of reality. "Hit men?"

"Ex-royal military with some covert ops experience is my best guess. My people should have some information on them by this evening. Tomorrow at the latest. Then we can see what connections we can draw from there."

"By *your people*, you mean...?" Again he didn't bite. "Fine, but I'd like to check on Willow and try to help figure out this whole mess."

Law's cheek wrinkled with a smile. "I know you want to help, but you'll do that by staying safe and tucked away."

Magdalena pulled her spine straight and leaned into his space. "Do you really want to be locked in a room with me, all day and all night?"

His gaze lowered to her mouth then lower still. When his green eyes returned to hers, a glower surrounded them.

She flashed a smile at their waiter and the young bloke walked over. "We need the check, please."

Chapter Twenty-seven

Good judgment passed Law on the highway, speeding in the opposite direction of Cardiff. With two hours motoring toward the first place Magdalena had been attacked, he had every opportunity to clutch the brakes or slide off an exit and turn the fuck around. But he barreled into the trim port city, Magdalena clutching his sides, because her instincts were correct in all likelihood. Other than the missing files at her father's house and her trip to the DRC, nothing tied the incident to Africa. A harder look at the inciting drama rocking his ordered world seemed the wisest course of action. A shit ton better than sitting in a hotel room wallowing in the mire of his own hell.

He was a first rate prick who deserved every smack or scowl Magdalena wanted to dole. If only she'd popped him hard enough to jar the fear from his skull. He'd thought the near miss at his flat had cured him. *That's what you get for thinking, chump.*

Three little scars had changed the game while he ran down field. He'd come to terms, lumpy and uncomfortable as they were, about the possibility of losing Magdalena. But a helpless child, with her wild hair and spray of freckles? He couldn't explain the aloofness of the reaper or the finality of death to a puerile mind, nor could he survive their untimely end. He wanted to be as brave as Magdalena, to love free and wide regardless of the potential fallout. For now, he'd have to settle for figuring the one solvable mystery at hand.

He circled the block twice, looking for potential threats, before parking the Harley between two dumpsters off the back alley and sliding off. Flipping open the saddlebag, Law retrieved a small forensics kit and extra magazine and shoved them into the pockets of his jacket. The thing kept him toasty on winter days and cooked him alive on summer ones, like today, but it was the best way to carry both his Sauers without notice.

"This way." Magdalena moved through the heavy metal rear access door of a newer glass, brick, and stucco building.

Hand on his sidearm, Law followed close behind, scanning the deserted corridors for any sign of trouble. The teenage girl with shorts as obscenely short as Magdalena's didn't count as a threat. At least, not to him. The stare his fiery little woman gave the gawking youth said otherwise. He smiled at Magdalena's back then kicked himself for branding her as his when he couldn't be the man she needed.

But Lord, he wanted to mark her. To make her his and never let her go.

"It's that one." She pointed at a neatly painted white door on the other side of the balustrade.

"Once we get in, stay behind me."

Magdalena slid the key into the door and regarded him with those soft green eyes. Fear and determination swam in their depths, along with a little sadness and something else. Love. He'd seen the look in a woman's gaze once before. Then, it made him invincible. Now, it humbled him like a puddle at her feet.

Why were the women he loved so damn fearless? Clara took on death with a straight chin. Magdalena saw the ugliest side of him and fought the skeletons away with her sassy mouth, tenacious spirit, and bare hands while he sat on the sidelines. It was in his nature to confront and battle the injustices in the world. Yet, he'd allowed his own fears the latitude to corrupt his life.

Determined to combat his weakness and face his fear, no matter the result, Law placed his hand over her delicate fingers. "Magdalena, I don't know how to love you." Her lips spread as though she were about to lay into him. "But—"

Both their heads snapped at noise from beyond the apartment's door. Like the squeak of a chair dragged or a heavy piece of furniture being shoved across a wooden floor, wood groaned against wood in an unmistakable sound of human presence. Law scooped Magdalena behind him and twisted the key. He pulled his Sig from its holster, flipped the safety, and grabbed the knob.

"Don't shoot Willow," Magdalena whispered.

"What does she look like?"

"My height, but skinnier. Brown hair and eyes."

Law nodded. "Watch our backs."

Her adamant nod tugged at his jacket, which she held in a death grip at the lower hem. Law turned the knob, clearing the latch, closed his eyes, and strained to hear any noise from inside the flat through the thin gap he created. He held the wood-finished handle of his gun at the ready, but eased his left hand up in a countdown for Magdalena. Three. Two. One. They moved with surprising grace, her tight against his back, through the doorway.

Law's sight adjusted instantly to the dim entrance, scanning right to left for the barrel of enemy guns. None presented themselves. Magdalena closed the door behind them, her white knuckles threatening to strangle the knob if it made a sound. As they moved deeper into danger Law swept the kitchen in silence, finding only a sleek modern arrangement of appliances and clean lined furniture in the living area beyond. Everything from the dishtowel hanging to the left of the sink and the magazines stacked on the small living room table rested pertly in its place. No huge pieces of furniture provided an opponent a vantage point against them. Still, irritation tickled his nape. Things were too quiet.

His pace increased, as did his wariness, as he cleared the first bedroom, a soft palate of lilac and white that seemed incongruous to the lightning rod of a woman behind him. But it smelled like the wild vanilla of her skin. The closet doors gaped open. Its contents littered the floor, but the articles weren't tossed as those at her father's house had been. These lay shoved in small piles in a deliberate path to the back corner. A mallet and red ball leaned against the far joint of the wardrobe. He discounted the mess as one Magdalena had created while trying to save her friend like she'd recounted.

The last bedroom sat pin neat, every last colorful pillow in its place atop the bed. By design, three paintings hung askew above the headboard. A rift between the windowsill and bottom frame caught his attention, but he held himself back. Law's gaze swung to the buttoned-up closet opposite the foot of the bed. He removed Magdalena's hands from his jacket and stayed her at the doorway with a raised palm. He pointed two fingers at his eyes then turned them out the doorway. With a hesitant gnaw of her lip, Magdalena's gaze left him and the ominous closet it bounced between and locked on the corridor.

Law holstered his Sig, opting to have both hands free in the close quarters. He eased toward the closet and wrenched the door open. He didn't bother using the paltry wood as a shield, but attacked the interior like a grizzly busting open a garbage can in search of a meal. Dresses and vibrant tops fell from the rod. Shoes cascaded from their neatly stacked boxes.

When he came up one bad guy short, a growl rumbled from his throat. *Someone was just here and you tipped them off, getting all sappy.* Law's gaze snagged the window and he launched himself at it. Fingers curled under the edge, he heaved the thing open. The same screech they'd heard earlier pierced the air.

Careful not to get his head shot off, Law peered out enough to see a dark iron fire escape snuggled to the side of the building. He leaned over the edge and watched a man jump from the lowest landing to the street below. The bloke took the fifteen-foot drop and hit the concrete below on the balls of his feet, curled into a ball, and rolled up from the crouch in one fluid motion.

Law admired the free-runner types. What they did with their bodies was nothing short of amazing, but fuck he hated chasing them. It always ended with a bullet in their ass and him sucking wind like an old geezer.

"Stay here," Law barked. But before he could leap onto the escape, the speedy chap veered into the alley, headed for the back of the building. "Damn." He turned into the apartment. "Lock the door behind me." With everything he had, Law propelled himself through the flat and into the stairwell. He took each set of stairs in a single leap, steadying each jarring impact on the lands with his grip on the railing.

Light but rapid footfalls sounded a story above his head and irritation tickled his spine. Magdalena hadn't listened. The accompanying breathy gasps gave her away, but he couldn't stop to reprimand her for putting herself in harm's way. Law doubled his efforts, putting as much distance between himself and Magdalena as he could while closing the span between himself and the man he pursued. He needed answers and it was bloody time he got them.

Sweat stung his eyes, but he didn't bother wiping it away. Two more bounds and he landed in the main lobby. Law turned to the back of the building and surged down the corridor he and Magdalena had entered minutes ago. He slowed only enough to shoulder the door and push through it.

Lightning flashed in his eyes so brilliant and painful he'd swear the sky opened and struck him down as soon as his feet hit the pavement. His skull threatened to shatter at the force. He gripped it with both hands, holding the shards together as the world tilted and he met the hard surface with a *thud*.

The *whack* of impact at his ribs gave Law the first clue that he hadn't been struck down by the thunder god. A hail of blows tenderized his gut and his body took over, balling into the fetal position. The brunt of each hit burned his belly and sent bile pitching toward his throat.

Law struggled to open his eyes, but they refused his commands like some critical nerve had been severed. Hell, he couldn't even see where the attack came from. Training overrode instinct and

Law focused on the senses he had to locate his attacker. Bits of gravel and sand crunched in front of him and the kicks originated from the same place each time, even the same damn foot—a foot covered with a steel toe boot.

Magdalena's gut-rending scream compelled his left eye open just enough to see her petrified form fixed at the far end of the corridor. Her face contorted in a broken expression of horror. Only still for a moment, she ran for him. Fear shredded his heart, making a mockery of the anxiety he managed before. Magdalena ran toward certain death. No matter what he tried, half beaten to his own demise he was no match for this son of a bitch. If he grabbed for his gun, the man would just as likely rip it from his grasp and shoot the two of them with it.

Law breathed as deeply as he could, kicked the man's left foot, and crawled to the door. Magdalena's face brightened then fell as he closed her inside. "Run," he hollered. But only a rasped choke escaped his lips. He collapsed the weight of his torso against the door and faced his attacker. And found two through the slit of his lid. The one he'd seen drop from the escape dusted the leg of his blue jeans. The other held Magdalena's cricket bat in his meaty hand.

The door jarred as his sweet Magdalena pushed against the door. Her screams filled his ears. And he regretted so much. Bringing her here. Acting rash and barreling into the situation without adequate recon or back up. Not being strong enough to take these fuckers out. But most, he regretted not telling her how much he loved her.

Chapter Twenty-eight

Magdalena shoved at the door, straining every feeble muscle she possessed. As it had five times before, the door opened only a crack before slamming shut. The *clack* of metal on metal rang in her ears as did her sobs. Tears streamed down her cheeks in rolling waves with every failed attempt to help the man she loved.

He'd closed her inside to save her, no doubt, but she would rather die fighting to save him than listen to the sickening *thuds* of the beating he endured. "Law," she screamed. "Let me out!" Magdalena balled her fists and beat them against the door. "Please."

"Please shut up!"

Magdalena pivoted, fists drawing back instinctually at the woman who'd caught her unaware.

A thirty-something gal in a wrinkled sleep shirt and bare legs shrank back against her opened apartment door. Her hands flew to her chest, palms out, warding Magdalena off. She'd never elicited such a response from another human being. She would have apologized, but she couldn't think of decorum with Law's life in danger. Desperation clouded self-preservation and every other civil tendency her father cultivated during her formative years.

"Does your flat have a window to the alley?"

Black jaw-length curls flopped back and forth. "I don't have anything worth stealing. I work two jobs just to afford this place."

"I'm not robbing you. My friend is being attacked in the alley. I need to help him."

"In the middle of the day?"

"Yes," Mags hollered, beyond frantic to be at Law's side.

"I'll call the police." The lady stepped into her flat, a flash of relief slacking her tight features.

Magdalena ducked past her into the unfamiliar layout.

"Hey."

"By the time the police get here he'll be dead. Please, where is the bloody window?" Mags ran headlong, not waiting for a response, fumbling her way through the maze of rooms.

"Last bedroom. End of the corridor," the woman's voice called from the entryway.

All the curtains were drawn tight throughout the flat and in the master bedroom the sheets lay tossed back. Magdalena bound onto the bed and shoved the thick fabric over the window to the side. A green wall greeted her. The dumpster they parked by nearly abutted the building, blotting out the sunlight. She smashed her face against the icy glass and peered down the back street. To the right, green blocked her view, but to the left she saw the tip of the Hog's handle and the sleek side fender.

"What in the hell are you doing?"

Mags turned to the woman, who had both hands shaking in the air. "Close and lock this behind me as quietly as you can and stay inside your flat."

"For sure."

With her swift breaths hushed by force of will, Magdalena unlatched the window and tugged. Inch by measured inch she increased the gap and thanked the contractor for installing stealthy new windows in this part of the building. As the window opened wider the sound of flesh smacking flesh filtered through, causing her lower lip to quiver.

Finally, the window yawned wide; she slipped one foot out and prayed it would fit between the dumpster and wall of the building. Her sandals scraped along the brick in what sounded like a break in the sound barrier. Magdalena froze for a moment, but the beating did not. So, she gripped the frame, ignored the woman's wide-eyed stare, and lowered herself toward the ground. Her stomach and elbows scraped the stucco sill on the way down, stinging only a microscopic fraction as badly as her heart did.

When her feet hit the pavement Mags shuffled like a real-life version of Gumby, the flat green chum she'd seen as a kid, away from the fight until daylight enveloped her. She hurried on tiptoes to the Harley, flipped open the saddlebag, unzipped her pack, and shoved her hand into the depths. Cold metal slid beneath her fingers and she clamped down on it.

Never in her life could Magdalena Wells have pictured herself holding a gun, much less preparing to shoot someone with it. Inside, her nerves quaked an eight on the Richter scale. But her fingers gripped firm and steady around the sleek wood-finished grip. She thumbed the safety down, filled her lungs with the humid air, lifted the threatening metal with both hands, and stepped out from behind the dumpster.

Two men stood over Law. One wrenched his leg back and slammed it into Law's stomach again and again. The other bastard watched, twirling a cricket bat in his hand like he itched to take a swing. Law's only saving grace was that he had arms big enough to absorb some of the blows and block his ribs from being snapped like dry twigs.

Never had she seen or imagined Law vulnerable like any other person. His thick muscles and armored heart created an illusion of invincibility. But the man she loved lay slumped against the door, a curled ball of susceptibility. Even in his weakened state he was powerful. He blocked her exit. Guarding her until the end.

"Stop!" Magdalena's voice bounded off the brick walls and reverberated in her head in a gritty pitch of demand. The word came from deep inside. Someplace strong, someplace she didn't know existed.

The punter's leg gridlocked on a back swing. In unison, two sets of eyes found her and narrowed as they registered the gun. Magdalena couldn't look at Law again, fearful she might accidentally shoot him or lose her bare-threaded composure and give the attackers the upper hand.

"Back away," she commanded.

The chav with the bat, her cricket bat, stepped forward. "The information we got didn't say anything about you knowing how to shoot. Your grip's pretty good for a first timer, but I don't think you have what it takes to pull the trigger."

"I can pull the trigger. The question is, can I hit what I aim for? I could try for your shoulder and hit your nuts. Assuming you have any," Magdalena taunted like she wasn't about to pass out.

"Fuck it," bat-boy said. "We were supposed to bring you in alive for some fun, but I like my sack where it belongs. How about you, Mac?"

The kicker fisted his junk and shook it, flexing the area toward Magdalena. "Yeah, I like em' attached all right. Shoot her and we'll find them some other entertainment."

Her breath caught. She hadn't expected them to have guns. She didn't expect *anyone* to have a gun, because she hated them. But a cold hand gripped her throat as bat-boy switched hands with the bat and reached behind his back.

Magdalena's hand tingled from the rabid grip she had on the weapon, but she adjusted the man in her sight and pulled the trigger. The thing exploded in a concussive sound that rippled through her entire body. It bucked wildly. The shot went wide, chipping away a hunk of brick in the building to her left. Her grasp loosened on the unruly beast and she readjusted in time to see the barrel of the man's gun and his zealous gaze squared on her chest.

Two gun blasts cracked the hot day. Magdalena had no time to react. She stood static. A perfect target.

The cylindrical metal hole she stared into did launch a bullet at her heart. It quavered and her gaze drew to the man's face. His intense stare washed vacant. The wrinkles in his sneer slacked. His life evaporated in the brutal sunlight and he collapsed to the baking ground, blood seeping from behind his ear.

Magdalena looked at the gun in her hand and the man on the ground, and then her gaze snapped toward the second assailant. Unlike the man who lay sprawled in front of her, he lay in a knotted heap against the wall. Beside him, Law pitched on his side. One of his arms wrapped around his middle. The other clasped his Sig, now resting on his thigh.

Emotions roiled inside her body, ricocheting and eviscerating her composure. The sobs she'd shoved aside only minutes earlier broke free as she sprinted for Law. His regal jaw set in a hard line. The flesh of his right brow split wide, oozing blood down the angles of his cheek. Swelling puffed the skin around it, sealing his lid shut in a macabre painting of blues, purples, and yellows. His left eye had taken some of the impact, bloating the hood of his eye to half-mast.

She skidded to a stop on her knees beside him, her hands shooting out to help, but only hovering. It seemed there was no safe place to touch him. "What can I do?"

"Start by flipping on your safety," he rasped.

"Oh God. I'm so sorry." She tried to stem the waterworks, but her sobs only transformed to hiccups. A flick of the lever set the gun on safety and she glanced at Law's gun. Of course, he'd already managed his weapon.

"Magdalena."

"Yes," she sniffled.

"Don't be sorry. You saved my life."

"I didn't. I—"

"You did. Now, stow your gun in my left holster."

Law raised his arm and muffled a groan behind his pinched lips. Magdalena lifted his jacket and snuggled the metal into the leather compartment. "Now mine," he said on a sharp breath. She repeated the task with a bit more difficulty since he lay on his right side.

"You're doing great, Magdalena. I'm going to need you to help me up."

"Okay, but where else are you hurt? If you have any broken ribs, moving you could puncture a lung."

"Staying here will get us in jail or dead."

Right. Her unwilling helper probably called the Met as she locked her window. Mags burrowed her head under the crook of Law's left arm, waited for his go-ahead, then pushed so hard her legs quaked from the effort. Together they staggered upright. Well, upright for her. Law hunched like Quasimodo. She gripped his arm for leverage and searched for an escape. There was no way he could drive the Hog in his condition.

"Do we hail a cab?"

"No. Bike. You drive."

"What?"

"I'll handle the clutch. You steer."

Magdalena couldn't speak for her shock and the use of every muscle and bit of coordination she had to keep pace with Law's shaky strides toward the damn motorcycle. Hiking his leg over the massive beast cost him dearly. His breath hissed in hasty pants. The beautiful lines of his face were mangled by blood, swelling, and wrinkles from a deep grimace.

He handed her the spare helmet and shoved his on with a string of vicious curses obscured by the hitch of his breaths. Magdalena shoved hers on, slipped on in front of Law, and hoped she hadn't just saved him to lose him in the wreckage of a multi-vehicle collision.

Chapter Twenty-nine

Even though Magdalena had been expecting it, her entire body jumped at the sharp knock on the motel door. Shit, she'd been counting down the seconds since she practically dragged Law from the motorcycle, into the room, and situated him in the chair next to her. He refused the bed and she hadn't had the heart to make him explain his reasoning. She just hoped his injuries weren't too serious. And that the obscure rural inn was far enough away from danger.

"Check first," Law croaked.

Bloody hell, she wasn't cut out for this clandestine shit. Her heart raced and the thing of it was she didn't know which life altering experience to attribute the constant and frantic thuds. Struggling to save Law from certain death? Firing a gun for the first time? Watching yet another man's life leave his body? Driving a fucking motorcycle through the crowded streets of London?

She attributed the current spike in her pulse to the gorgeous, yet menacing woman towering on the other side of the door. Jet hair barely brushed her shoulders and clouded grey eyes sharp enough to pierce Magdalena's sensitive skin stared back through the peephole. She swallowed past the swelling of her throat and looked at Law.

"Is she bloody huge?"

"Tall. Not fat."

"Right." She opened the door and the Amazon breezed past her, a bright lipstick orange-red mouth creased in a determined scowl. Slaughter, *if ever there was an apt name*, plopped the duffel bag she carried onto the bed and dropped to her knees beside Law.

"Next time, listen to me, would you? God damn it! If you'd had back-up this wouldn't have happened," Khani snapped. Before he could answer she rattled on. "That's one hell of a shiner you've got there. You know your mum is gonna kill us both for it?"

Onyx flashed in the lamplight then those stormy eyes were on her. Mags preferred obscurity to the direct poke of Khani Slaughter's gaze. "You're the one who got him into this mess in the first place?" Though phrased like a question it sounded more like an accusation of high treason.

"How about you take care of him first and grill me later?" Mags said with surprising grit.

"Fair enough." Khani turned her thickly lined eyes on Law and propped his chin on her folded index finger. "Looking at about ten sutures, give or take two, and a gnarly scar through your brow."

"Add it to the collection, doc," Law said.

Khani set out several packets of hospital grade supplies, stalked to the sink, and scrubbed her hands before scooting the other chair between Law and the bed with her knee-high laced boot. Over her shoulder she flashed Mags that daunting gaze. "You might want to go take a walk or go shower for this."

Magdalena shook her head. The Amazonian couldn't make her leave, unless she physically removed her from the room.

"Your lunch." Khani shrugged.

Law's swollen-lidded eye prodded Khani. "She's stronger than she looks. Braver than me, and you. I'd be dead, if it weren't for her."

Magdalena's chest squeezed at his praise, until Khani cleaned the gnarled wound above Law's eye. She hung back, giving Khani space, because of her own discomfort with the stranger who had such close ties to the man who held her heart. But when Law ground his jaw so tight the muscles in his face bunched, Mags no longer cared about anything other than comforting him. She walked to the far side of Khani's work station, clasped Law's left hand in her own, and hung on for dear life.

Every prick of the needle had Mags clamping down on Law's hand in encouragement, but by the fourth suture she knew he comforted her, not the other way around. Just when she thought she'd do him more good by going to take a shower, Khani hit a nerve and he seized her hand in a strangle hold. She squeezed back, lending her abiding love and ready support.

It seemed an eternity before Law lay passed out on the queen-sized bed, the hole on his brow stitched and tidied. Khani had checked his ribs which, judging by the breaths he hissed and sucked, hurt more than the closure, and given him the all clear. She ordered him two days rest, four if he could possibly manage.

"You go get cleaned up," Khani said. "I'll keep an eye on him."

Reluctantly, Magdalena left him. She showered in record time, dressed in her last clean tank and pair of boxers, and returned to the room feeling more awkward than ever. Like the first day of school the summer after she had gotten boobs hadn't been enough embarrassment to endure a lifetime.

"Thank you," Mags whispered. "I don't know what I would have done if..."

Khani shook her head. "I'm sorry. I was an ass. Law is my family. Not by blood. Thank fuck. But by bond. He's like my brother and I get a little overbearing sometimes. Thank you for whatever it is you've done for him."

Mags quirked a brow.

"He's different, besides having the shit kicked out of him. And it's a good different. Make sure it stays that way."

"What is it with you two and threats?"

"Sorry, I work with a bunch of men. It comes naturally. Anyway, I brought you each some clothes. Life on the run sucks."

"So I'm learning."

"If you think of anything else, call me. We're following the money on the assassin from the park, but it's taking a while. Tons of offshore and dummy accounts to work through."

"Assassin?"

Khani's expression lightened. "We'll figure it out and get you your life back soon. I promise. If you want to get some sleep, I'll drop food by this evening. Oh, I packed some granola bars, nuts, and fruit in the bag too."

"Sleep?"

"Yeah, take it while you can get it."

After locking the door behind Khani and thinking about sleep, Mags found her lids unusually heavy for mid-day. Then again, these past few days had been anything but typical. She crawled up the far side of the bed and rested her head on top of the covered pillow. Law's chest rose and fell, expanding his fresh white tee in a shallow but steady pace. Magdalena locked on the movement, thankful for each breath he took, because she'd sworn they'd both taken their last today.

Chapter Thirty

"Why are you up?" Mags bolted upright and rubbed the sleep from her eyes. Law stood at the small rectangular table by the window. Tiny rays of daylight glistened from the edges of the heavy curtain lighting the room and the purple and fuchsia shoe prints staining his bare abdomen. He laid his phone on the table and walked to the foot of the bed in a surprisingly even gate, given his earlier hunch.

His mouth curved in a smile and the perfection of his expression made her want to weep. He winked. "A man has to pee and shower."

"You should be in bed. They beat…" Her voice wavered.

Law shrugged. "I've had worse."

"Not helping my piece of mind."

"Checked on our breakfast too. It'll be a couple of hours. Khani's pulling a bullet out of Street."

"Breakfast? He got shot?"

"Yep. You slept smooth through the afternoon and night, tart. And the kid needed his edges dulled. Better shot than killed. He'll be fine."

"I'm not cut out for this shit." Mags flopped back on the bed and rubbed a hand over her heart.

"You're actually a little too good at dealing with it."

Law sat on the edge of the bed and she rolled toward him. The swelling in his face had diminished over the hours, leaving only a streak of violet over his left eye. His right hosted a brilliant starburst of color at his brow. Both his hypnotic green eyes studied her in the morning light. He lifted the hand at her chest and his warm fingers eased away her creeping sorrow.

"I don't know how to love you."

Magdalena's heart cracked. She felt the fissure form under the space where her hand had been. She tried to pull away, but his grip tightened. "You said that yesterday. So, just stop. Please."

"But I didn't finish saying what I needed to say. What I need you to know. I don't know how to love you, Magdalena, but I do."

Mags held her breath as he shifted toward her. A grimace echoed on his face then faded into a smile that zinged from her heart to her toes. His other hand cupped the nape of her neck.

"And, if you'll let me, I'll practice every day, for forever, until I get it right."

Her lips spread in a gasp. A quiver shook her lower lip. "You're gonna want to run away."

"You won't let me." He smoothed his thumb over her mouth.

"Damn straight," she agreed.

Law pulled her up to sit with him. Mags marveled at the change in him. Gone was the wall he'd hidden behind and in her lap dropped everything she'd never known she'd wanted. A dangerous man with the ability to pluck her heart right out of her chest without words. A man who made her stronger than she'd ever known herself to be. A man who saw the best in her when she was at her worst, who saw her worst and opened his arms to embrace it.

"What about my scars," she asked. "They scared you right out of my arms last time."

"We both have them, Magdalena. I can handle yours, if you can deal with mine."

He stood and his hands went to the button of his jeans. Magdalena's lungs constricted as though the air had evaporated from the room, but she panted her impatience.

Her nipples peaked beneath her shirt. Like the fire of her need had only been banked since their last encounter, it roared to life, melting her and coating the lips of her sex in desire. He hadn't even unfastened his pants and she was ready to come from the sight of him, from the pent-up angst of their denied hunger. Battered and bruised, he revved her to red without trying.

Those sure hands and deft fingers opened his fly in a blink. The flaps fell wide, revealing the beveled edge of his lower abdomen. Smooth skin wrapped tight around the curve of muscle that V'd to a short-cropped patch of dusky hair. Magdalena shifted to her knees, trying to glimpse lower still. When their gazes fused, Law shucked his pants, kicked them off his bare feet, and stood with his hands at his side.

His flame-green eyes seared her with the reflection of her burning passion and the mixture of his hunger and vulnerability. Again she took the pleasure tour of his body, roving the contours of his ripped arms, abdomen marred by contusions, and the cut at his side. Only this time she added the densely corded muscles of his legs to the visual indulgence.

A hollow in the relief of his left thigh caught her gaze just before it alighted on the heft of his erect sex. Over his hamstring, scar tissue knotted the skin of the indention with pink threads that ran a jagged line nearly a foot in length. Beside the distortion a web of rose-colored flesh crawled out the center point in a misshapen circle.

The scars he spoke of were physical, not just emotional. If she let herself, the sadness over the suffering he'd endured would engulf her in a tidal wave of misery. But this was the best day of her life. The man she fully expected to love forever and never touch had told her he loved her, and offered himself to her, flaws and all.

"Law," she said, meeting his gaze. "I love and accept every part of you." Her battered warrior smiled and she returned the radiant beam with her own. "And," she added, "I plan to take my time getting personally acquainted with all of you."

Law's fists tightened. The squint of his brow smoothed away. His tongue swept over his lips as though in preparation for a feast. The air between them crackled with sexual awareness. Magdalena giggled a moan as the length of Law's silky cock bobbed in agreement. Veins splayed over the wide column, hugging tight beneath the flushed skin.

"Sounds like the best plan ever, but now it's gentlemen first."

He walked toward the bed. Anticipation fluttered her heart. His fingers caressed her brow, down the round of her cheek, and over the wetness of her lips. He pulled her chin forward and she went willingly, giving him anything and everything he requested because she belonged to him. Before he knew it, even before she'd known it, she'd given him her heart. Now she gave him her body.

Law pinched the hem of her shirt with his eager grip and slowly pulled the fabric up her sensitive skin. Every inch revealed shot a wave of adrenaline through her already amped system. The collar collected her hair off her back, and then dumped it as the shirt came free. He tossed it to the floor and shook his head.

"I am the luckiest damn man on the planet."

His mouth worshiped hers with light grazes. The smell of his skin, a blend of soap and sex, permeated her brain, making her achy all over. Her breasts weighted and begged for praise. Her sex throbbed, needing the fill of him all the way to her cervix, and she had no doubt he'd get it there or that he'd get her there without much effort. But he seemed determined to take his time, nibbling and sucking her lips in turn.

Those agile hands of his didn't caress her skin. His hard chest didn't mash her supple breasts or abrade her rigid nipples. Only their mouths mingled. He nudged her chin up with his wandering lips and her head sank back, enjoying the feel of his hot breath on her exposed neck.

"You know," Law mumbled as he nipped her ear. "There's a picture in the living room of you wearing a short green skirt and tiny white top."

"Mmmhum."

He kissed a line to her collar bone, across her upper chest, and to her other ear. "Your feet are in the sand and your skin is red from the sun," he whispered.

"From my trip to Saint Tropez after graduating the second time."

Law licked a small line below her lobe and blew. Magdalena moaned at the astonishingly erotic sensation coursing through her body. It had been a long time since she'd had sex, but in all the sex she'd had, she'd never been loved. No one had ever made love to her. And the phenomenon heightened every touch to the point of exquisite pleasure and pain.

"I fantasized about reaching under that skirt, slipping the panties off your pert ass, kneeling at your feet, and sucking your pussy until you could no longer stand."

Magdalena teetered at the blazing image he painted in her mind.

"Easy there, tart." She caught the edge of his curved cheek in her periphery. He took her mouth in a hot kiss, licking deep and curling his tongue around hers in a possessive embrace before sliding out and traveling south. His cheek nuzzled the side of her breast then he licked out, flicking her stiff peak. "Sometimes I'd turn you around, flip your skirt over your sweet cheeks, pull your panties to the side, and slide my dick inside your hot cunt. You'd arch your head back and moan my name."

"Law?"

"Yes?" He suckled her right nipple into his mouth. His hands lifted toward her breasts and Magdalena rejoiced, until he fisted them and lowered them back to his sides. He switched to her other swollen bud. "You were saying?"

She moaned and growled. "If you don't put your hands on me, I'm going to die, and if you keep talking to me like that, I'm going to come."

His gaze rose to hers. "I can handle the latter."

He hugged her sides with his palms just under her breast and ran them over the curve of her waist. "Other times, I'd slip my hand into your panties. You'd be so wet you'd slick my fingers before I even guided them into your slick pussy. I'd massage your clit and you'd beg me to fuck you." His hands glided over the cotton of her boxers and curve of her ample butt and back around to her hips.

"And did you fuck me?"

"Sometimes, yes. Other times, I'd work you with my hands and make you come. Three or four times."

"Jesus," Magdalena gasped.

"Even in my fantasies, you were a fireball. By the third orgasm you'd demand I suck my fingers clean, so I'd taste you on my tongue and know what I was missing."

Every muscle in Magdalena's body tensed, needing release, begging for it. His fingertips delved behind the edge of her boxers and she panted, rocking against him in an unconscious effort to lure him closer.

"Fuck me, Law. Please." His fantasies were pretty damn accurate. She'd beg. She'd bargain. She'd do just about anything to get his cock inside her. To rub against him and ease the ache building in her core.

"There will be plenty of time for fucking, Magdalena. Right now, I'm going to love you."

"Can't you love me faster?"

"No." He smiled. *Damn him.* "If I love you any faster, I'll cheat us both by coming on your belly."

"It sounds like you've been getting off quite a bit lately. Though, we've been together a lot and I've missed my pleasure expeditions."

"Pleasure expeditions?"

"Me time. Jerkin' off. Pettin' the parrot. You know."

Law toppled her with a kiss, guiding her to the bed with a hand on her nape. He didn't crawl atop her, but knelt to the side. "Magdalena, I haven't pleasured myself in far too long and it's been way longer than that since I've been with a woman."

"How long?" Mags had a sudden and irrational fear he hadn't had sex since Clara. But he was such a virile man and ardent lover. Surely, it hadn't been that long. Thought she was anxious for the answer, she appreciated the ripple of muscles beneath his tanned skin as he sat back and braced his hands on his thighs.

"Eight years."

Her mouth gaped then closed only to gape again. Then she remembered a conversation they'd had about his motorcycle and how he'd never had anyone on it but her. She asked even though she didn't want to hear the answer. "Since Clara?"

"Yes."

The answer pricked her heart and she hated that any part of her was jealous over a dead woman. But she wasn't just a woman. She was the woman Law loved. The one he'd be with, if death hadn't taken her away. The pain must have shown on her face, though she hadn't meant it to. Law didn't deserve her grief, but he accepted it all the same. He stretched out next to her, snuggling his body against hers, and cupped her face in his hand.

"After she died, I shut down. Not because we had an epic love. Those take a lifetime to form and we didn't have that kind of time. But I played the game and lost big. I never thought it was worth it to gamble another hand. Made it a few years like that too.

"Then I moved in with Baine and saw your pictures plastered throughout the house. Heard the colorful tales of Magdalena, the wild cat next door. I saw the way your father's face lit up when he talked about you, and how Baine's did too. And I was terrified to meet you."

"Terrified?"

"Yes, I hadn't even met you and you stirred a longing I'd banished to the pits of hell. So, when I knew you were coming to town I took assignments or made excuses to hide out. Why do you think I still have my flat?"

"Seriously?"

"I fall hard and fast, tart. And I knew if I ever met you, I'd be doomed."

"You make it sound so horrible."

"Just the truth. The moment I plucked you off the floor you stole my heart, no matter how much I tried to deny it."

Magdalena wrapped her hands around Law's neck and pulled. Their lips sealed together in a desperate kiss. She ate at his mouth and laved at his soft pout. The pulse at his throat pounded against her thumb, driving her to take more and give it all. Her palms roved the granite of his shoulders and arms. She arched off the bed, abrading the tips of her nipples across his chest.

One of his hands braced the bed while his left snugged the bow of her spine and anchored them together. The plump mushroom of his cock head prodded Magdalena's clit. "Law, yes. Right there. Please." He groaned into her mouth and rolled his hips. Imagines of the wide burgundy bell jolting her dissident flesh filled her mind as she gripped his lats and bore into his fierce gaze.

The tough calluses raked over her lower back and the buxom curve of her ass as he slipped his hand behind the fabric of her shorts. His digits skimmed the crack of her bottom and strummed the swollen lips of her sex.

"No panties," he growled. "Dammit, Magdalena."

"Sad it's not like your fantasies?" He bit her lip and slipped it into his mouth. She moaned against his lips. A fresh rush of desire dampened his fingers and she wiggled her hips, hoping to guide them inside.

"You were my fantasy. Not your panties. Now, you are my reality, and you're so much sweeter than I could have ever imagined. Honest. Brave. Loving. Hot and wet. You're so ready to be mine."

"I am yours," she moaned.

Law grabbed the hem of her boxers with both hands and drew them down her legs. He bit his bottom lip as he studied her head to toe. In that long minute, Magdalena held her breath. She'd never been self-conscious of her curves, but he was so fit, without an ounce of extra skin or fat on his body. He brushed a hand over the swell of her hips and smiled.

"Perfection," he whispered.

She never wanted to be perfect. But Law saw her that way. "Thank you."

He shook his head. "No. I worship at your altar and thank you for the life you returned to my existence and for the love you give me."

Law licked the tear away that tickled her cheek and levered his body over hers. Magdalena wrapped her arms around his neck, squeezing him tight. His hands coursed down her body, hooked the back of her knees, and opened her legs. The weight of his head pinned her shoulder to the bed.

"I don't have any condoms. I didn't even think about them. Haven't needed—"

"It's okay. I'm still on the massive dose of birth control they required from my trip. I was tested before we left and haven't been with anyone."

"I'm clean...practically revirginized," he groaned.

"God. That shouldn't make me so hot, but it does." She curled her legs around his waist, careful to avoid his cuts and bruises. "Love me, Law."

"With everything I have."

His arms slid beneath her shoulders and around her waist, and he held her to his chest. Safe. Secure. On the sharp edge of satisfaction. Their gazes locked as the blunt tip of his penis gently buffeted the slippery folds of her vagina. Exquisite pressure built as his hips undulated, teasing her entrance with the barest inch of his width. His rock hard flesh stretched her, forcing her to relax and open for him. She hitched her legs higher on his back and his mouth fell open in a sigh of ecstasy.

"Magdalena." All across his body muscles played, bunching and releasing as he slowly worked his cock deeper. The thrum of his length massaged her narrow channel until her clit nestled at the base of his shaft. Law reared, lifting them both and supporting them on his knees with the strength of his powerful body.

The shift in position stuffed her so full of his dick she swore at the biting pleasure as he pierced her womb. He rested his forehead on her brow, panting with her, his jaw tight in his own delicious pain. Then it struck her.

"Your injuries..."

"All I feel is need." His eyes flashed flames of passion that melted her short-lived hesitation. The satin of his lips wore hers in a tender kiss, tugging her heart right out of her chest.

"Then feel this." Magdalena clung to Law's sturdy shoulders and lifted herself to the tip of his penis then plunged back to his root.

Law gripped her ass with both hands and repeated the move. His cock stroked her while his vulnerable gaze loved her with utter abandon. Sweat slicked their bodies as heat, primal and blistering, broiled between them. Her full breasts bounced in time with their mating thrusts, abrading her flushed red nipples on the slabs of his pecs.

A storm gathered as Law thrust into her sensitive flesh, ground his wet pelvis against her swollen clit, and retreated to complete the decadent cycle again. She wasn't the only one caught in the tumult. Law's eyes shut and his head strained toward the sky.

"I'm about to come inside you, Magdalena."

The hoarse admission of his blatant satisfaction forced a deafening clap of thunder to roll through her body. "Yes. Law. Yes. Yes." She panted in hedonistic fashion as she came, fisting his cock as her muscles spasmed, showering his length with her release.

"Oh fuck, Magdalena." Hot semen gushed deep inside her. The muscles in Law's neck strained. His fingers gripped her mounds, locking her against him as he filled her.

Mags collapsed in blissful surrender, draping her arms over Law's shoulders. Their chests heaved together for a moment, but Law collected his exertion into steady, even breaths in no time. He kissed a trail from her lobe to the crest of her shoulder. His arms slid to her middle and he squeezed. A smile curved her lips.

He laid her back on the bed and snuggled atop her, never leaving the shelter of her body. Law's green eyes sparkled and he flashed a lopsided grin of unadulterated mischief. Her nipple screamed back to life as he pinched one aching bud between his thumb and forefinger. His tongue licked over the tender skin then rolled it like a jeweler examining a fine diamond. She arched against him.

"Aaaaah."

"Tell me how it feels," he demanded.

She shook her head and watched stars burst behind her closed lids. Holding himself on his elbows, Law caged her jaw with his other hand, opened her lips, and plunged his tongue inside. He tormented her mouth with long sweeping strokes while he increased the hold on her ever-responsive peak. When he withdrew from her mouth her eyes flew wide. Mischief darkened to determined lust over his beautiful and battered face.

"Describe everything, Magdalena."

"You're pinching the hell out of my nipple. And it should hurt, but it's a totally unique sensation. It makes my pussy pulse, like my heart beats around your cock."

"Excellent." He nibbled her bottom lip then released it, his gaze focusing on her breasts. The grip of his fingers held firm while he cupped her other breast in his right hand.

"I expected you to pass out on top of me from our orgasms," she panted. "But you're staring at my chest as though you've never seen tits before. I don't know what to expect from you, and you're making me talk about everything. It's the best damn aphrodisiac. If you rocked your hips, I'd come again."

"Can't have that just yet."

He fondled her weighted breast with his hand before sucking it into his mouth. Her clit throbbed and she grabbed his head, pulling him closer. "You're forgetting something," he mumbled.

"Damn you." She groaned, remembering her orders. "It feels fucking amazing. Your mouth is so hot and your coarse tongue is licking me raw, in the best way. My clit is trembling like you're sucking it instead." Law released her breast and nipple and she gasped at the sudden rushing return of circulation. He arched a brow and she spoke in a rush. "They burn, but it feels so good." Magdalena's chin arched toward the ceiling at the tingle.

"I'm saving your little pleasure nub for later. But, trust me, it won't feel like it does now." He bit a path up her neck. "It'll feel a hell of a lot better." He rolled his hips, pulled out and rammed his thick cock home over and again.

"Yes," Mags begged. "You stretch me wide. Fill me so perfectly. I can't... Oh, Law. I'm com—"

Law's roar filled her ears and hot bursts of his release seeped out of her filled pussy and down her ass. He continued to pump into her, milking their extreme satisfaction until they both collapsed onto the mattress. Using the discarded boxers, he cleaned them both. With a roll, he cocooned her sweaty body in his arms and pillowed her head in the crook of his shoulder. Under her hands his heart galloped.

As she stared into the green, yellow, and grey fissures of his eyes, hers grew heavier and heavier. She fought against the darkness, but was pulled into the most contented sleep of her life.

Chapter Thirty-one

"So, about that titty fuck you offered," Law whispered.

Magdalena's sex-sleepy eyes rushed wide. The red of her kiss-swollen mouth curved into a wide smile and her belly shook against his arm. Rich laughter assaulted his already loopy senses and had him joining in the revelry of their addictive and terrifying love.

"You're voracious."

"Suddenly, I am. It's all your fault." He attacked her exposed neck with a hail of kisses, tasting salt and sex on her skin. His cock lengthened, but he tried his best to ignore it. Hell, he hadn't confessed his sentiment so he could fuck her to death. Not that she complained. The little minx tossed a thigh over his hip in immediate invitation. "If I'm voracious, you're salacious, tart."

Law shifted their bodies, stalled Magdalena with a wearing kiss, then scooped her into his arms. His middle protested, quaking tremors of agony through the organs behind his dark blue skin. But the gleeful expression on her freckle sprinkled face numbed his pain and empowered him like a B-12 shot, only better. He stood and carried her toward the bathroom.

"As much as I'd love to explore your perfect rack and delicious pussy, if I don't get some food in me I won't be able to function. Are you hungry?"

Her gaze glazed like a donut, syrupy and sweet. "Just for you."

"Wicked woman."

He crushed her to his chest to fit them through the narrow bathroom door, but held her there past the opening, strengthened by her eager embrace. Her delicate arms cinched around his neck, holding him in a fierce hold. When she leaned back, he pecked her nose then set her on her feet on a thin motel towel in front of the tub. He adjusted the water temperature in the shower before ushering her under the warm spray.

The lion's mane of her unruly hair, which absolutely fit her personality, slicked from the weight of the water. The artificial rain washed away the glimmer of seduction in her eyes and stiffened her bottom lip. Law ran his hands over the slick tresses, returning to cup her cherub face.

"It's catching up with you." She launched into his arms and gave decent effort at expelling the air from his lungs. Her head nodded against his chest. "I've recently learned, from a brilliant and stubborn woman, talking about what's on your mind can help ease fear's nasty grip."

She sniffled, her small body wracking. Law pivoted, giving the stout spray his back, and hugged Magdalena closer. He couldn't help but feel grateful for the drama that had brought them together. But bullets flying and bodies hitting the pavement was a normal day at the office for him. The gentle woman he loved handled the situations so well, too often he failed to remember this demolished her world. A bully beamed her dollhouse with a tire iron and the hits just kept coming. Her tears ripped his heart out.

"Magdalena. Please, talk to me."

"I almost lost you." The words came in a sob.

"Nah. I was just waiting to make my move. You were so damn brave. Stupid. But brave. You made it a fuck load more nerve wracking, but you provided a perfect distraction."

"Stupid?" She leaned back to toss him a counterfeit glare.

"Hell yes. You should have run as fast and as long as your body would carry you in the opposite direction and called Baine. Like I told you to do before." He wiped her tears away with his wet hands, exchanging liquid emotions for water.

"The thought never entered my mind." She batted her long lashes and he lost himself in the sea of her eyes. "I couldn't leave you."

Her words whispered to his abused heart, coaxing it from the deep dark corner it huddle in like a battered mutt. He pressed his lips to her sleek hair. "I love you." She smiled at that, and the grey recess of his mind lightened further.

Law held her close and grabbed a tiny bottle of shampoo, depositing a liberal amount onto his palm. He massaged the light flower scent against her scalp with sure strokes. The unrelenting grip she'd locked around his middle softened, becoming long leisurely strokes of her fingers along the receptive skin of his lower back. Worry fell from her face, which smoothed in tranquility. After working to the tip of her strands, he turned her into the warm spray and sluiced off the collection of bubbles.

Next he snagged a washcloth, wet it, and worked a small corner of it over her face. Her head lazed at his ministrations. He cupped her nape and whispered.

"Do you trust me?"

"Mmmm," she sighed.

"Close your eyes and hold your breath."

She sank deeper into his hold, lowered her lids, and filled her lungs. Law dipped her backward under the spray. The droplets rained on her hairline and tumbled over her face, rinsing away the grime of their lovemaking. He held her there a moment longer then pulled her out of the stream, still dipped in his arms. His mouth lowered to hers and he ravaged her lips.

"God, Magdalena. You are everything to me."

Law finished washing her, paying special attention to her most intimate parts, then cleaned himself with practiced efficiency, gliding over his junk only enough to get clean. It wouldn't take much to send him over the edge again. He had enough trouble keeping Magdalena's wily hands off his raging hard-on until they got out of the shower and dry. Her grumbles tickled a smile onto his face.

"I'm starving to death," Law griped as he gripped her toweled hips and walked her backward out of the bathroom to a vanity similar to the one they'd fooled around on in the B & B.

"Shouldn't Khani have been here by now? I mean, you talked to her nearly two hours ago."

"Three hours ago, you sex addict."

"Me, a sex addict? If I am, it's because I'm following your lead, zealot."

His brow furrowed. Khani should have been there an hour ago to be precise, but he couldn't worry about the extra time with a greedy Magdalena all to himself. "Addiction is all about instant gratification. I'd like to think our satisfaction builds."

"There are granola bars in the bag she brought last night. I had one last night. They're good." Magdalena ignored his taunts, but the amusement in her quirked mouth hinted at her cunning.

"I had two already this morning. I need something warmer."

"We don't have to wait on her. We could go get something ourselves. I mean, I can drive a motorcycle." She grinned. "So, we can go wherever."

"I want to go south."

"Why? Isn't there someplace we can go around here?"

The artificial countertop wasn't nearly as nice as the previous one, but it would do just fine. He lifted her onto the surface and she drew a knowing breath. His eyes narrowed, pinning her gaze as he tugged the terry cloth from her breasts and fanned the ends open. He hooked both hands behind her knees, yanked her lush ass to the edge, and spread her legs wide.

"Because it will be the best thing I've ever tasted." He knelt between her lush thighs and inhaled deeply, running the tip of his nose up the length of her milky leg. She gasped and the bare lips of her pussy clenched. His attention excited her and it strangled his dick against the cloth around his waist. The white of her skin turned pink at her core. Her plump lips hid her clit and smooth opening from him, but proof of her arousal glistened at the edge of her folds.

"Imagine being starved, Magdalena." His voice was husky in his own ears. "Denying yourself of all desserts, but obsessing over one perfect chocolate sundae for years." His lips whispered over her mons. "Vanilla ice cream. Chocolate sauce.

Whipped cream. One day soon, I'm going to put that on your sweet cunt and lick it off."

Magdalena's belly quivered and she panted before he'd even touched her. So damn responsive. "But today, I'm going to enjoy you on my tongue. No added flavors. Just you." He licked the crests of her lips. "Tart?"

"Yes."

"I want you to come in my mouth. I want to taste your excitement."

"Law."

She moaned his name as he flattened his tongue and glided it across her heated flesh. The tang of her arousal danced across his taste buds, spurring his own insatiable lust. He held her thighs wide and dove pointed strokes between her smooth creases. With tender laps he coaxed her sensitive bundle of nerves from its hiding spot, watching in rapt awe as it engorged with the rush of her pumping blood.

Law moved closer, wrapping a hand around her waist and pulling her to his eager mouth. His other hand skated up her belly to toy with the peaks of her breasts. The world fell away, a dangerous thing in his experience, but he couldn't muster the energy to care. Every sense he honed over the years focused on expert possession of Magdalena's mind, body, and heart.

He peppered her clit with light, rhythmic brushes of his tongue until her hips rolled then rocked, seeking more. Law unbound his hold on her soft midriff and hip then rubbed his fingers over her wet cleft. She murmured an incoherent plea.

"You want my fingers, Magdalena?"

"I want..." she swallowed, "...your cock inside me."

Law swirled two fingers at her pulsing entrance, teasing her mercilessly. He eased from loving her hypersensitive nub and licked her off his lips. "You'll have my dick as deep as I can burrow it into your hot pussy. Just not yet."

Magdalena bit her lower lip and moaned. He thrust two fingers into her silk channel to the base and curled them repeatedly against the gathering of nerves in the front wall of her vagina. Her moan grew to a mew and her head shook back and forth. God, he loved the blush of her cheeks and the grip she fastened to his hand, holding it against her mounded breast.

"Are you ready to come, Magdalena?"

"Yeeesss."

He sucked her clit into his mouth and wound it in small circles over and again. Her hands gripped his forearm as she fucked his mouth.

"Law. Law. Law. Oh. Yes."

His tongue and fingers coaxed every last drop of desire from her body and he lapped it with hungry swipes. He kissed a line up her body then hugged her. She sagged into his embrace, her head listing to the side as she eyed him speculatively.

"How in the world did I get so lucky?"

"Tart, I was a total bastard to you and there's some faceless man trying to have you snuffed. I don't know that lucky is the proper term for what you are." He tapped her nose. "How about, for now, we stick to passionate and gorgeous."

Her little nose crinkled.

"What was that about?"

She shrugged and her breast nudged the head of his steel hard dick, still bound by his towel. He eased back in an attempt to calm the painful bulge. Her fingers slid into the top of the cloth and yanked, shedding the fabric from his waist. His thick length sprang free and carnal craving gripped him by the balls, making his knees weak. Magdalena's hands shot toward his bobbing cock, but he caught her wrists.

"Hey, why are you retreating? It's my turn."

"I didn't give you head so you'd get me off, tart. I ate you because I needed to. Besides, you have to explain your wrinkled nose."

"First, I need to get your dick in my mouth. It's possessed my dirty mind since I thought about dropping to my knees the first night at my father's and licking you from head to head and everywhere in between. Second, I don't need to bare my insecurities to you."

"First," he shot back, "I'm so going to fuck you senseless for searing that image in my mind. Second, why not? You've bared your heart to me and your worship-worthy body."

"Because I act like it doesn't bother me, and most of the time it doesn't, but sometimes... I don't know. Here, if you don't have legs up to your tits, and tiny flat ones at that, you're considered less than desirable. It sucks. I want to be comfortable with me."

"Tart, I've never met a woman who is more self-assured or has a body of such mind fucking perfection. One inch of your creamy skin or quirk of your smile and I'm crazy with lust."

"Then come and give me all you've got."

Magdalena hopped from the counter and curled her finger twice.

He stepped, bringing them chest to face. Her tongue snuck from behind her lips and lashed wildly over his nipple. A thrill shot down his body to his big toes and his hands fisted at his sides.

"Fuck, I didn't know those things were sensitive."

Her mouth curved around her working tongue. After a few more whips of his beaded disk she dropped to her knees.

"Spread your legs."

When he didn't move Magdalena tore her lusty stare from his package. Her lips pursed at his quirked brow.

"Trust me." She coaxed him using the same words he had on her.

Law moved his feet a shoulder width apart.

"A little more."

He gave her two, but would budge no more, having no idea what was in that head of hers. When she fisted his cock it lined up perfectly with her red swollen lips. She licked them as she studied, running her fingers gently over the smooth skin that wrapped around his bulging appendage. Suddenly he didn't give a shit that he was wide open and vulnerable to her probing hands.

Law's mouth gaped on a groan as Magdalena's mouth stretched over his feverish dick. Her slick heat welcomed him to the back of her throat, taking half his length. She fisted the rest in her gentle hands. Slowly she eased off, popping her lips off his tip, then mimicked the lashes she'd flecked on his nipple. The carpet bunched under his curled toes and every muscle in his jaw flexed, arching his head enough that he caught their reflection in the mirror.

Veins raised over his shoulders and arms to his clenched fists. Sweat glistened between his pecs and across his abdomen. Magdalena's half-dried hair danced against her back, caressing the skin at the curve of her hourglass waist. Her head bobbed and white-hot yearning temporarily blinded him. He closed his eyes against the radiance and struggled to calm the hasty and consuming need to fill her mouth with his seed.

He was about to demand she slow her rabid pace, but she released her grip on his base and swallowed his tip down the back of her greedy throat. Stunned, he could only gasp at the sensation. One of her hands bit into the toughness of his tightened ass, urging him deeper. She drank him root to tip while her other hand cupped his heavy sack and cosseted it with sure tugs.

"Magdalena. Not yet."

His demand sounded more like a pitiful plea, which she ignored, increasing her efforts to drive him over the edge. A muffled moan left her throat, vibrating his cock in her strangling tight channel. Law exploded in a growl, losing all control. His hands fisted into her hair, pumping her pretty mouth over his spasming cock.

Magdalena's keening sounds continued, spurring him on. The first hot spurts of semen shot from his tip and she milked him, taking everything he had. His body quivered in spent ecstasy, leaving him weak and at the same time empowered. She slid off his still erect penis and licked her lips like the little devil she was.

In methodical paths she kissed him from toe to torso, paying no special attention to his scars, but neither avoiding them, accepting all of him in one more perfect show of affection. When she finally stood, Law pulled her against his chest and squeezed her supple body to his.

"I love you, Law."

He scooped her into his arms and welded their mouths together, mixing their essences in a consuming kiss.

"I'm going to show you just how much I love you, tart."

Law turned Magdalena to face the mirror, pushed her chest forward, and palmed her hip. The rounds of her delicious ass plumped in front of his saluting dick. Her back bowed in a sweeping curve that made his mouth water with the yearning to lick it.

Her eyes rounded. "Again?"

"I'm just sorry I'm busted up."

"Doesn't seem to be slowing you down any."

"If I loved your body as many times, in as many ways, as my brain invents, you'd never walk right again."

Magdalena dragged her bottom lip through her white teeth and arched deep, rubbing her boobs against the countertop, and nestled her hot slit over his rock hard penis.

"Magdalena."

Law twined his hand in her unruly hair, anchored the other at her hip, and thrust deep. Her mouth fell open on a cry that flash froze him until the set of her shoulders gentled and the strangle hold she had on his dick relaxed. He pulled from her core and slid gently back home. Magdalena wrapped him in her wet satin embrace and welcomed him farther inside her than he'd ever been.

He leaned over her back, covering her body with his own. Law sidled his face next to hers and with the help of the reflective glass bore his gaze into hers.

"I love you," he said.

He kissed a line across her cheek and down the curve of her back as far as he could, settling in to measured thrusts. His legs burned as he crouched, keeping them in line. He enjoyed the heat of their union, rolling his hips to hit the perfect spot. It would take time to learn her body, and he could only look forward to the education with unmatched excitement.

Law's blonde beauty moaned. He ground hard against the tender point that stirred her passion then pounded with unrelenting strokes. Magdalena's hands, splayed wide on the counter, squeaked as they slipped from the force of his primal desire. She planted her hands on the mirror, framing the picture of her flushed face. The heat from their sweat-soaked bodies formed steamy halos around her fingers on the cool glass, framing her heavily lidded eyes. Her new position allowed him a prime view of her bouncing rack. It was enough to break his control and pitch him into the yawning chasm of bliss.

"You're so beautiful."

Her answering moan let him know he wasn't the only one with broken restraint. Law released the last vestige of discipline, giving himself over to the ferocity of their lovemaking. He rammed balls-deep until they both screamed their release in panted growls.

Magdalena rested her head on the counter and he collapsed onto her back, holding his weight from crushing her with shaky legs. Their sweat and breaths mingled as their hearts drummed the ancient beat of lusty love.

"I think," she gasped, "we need another shower."

"I can't be sorry about it."

"Me either."

Her giggle shook his head. The peals brought a dopey smile to his face. Law disengaged from her tight body and pulled her into his arms. She came willingly, knotting her arms around his neck and legs around his middle. A sting in his battered torso reminded him of the precariousness of their situation, but he blocked it out a moment longer, reveling in the magic of Magdalena.

"We have some stuff to figure out, but we'll do it together," he assured.

Her brilliant smile was all the answer he required. But too soon it fell and her brow pinched. "Oh Lord."

"What is it?"

"Willow. I need to talk to her, to make sure she's okay and find out what the hell she's involved in. But first, we have to make sure we're not wanted by the Met. We left two dead bodies in our fumes."

"My Hog doesn't fume."

His attempt to lighten her clouding mood worked a bit. She bopped his nose with her index finger.

"Be serious."

"All right. Seriously, I'd like to find Willow myself. If this has nothing to do with Africa then it has a hell of a lot to do with her, and I want answers." He brushed a hand over her mass of hair. "We're not fugitives from the law. Khani took care of it."

"How do you know? And how does she have so much power?"

"Trust me, tart."

He smacked her bare ass. She yelped then narrowed her gaze. Law muted her tirade with his lips over hers. She'd just slipped her tongue into his mouth when a sharp knock echoed through the door.

Magdalena gripped his shoulders and reared back.

"Shh, it's okay. That's probably Khani with our food. Finally. You go get that shower started and I'll get the door."

Chapter Thirty-two

It took some cajoling, but Magdalena ambled warily toward the bathroom. Law waited until the door closed behind her apple-round bottom then he lunged for the Sig he'd stuffed under the mattress last night and headed for the far corner of the window. He peeked into the tiny crack of light between the curtain and frame and saw his adopted sister shift from one foot to the other in uncharacteristic fashion. His grip on the gun tightened as he flipped the safety and surveyed the surrounding area without shifting the thick fabric.

Few vehicles occupied the motor court of the small motel they'd chosen on the outskirts of the city. He'd have liked to have gotten them farther away, but had begun to press more and more of his weight onto Magdalena's back, unable to fight the fragility of his battered state any longer.

Khani's smoky-grey Benz sat beside his Harley. The car slung low on the pavement like a leopard waiting to unleash its power. A delivery truck parked by the registry office drew his hard gaze. When the portly transporter rounded the truck's rear with a handful of envelopes, he studied the other cars in the lot. None carried passengers or hid ready gunman. Not that he could see anyway.

Law snagged his blood-crusted jeans from the pile of his dirty clothes and slipped them on. He opened the door, hanging back in the low-lit room, scanning the office windows and cars for movement.

"You looked properly fucked," Khani said by way of greeting.

He flashed her a grin, still watching her back.

"And overly cautious." Khani shook her head. "You think I'd have knocked on your door, if someone was following me? Give me some credit, Pierce."

Law stowed his Sig in the rear waist of his pants and shrugged. "Sorry."

Her normally impeccably styled hair sat high atop her head in a messy bun. The artful painting of make-up smudged about her eyes. Not like she'd been crying, but maybe sweating heavily. Her cheeks flushed a high rose. The swell and hue of her lips resembled Magdalena's well-loved mouth. Someone had kissed off Khani's wild lip color of the day. Law's money was on the rookie she'd taken an especially long time pulling a bullet out of. Guess he wasn't hurt too bad.

"I'm not the only one. Properly fucked, that is," he said with a grin.

She thrust a plastic bag with three takeout boxes into his hand. "Oh, I'm totally fucked. Fucked up," she growled.

"Want to come in and talk about it?"

Her face contorted into a sneer.

"Never mind. I'm here, if you need me."

"Yeah, and you better stay put this time. I have two men on your room." As if just remembering, she shifted uncomfortably in her mussed clothes. "Give me an hour to get my shit together and we'll reconvene."

"They're not close."

"No, sniper and spotter."

He nodded. "We need to start with her roommate this time. Willow May Wren."

"I'll get a dossier worked up and have it ready. One hour."

Khani turned and walked away, but her no-nonsense strides hunched at the shoulders. Damn. She'd screwed a subordinate and herself in the process. Possibly her career, but most assuredly her own strict moral code. Khani was no saint, but when it came to her job she had impeccable scruples. Had.

When the rumbling car shot past, Law touched his finger to his bowed head then locked the door's bolt and metal latch. It wasn't much protection, but the guys at the highest of three rolling ridges toward the east reassured him. The Base Branch snipers were the best in the world. Just like their agents.

Law deposited the bag and its mouthwatering contents onto the small dresser and ignored his protesting stomach as he walked toward the bathroom. When the knob twisted from the interior his hope to catch Magdalena wet and ready fell. She exited in a rush and assessed the room with two brisk rakes of her lovely gaze.

"I think that's a world record for water conservation. Did you even get behind your ears?"

The worry in her furrowed brow smoothed as she pinned him with her gaze and unsuccessfully wrestled back a smile.

"Nosey reporter." Law lowered his head, brushing his lips over hers.

"Journalist. Nosey journalist."

She mumbled against his mouth, her hand shoving at his chest. He tucked her in his embrace and stood, lifting her feet off the ground. Her giggles warmed his belly and spread a grin across his face.

"You're still wet."

"I'm always ready for you." She snugged her arms around his neck and kissed his bruise and the forming scar on his brow. Her gaze snagged on something behind him. Her tongue darted out to lick her lips. "Except when there's a bag of warm breakfast singing a siren song to my concaved belly."

It was his turn to laugh. He hugged her tightly and set her on her feet with a light smack on her towel-covered cheek. "Go eat. I'm going to grab a shower then join you. Save me a little."

"You better hurry." Over her shoulder she winked.

He did hurry, giving her world record cleaning a run for its money. Law was ready to sit across the table from Magdalena and drink her in as he ate the hell out of his meal. Only he didn't find her putting a dent in the mountain of food Khani brought.

The box sat, opened but abandoned, on the table. The television warbled from the dresser and Magdalena sat on the edge of the bed, her feet propped on the railing, typing furiously onto the laptop's keyboard. Her hair hung wet on her shoulders, and a crop of gooseflesh grew on her skin.

"I saw him," she said.

"Who? And where?" Immediately, his grip firmed on the gun he'd brought with him into the bathroom.

"The weasel. On the TV."

Law plucked a towel from a short stack and hurried to Magdalena. He knelt at her feet and spread the cloth over her shoulders, lifting her wet hair atop it. She continued assaulting the computer with rapid strikes of her fingers which no longer seemed so delicate, but skillful and determined. As tenacious as the woman they belonged to.

"What are you looking for?"

"He was in the background at a press conference for the Prime Minister."

The hunger in his gut twisted, forming an entirely different and unwelcome sensation. His phone vibrated on the nightstand and he reached for it, if for no other reason than to give his brain a second to catch up. Khani's encrypted phone number showed on the I.D. and he hit the screen to accept the call. The question she asked in lieu of a greeting had the one-two punch effect of rendering him momentarily mute. He dropped the phone from his mouth and stared at Magdalena. After a second she met his gaze and stilled.

"What?"

"Did you know Willow's father was the Minister of State for Trade and Investment, the Lord Wren?"

"Oh my God." Her hands froze on the keys and her shoulders slumped.

"Your hour just got cut in half, Khani. Get here as soon as you can. Magdalena saw the dick that started all this at a press conference for the Prime Minister."

Law hung up before she had time to gauge or ask questions he didn't know the answers to, yet. He shoved the computer and phone to the side and grabbed Magdalena's ice-cold hands.

"We've been friends for so long, he's just always been Willow's dad to me. Not some power wielding government official. I've never even met him, busy as he is."

"It's no coincidence Willow's dad is a member of the House of Lords and you saw the perpetrator in the press core, so near the Prime Minister."

"Law, he wasn't with the press. He was in the background with the Minister's staff."

Chapter Thirty-three

They dressed in a rush then Mags sat back at the computer scouring the Prime Minister's official site for the weasel's picture, his name, and business relation to the head of state. Law sat beside her studying the pages she clicked and scrolled through, offering bites of maple-syrup-covered waffle and fried chicken. Despite how her stomach grumbled its appreciation, she couldn't taste the food she chewed and swallowed to appease the insistent man.

The same sharp knock from earlier made her heart leap. Law left her and answered the door with gun in hand. She glanced at Khani Slaughter only long enough to toss her a nod of hello before finding the events gallery and scrolling through a myriad of faces. The pictures ran the gambit from summits to formal meetings to full out galas. People shook hands. Patted shoulders. Smiled widely. Some wore finery. In other pictures, business dress was the call. Luckily, each formal picture where people stood in rigid lines in succession of shortest to tallest and skinniest to fattest came with its own legend stacked neatly beneath.

The bed dipped on her left and she canted her head to Khani. The sharp woman wore head to toe black, from her hair to her trim fitted pantsuit, with the exception of her moss-green eye shadow, orangish-red lip stain, and similarly colored stiletto sling-backs. The color popped her off the strictly business page. That, and something in her storm-clouded eyes said she was much more than a businesswoman. She already bore witness to her calm under pressure and skill with a needle and thread.

Magdalena thought Khani had such a pitifully tiny list of things she couldn't do that her can-do list overshadowed it by miles and miles. Proving her right, the raven haired beauty pulled a laptop from her case and ticked her fingers across the keys with speed and accuracy rivaling her own.

"Maybe I can help," Khani offered.

"I'm scrolling through a million pictures looking for the guy. He has dark hair, is tall and rail thin. He looks like the human version of a weasel."

"Like the long rodent?" Her upper lip curled.

"It's carnivorous. Non-rodent, but you've got the jest."

Law sat on her right, continuing to feed her, while Khani quickly maneuvered to the site and discovered just how many pictures they had to click through. She groaned.

"Screw this." Khani handed her a piece of paper and a pen. "Write down the station you saw the guy on and when."

She wrote the info and handed it to Khani. "What good will it do?"

"Lots of people owe me favors. I'll collect a few," Law's friend said.

"I suppose I owe you a few already."

Khani looked past her at Law and smiled. "Nah, family doesn't count."

"But I'm not your family," Mags said.

"Not yet," Khani sing-songed.

When Law stuffed his cock inside her, damn near to her throat, and talked shamelessly about all the naughty things he wanted to do to her or described what he did to her, Magdalena hadn't blushed a bit. But heat crept up her neck and over her face at Khani's words. Though she could see him out of the corner of her eye she didn't dare look at Law, afraid to see the same blush across his cheeks, or worse, horror.

Mags trained her eyes on the computer screen and sifted through the pictures. Whether it was a waste of time or not, with the type of power and technology Khani had at her disposal, she needed something besides her ripped lover to keep her gaze and mind busy. Khani stood and paced while barking orders into her phone. Magdalena clicked and scrolled until her hand, wrist, and forearm cramped then did it some more.

"We'll have the footage within the half-hour," Khani said. "Then we can run facial recognition on him. If the guy does work for anyone in the Cabinet, his information will be in the system."

"Then I'll go pay him a visit." Law's voice hinted at a smile on his lips, but Mags didn't look.

"I don't think we'll need the footage."

She stared into the black, beady eyes of the man who'd assaulted Willow. In the picture his hair sat neatly quaffed atop his head, not slicked back in the greasy rendition it had been at her flat. He smiled brightly at an attractive young woman, clutching a stack of books. Magdalena's heart churned, wondering what he'd done to that poor girl, what he'd done to other unassuming women.

Law's hand settled over hers, stalling her quakes. "I'll get him. Don't worry."

Khani sat beside them and hunched toward the screen. "He looks like a bastard and a weasel.

Click on the enlargement." She did and they all leaned closer to the screen. "That's the Minister of State for Schools, Livingston Hues, beside him."

Magdalena's breath caught.

"What?" Law asked.

"The banner in the far left-hand corner. The Council for Higher Education."

Law cussed and Khani's fingers worked her computer like Elton John did the piano.

Mags took her hand back to join in the search. She didn't know what Khani sought, but she went straight to the Council's website and read aloud. "The Council for Higher Education. An international non-profit organization dedicated to fulfilling higher education needs for the less privileged, connecting US and UK foreign exchange programs at the college level, and fostering the non-traditional student's needs through low-cost childcare and work-study programs.

"Director: Livingston Hues. Co-Director: Haltman Weaver. That fucking prick."

His *I'm a wonderful guy* smile shined below his title.

Khani leaned around her again. "You can keep her. She's hot, smart, and she cusses like me. What's not to like?"

"Focus, Khani." Law shook his head, but Mags caught the curve of his mouth.

"Yeah, work your magic." Mags agreed and pointed at the two men. "We need to know everything there is to know about this organization. I have a puke-worthy feeling that this has everything to do with what happened to Willow."

"Before he knew I was there, this guy asked Willow if someone else had told her he gets every part of her. Weaver said, *he*. It could be Hues."

"It could be any one of a million people," Law interjected. "But this is a great place to start digging."

"I'm in their financials now," Khani said.

"How did you—"

Law quieted her question with another bite of waffle. She wouldn't get an answer anyway, so she opened for him. For the first time since Khani had made her red as a blood rose, Magdalena looked into Law's vibrant eyes. He heated her with a gaze that saw right through to her wild thoughts about one day becoming part of his family. Coming home from a hard day's work or welcoming him home from a long day's whatever the hell he did. Snuggling up to him every, or most nights, for sleep. Cuddling up to him in the mornings for a little pre-dawn hot and hard.

"I want that, you know." Law said with a wink.

Magdalena's heart shimmied and shook inside her chest, but she didn't say a word. She didn't know what to say. Didn't know if he was talking about what she was thinking about. Khani saved her with an exaggerated cough.

"Who needs to focus?" Khani slanted her head at them both. "Oh, give me some of that. The chicken." She nodded with rounded eyes.

"I'm the muscle behind this mission." Law shrugged.

Both of the women nearly choked on their tongues. "And the muscle happens to have a lovely brain. So, how about we put it to use?" Mags said.

With the three of them working it took five hours and lunch, but they connected The Council for Higher Education with three offshore accounts. Twelve prominent colleges had signed contracts with the company. Its donor roster read like the roster for a top tier multi-government summit. Hundreds of millions in illegal donations funneled through the books with only an easily breakable facade of actual donations or good achieved by the group.

"So, we still don't know what all this has to do with Willow and her father." Magdalena paced as she reiterated the obvious.

"No, but we know who has the answers," Khani said.

"And you know just the person to get them out of him," Law added.

Chapter Thirty-four

"You're not going without me," Magdalena shot back. "This is my mess and I intend to see it through."

Law's thickly stubbled jaw flexed as he shook his head. "It's not your mess. It's Weaver's mess and I am fully prepared to make him a weeping, bloody mess in order to get the answers I want." He stepped toward her and brushed his fingertips over her bare arm. "You've already seen too much. You already know too much about what we do.

"For Christ's sake, tart, you've already seen me kill four...no, fuck, five men. I won't expose you to any more ugliness. You deserve beauty and happiness. So does the lady you're staying with."

Magdalena turned to Khani who gave a wane smile and shrugged. Fear rattled inside her chest like an old-world, chain-shaking ghost. It irritated her battle worn heart and set her stomach on perma-queazy.

"If you leave me here, I'll go insane," she promised.

"Oh, come on. Slaughter isn't that bad," Law crooned.

Magdalena filed her gaze to a point and he stepped closer, planting a kiss on her forehead. "You worried about me, tart?"

"What if...you need help," she said in a pitifully wet voice.

"He won't be alone," Khani offered in cool dispassion.

That earned her a head tilt from Law.

"Besides your snipers, everybody is on assignment."

"Incorrect," Khani said.

"Oh, come on." A burst of heat radiated from the thick chest nearly touching her own. "He's shot, stupid, and a son-of-a-bitch."

"Word from the old guard is, Street is about as hot-headed and reckless as you and Baine were when you started. He's anything but stupid. The bloke tested off the charts. So, he's probably smarter than the three of us combined. Sure, he needs to be reined in, which is why I'm sending him out with a grandpa like you. As to the son-of-a-bitch, there are many bitches in this world. Myself included."

Magdalena didn't get all the nuances of Khani's address, but Law did. He exhaled in a rush. His wickedly warm breath blew over her breasts, turning her nipples to shameless peaks. "Are you happy now? I have to baby-sit a James Bond Einstein Casanova."

"Don't break a hip," she teased.

Before she could move he placed both hands on her cheeks, wrapped his fingers around her nape, and pulled her to his mouth. His lips bombarded hers with firm strokes, slanting over her slackened chops from every angle. With an artful maneuver he opened her mouth with his own and slipped his tongue inside, sliding it against hers with instinctual perfection. He broke the kiss as quickly as he'd started it.

"I might. With you. When this is done," he growled. Law touched a kiss to the end of her nose, turned around, and left her in muted fury.

Khani allowed her to brood for a handful of minutes, pacing like the caged animal she was, but too soon she chimed in. "It'll help if we're productive while he's gone. And wearing a trench into the carpet isn't time well spent. So, how about we brainstorm while you patrol?" Mags nodded her concession. "Excellent. We can try and piece together the financials a little further and form a clearer picture of the power flow through the shell company. We can also—"

"Can you run your facial recognition on this girl?" Magdalena scrambled to the computer and clicked on the second of twenty windows opened on her screen. Up popped the picture of Weaver with the young co-ed.

"Sure, but why?"

"Look at the date stamp. This picture was taken close to the company's inception, four years ago." Magdalena clicked on the next few windows. "She's in several pictures at different events, like she was the face of the company. Their spokesperson. She knows something. I'll bet my Lula polka-dot Sophia Websters on it."

"What size do you wear?"

"A three."

The twinkle in Khani's eyes dulled and she pursed her lips. "I wear a seven, tiny toes." She straightened the leg crossed over her other and preened her sizable shoe for Mags.

"I'll buy you a pair. Please, just look her up. I can't stay here and do Internet searches while Law is out there risking...everything."

"You win. Only because I hate waiting around too. More than you'll ever know."

They purred to a stop in front of a small country cottage thirty-five minutes from the hotel nearly that many minutes later. It hadn't taken Khani long to run the facial diagnostic and locate Jessica Watts.

"Let me handle this, okay?" Khani's voice hovered in that non-emotional tone of authority.

"Not a chance. You order trained killers around for a living and intimidate the hell out of us common folk. Did you see the way the man at the petrol station eased off? You'll scare this women into her shell before you open your mouth."

Something passed over Khani's face that made Magdalena's stomach ache. Maybe Khani was a hard ass, but it didn't mean she didn't have feelings all the same. "I'm sorry," she whispered.

"You're right. There's always a curve with civilians, and you're a journalist. This is your area of expertise. So, have at it."

"Thank you for not calling me a bitch...or a reporter."

They shared a small giggle before exiting the car and walking up the pea-gravel path. Mags knocked on the paint-chipped front door and stepped back by Khani, hoping she exuded enough warmth with her smile to assure whomever answered the door. Khani leaned in and whispered.

"A small kid lives here too."

"How do you know?"

"Wind chimes." Khani's head canted toward a line of hand-painted sticks hanging lengthwise tied to a much longer stick.

Mags nodded. Only a parent would be proud enough to hang the precious monstrosity nearly front and center on the house. Finally the door opened. A shrunken old woman with a shock of white hair stepped forward.

"Can I help you?" The older woman sized them up with obvious rakes of her blue eyes.

"I hope so. My name is Magdalena Wells. I'm looking for Jessica Watts. She and I were both members of Sigma Tau Delta."

"Well, miss, I don't know what that is," the old lady said.

"I'm sorry. It's an academic honor society," Mags offered.

"Oh, well, come on in and don't mind the mess."

When they stepped through the door Magdalena looked for the mess, as anyone would do when told not to do something, but found none. A meager and tidy farmhouse stretched before them. Wood planks hung a few feet above their heads and stone floors sat beneath their feet. Colorful rugs added comfort to the hard space and the light blue walls brightened it too.

"Call me Grams," she said, directing them toward a well-worn sofa in a den big enough for a flea circus. "Take a seat. I'll get Jess and bring some tea."

The lady walked toward the back of the house and, from the sound, opened an exterior door and hollered. "Jess. Company." The door shut and the house shuddered. Mags cut her gaze at her partner in crime and found a smirk on her face.

"In with Grams. Nice work," Khani praised.

They listened to Grams skirting about the kitchen, rifling through cabinets, turning on the gas stove, clinking ceramic together. After a weighted minute the back door opened and closed again with the same rattle of the ancient frame. A woman stepped into the room like she approached a firing squad, her steps hesitant and threatening retreat at any sudden move.

Magdalena smiled, but kept quiet, giving
Jessica time to settle. But she didn't take a seat.
Her sandy-blonde hair hung in a loose braid down
her back. Wisps had fallen from the intricate
working and danced at her strained neck. Others
clung to her dewy brow. Jessica held her breath for
several beats while she eyed them with wary
sapphire blue eyes that went wide perusing Khani,
but softened a bit when they studied Mags.
Jessica's gaze darted toward the kitchen and her
back straightened.

"What do you want?" Her whispered voice
held a steady tone.

"We'd like to talk a bit about The Council for
Higher Education." Mags matched her quiet-yet-
assertive inflection then watched the color drain
from Jessica's rosy cheeks.

"Are you...police?"

"No," Mags said.

"Reporters?"

"No," Mags answered honestly. She was a
damned journalist.

"You're with them," Jessica said in a squeak.

"Absolutely not." Mags shook her head. "My
best friend got involved with them somehow and I
need information, so I can help her."

Jessica's braided tail thrashed back and forth
at her denial. Tears streamed down her cheek. The
back door opened wide enough it smacked into the
wall. Jessica gasped a moment before the speedy
patter of small feet rolled across the floor like
thunder.

"Mummmmy! You didn't find me forever. I
don't wanna play hide and seek any more. I'm so
hot. Can I have a drink?" The little boy spouted all
the way through the house until his arms wrapped

around Jessica's shorts-covered thighs, hugging her with squint eyed abandon.

Magdalena's heart broke, just a little, at the bond she so desperately missed. No one could hug you like your mum could. Not even Law, though his hugs spun a magic all their own. Unlike his mother, the little boy's hair shimmered almost purple in the streaming light. His dark locks cropped above his ears.

"Dylan," Jessica whispered, "where are your shoes?"

"I planted them in the garden. Tommy said they would grow a stinky tree." His tiny shoulders shrugged before his gaze finally caught on her and Khani. He gripped Jessica's legs with his pudgy hands and hid his face.

"Hi, Dylan. I'm Magdalena, but you can call me Mags. And this is Khani." She pointed.

"Wow, she's tall, and you're little like me," Dylan said.

His mother scolded him and sent him to Grams for a drink, but Mags chuckled at the kid's unreserved expressions. To her surprise, Khani laughed too.

When Dylan left, Jessica stepped toward the door. "I am really sorry for your friend, but I can't tell you anything."

"I can see you're afraid of them, Jessica. But you can help us put them away for a long time," Mags offered.

"I can't. I won't lose...what I've worked hard to protect." Jessica lifted her hand, showing them the door.

"Dylan is Haltman Weaver's son," Magdalena said above a breath, careful no one in the other room could hear.

Jessica slapped at the torrent cascading down her face. "He is my son." She stabbed a finger at the door, and mouthed ferociously. "Leave now."

Magdalena opened her mouth, but Khani grabbed her arm and hauled her off the couch and toward the door. She was two steps onto the gravel walkway before she formed a rebuttal. But again, Khani stole her breath. This time, the warrior's arm shot out like a snake strike, stopping the door about to be slammed in their faces.

Khani bowed her head. "Did Weaver rape you?"

Jessica swayed on her feet and grabbed the doorframe for balance. She whimpered like a wounded animal then sobbed, "No."

Are you kidding me? If that didn't look like a yes, Mags didn't know what did.

"Did he coerce you?" Khani's voice dropped to a whisper.

Jessica covered her beautiful splotched face with both hands and nodded.

Chapter Thirty-five

"I wish she'd told us more. We have to find Willow. I know she was forced one way or another. She wouldn't allow someone to abuse her like that and she wouldn't push me away, unless someone had something over her."

"Or her dad," Khani allowed. "And she told us enough, for now. Once she realizes they're no longer a threat to her, she'll talk. At least she has her priorities in order."

"Damn them," Mags growled. "You know, I'm not a naturally violent person, but I hope Law beats the ability to sport wood from that weasel."

"Here. Here." Khani turned the car onto the highway then tapped a button on her sleek leather steering wheel. After a beep, she said, "Lima. Echo. Oscar. Papa. Alpha. Romeo. Delta. One. Nine. Nine. Four."

After a series of beeps an operator answered. "Voice confirmation complete. Director Slaughter, how may I direct your call?"

"Grizzly."

"You've got the bear. How can I help?" An American voice fit for phone sex or battle cries steamed the car windows, but Khani didn't seem to notice. She plowed ahead, all business.

"I need an address for the Minister of State for Trade and Investment, the Lord Wren. And I need last activity for his daughter, Willow May Wren."

When Grizzly chimed in again, they'd only passed a handful of trees on the forest-bordered thoroughfare. "His address is uploaded to your GPS. You'll arrive on his doorstep at five p.m. Would you like me to make you an appointment, or is this a surprise visit?"

"A polite ambush," Khani said.

"Sounds fun. Willow Wren's last banking transaction is a debit at Haskel's Pizza at eleven fifteen a.m. on July eleventh."

All the air left Magdalena's lungs in a rush.

"You're a gem, Grizz," Khani lauded.

"Back at ya, Lep," he agreed.

As soon as the call disconnected, Mags hyperventilated. Her chest convulsed in panic. Khani slammed on the brakes. Horns blared. Instantly, her breathing evened as she braced both hands on the dash and waited for the impact.

"Now, isn't that better?" Khani eased on the gas and carried on with her skillful drive through growing city traffic. "Freaking out isn't allowed. You've done really well, so far. Don't make me regret our little escapade."

Mags bobbed her head.

"If she's at her dad's place, like her note said, there's no reason for her to use her bank account. Pops has plenty of it."

"Right. You're right."

"Tell me about the restaurant."

"It's local, only a few blocks from our flat. Has great calzones and a mellow crowd."

Khani kept up with the open-ended questions and demands for information, most of which was irrelevant. Who really cared what type of fingernail polish Willow wore as long as they found her, safe with her father. It didn't take Mags long to realize the woman kept her talking to keep her from losing her shit again, and a place in her heart warmed for the cool, take charge giant. In no time at all they parked in front of Lord Charles Wren's red brick home on Lord North Street of Westminster. The irony sat bitter on her tongue.

Magdalena hopped out of the car and watched as Khani unfolded with cat-like grace, her call sign absolutely fitting.

"How do you want to play this? Will's my friend, but upper crust aren't my people," Mags asked.

"You grew up at Baine's estate," Khani countered.

"Yeah, on the estate as the help. None of his family made me feel that way, but we went to the same preppy school. And *those* ass-hats never let me forget it."

"Well, I grew up in the slum. So, they aren't my people either." Her bright lips drew into a half-smirk half-smile.

"Could have fooled me."

"That's the idea, anyway."

"We all have them, don't we," Mags sighed.

"Secrets? Yeah. Some more than others. Let's see what the Lord Wren has in his closet."

They fell in step together, ambling the short distance to the painted black door. Khani overlooked the gold lion's head doorknocker and bare-knuckled two strong beats on the wood. A spin later, a boy-toy butler opened the door. The twenty-something chap sported a fine tan, lean muscles, and impeccable bone structure. With his wide shoulders relaxed at a casual slant, he looked more model than houseman.

His smile required sunglasses. "Hello," he rasped. The come-hither furl of his brow and gentle purse of his lips was too much. Holy hell, he gave butlers a bad name and that set fire to Magdalena's britches in an irritating, stop, drop, and roll, kind of way. "What can I help you beautiful ladies with today? Or, any other day?"

Gross. *Just disgusting.*

"I'm looking for my roommate, Willow," Mags said to keep from laying into the guy, and not in the way he wanted.

"Oh, Magdalena," the guy nodded. "She didn't tell me you were gorgeous, but I should have known. You obviously keep fit company." His head inclined toward Khani, inspecting her head to toe. "Are those the new Charlotte Olympia's? They are sublime."

"Thanks," Khani said. "Willow?"

"Sorry, I get carried away sometimes. She's not here. I'm Roark, by the way."

"Roark, do you know when she'll be back?" Mags raised her hand, pulling his attention from Khani's shoes. Maybe he wasn't sweet on them after all.

"She stayed here two nights, but left yesterday with a friend. Said they were going out of town for a few days. I didn't know she had a thing for older guys." He sighed.

"Older guys," Mags squeaked.

"Yeah, he may not have been much older than Charles." He tsked. "Lord Wren, I mean. But the guy certainly doesn't take care of himself like... Well, he had a paunch and white hair." He flopped his shoulders. "Who am I to judge?"

Magdalena took the direct hit with no time to feint to the side for a glancing blow. The news charged her with relentless force, knocking the wind from her lungs. She gripped the door before she got intimate with the stoop or garden basket perched on the window to her right.

Khani took over. "We need to see Lord Wren." When his brows lifted she added, "Please."

"Step inside and I'll see if he's available."

Khani grabbed her arm and helped Mags up the tiny step. They murmured their thanks and cooperated, clopping their heels and sandals on the checkerboard black-and-white marble of the vestibule. Both watched Roark stroll away. Magdalena whispered. "I'm so confused. And on the verge of vomiting. They have her."

"It's most likely, but they won't for long. We've got one of their own. Law sent me a text."

"Is he okay? What does he know? Did he find Willow?"

"Shhh, he texted green. It means operation in progress, which means he's more than fine. Pull it together and tell me why you've not been here before."

"Will and I met at school."

"I'm formulating my deduction about what Wren's secret is," Khani conceded. "But I'll reserve, until after we meet with the man."

"You're confident we'll be seen."

"Absolutely."

Not a minute later they were ushered through a modern traditional home with enough recessed and colored lighting to remind Mags of an alien ship. Not that she'd ever seen one, even in films really. A professional decorator, no doubt, had dressed the office they entered in bright white and muted hues of grey like the rest of the house. Thanks to Khani she walked through it on steadier legs.

The Lord Wren sat behind a glass-topped desk and rose when they neared. His chiseled jaw jutted forward and his sturdy shoulders carried the weight of responsibility nicely. The rolled cuffs of his dress shirt, loosened tie, and three unfastened buttons at the top revealed sculpted muscles of an obscenely fit man in his fifties.

"Ladies, I am Charles Wren. It's nice to meet friends of Willow." He extended his hand and shook each reciprocating hand in turn with a sure grip. "Would either of you like something to drink?" When they declined the offer, he bowed his head at the man standing behind them. "Thank you, Roark."

Wren's gaze followed the man from the room then returned to them. He cleared his throat. "Please, have a seat, and tell me what it is I can do for you."

"How well do you know Haltman Weaver and Livingston Hues?" Khani asked.

"I'm confused." His lips thinned in tandem with his brow.

"What do you know about The Council for Higher Education?" Khani pushed on.

"I work occasionally with the two men and I know The Council does good in the education community, giving scholarships and the like to those less fortunate. Now, I thought you were here to talk about Willow. Maybe a surprise birthday party or some such thing. Why are you asking about two of my colleagues and their philanthropy?"

Unwavering, Khani forged ahead. "Do you have any secrets to hide, Lord Wren?" His posture took on the air of a corpse, stiffening from the tips of his salt and pepper hair to his toes. "I can see you do, and I believe Hues and Weaver have used that secret to blackmail your daughter."

"What?" He leaned forward, gripping the edge of his glass desk. "How? I don't understand who you are, or what you think you know, but I have nothing to hide and my daughter is just fine. She was here two days ago."

"I am a personal friend of the queen with level Zeta clearance. This is Willow's flatmate, Magdalena Wells."

Apparently that clearance business meant something to Will's father. His eyes took on the characteristics of a hot air balloon, swelling with surprise and threatening to lift right out of his head. He didn't break his gaze from Khani to acknowledge Magdalena's friendship with his daughter.

"I thought...that clearance level was myth," Wren stuttered.

"We'd like to keep it that way," Khani said with an edge.

"Lord Wren, Willow is a dear friend. She's been my anchor for the last several years, but more than that, she is a great person. Dependable. Crazy talented. Loyal. Honest." His gaze found her and two prideful curves bookended his mouth. "I've been away for twelve months on a foreign study mission. When I got back I stumbled onto a scene that was so unlike Willow I immediately knew something was wrong. There is no doubt in my mind that Haltman Weaver holds something over your daughter to make her bend to his will."

"Bend how?" Wren's voice resonated with authority.

"He sexually assaulted Willow." His entire body jerked as if he'd been shot. "She refused to talk with me about the incident, but I could tell she hadn't willfully consented."

Wren's entire body vibrated. He tugged at his already loose tie then his hand shot to the phone on his desk.

"That would be an imprudent course of action," Khani said.

"If what you say is true, then they chose the imprudent course. Not me. I'll take everything they hold dear and smear it all over Parliament." Wren seethed.

"Put the phone down. Now." The control in Khani's voice brooked no argument. To Magdalena's amazement, Wren complied. He looked at his hands in stunned amazement then at the woman who'd given him an order. "I have a man on the job in a much better position to handle this without sullying you or your daughter's good name."

Chapter Thirty-six

Sure, he wasn't one hundred percent. His side hurt like a whale had beached itself on his flank then died, weighing down the ninth and tenth ribs with mind-bending pain. A devil of a headache stabbed him between the eyes. Still, Khani didn't have to screw him with Street just because she screwed herself with the kid. He'd much rather be staring into Magdalena's sultry face than waiting inside Weaver's flat, catching King Street's, *what the hell kind of name is that,* astute gaze. The kid in a man's body considered Law like he were a Taylor series function to calculate.

At least Street could move his hulking body like a silent wrath and flatten a bloke with one pop of his fist. Had Law been alone against the six-man security team spread over two roofs, the front and rear building entrances, and inside Weaver's flat, things could have gotten messy.

Now all they had to do was wait for the weasel to stroll through the door, which, according to the chatty chap bound and gagged in the master bedroom closet, they expected within the hour. Waiting didn't usually bother Law. He'd waited seven hours in Columbian mud for his target to arrive, twelve days by Clara's bedside for her to take her last breath, and nearly a decade to resume living his life after. But instinct and Street's knowing gaze told him the kid was about to cross into unwelcome territory.

"Do you love her?"

Sometimes Law hated being right. "We're on the same team, but it doesn't mean you get to juggle my balls."

"I'll take that as an affirmative." Street's voice whispered over the room that separated them, but his amusement made the journey on an easy chuckle.

"Take it as you're going to end up with my boot in your mouth, if you don't shut it." Law growled.

"Am I sensing some pent up frustration?"

"You're sensing your death, if you fuck Khani over. Career and family mean everything to her. Don't take one away because you can't keep your dick in your pants."

"Ever heard the term it takes two to tango?"

Irritation inflamed Law's skin. It screamed for relief or release from the stony pose he'd taken twenty minutes ago. The perfect reprieve would be going rounds with Street. The kid was big, but Law had shaved Baine to size a time or ten. He had no doubt he'd do the same with Street, but banked Scouse bled through the kid's accent, just once, in a phrase he'd used while knocking a tooth out of one of the guards who tried to sneak up on the bloke. Law didn't know Street's background, but the way he rather skillfully hid his Liverpool roots spoke to the kid's intellect and street smarts. In a fair fight he'd go dirty every time, which is what separated the men from the boys. Maybe he'd have to refer to him as a young man.

Two pairs of footsteps tapped in the hallway, moving quickly toward the door. Neither Law nor Street made a sound, their back and forth forgotten for the time. A key slid into the lock and the door sung wide, pouring a rectangle of artificial light into the dark foyer and offset living area.

Law breathed as steadily as if he were relaxing on the couch catching a one-sided game. When a woman's voice split the air with a sob his breath suspended in his lungs. A slender figure stumbled into his line of sight, grasping the side of an antique entry table four feet from him.

"What is it with uncooperative bitches? One won't put out. One won't die. And now you. Oh, you'll give me what I want or I'll splash your mum's affair with her intern all over the news. She'll lose her job and you'll have to quit school. Waitressing won't get you through Oxford, will it?" Haltman Weaver tossed a key into a ceramic bowl on the side table from which the young woman retreated. His jacket came next, sailing through the air and landing on a wing-backed chair at the den entrance as he kicked the door shut.

The room plunged into inky darkness, but Law watched Street step out from behind the parting wall and nail Weaver square in the nose. A startled cry left the man's mouth a moment before the crunch and subsequent silence replaced it. But the young woman took over the shrill exclamation.

Law stepped forward and wrapped an arm around the girl's waist, pinning her arms to her side. With his other hand he pinched a nerve at her nape. Her panicked holler faded and he cradled her weight. Weaver, on the other hand, hit the floor like a wet stack of newspapers.

"What the hell?" Street barked. "She wasn't a threat."

"One, never underestimate a woman. Two, she's easier to deal with unconscious. Three, take her home. To her home, not yours."

"Screw you. I'd never take advantage of a woman. I may be a lot of things, but a fuckwad isn't one. And I'm not leaving until I have a crack at *that* fuckwad. His guy shot me yesterday."

"Well, you can catch her or let her hit the ground." Law released his hold on the woman and smiled as Street scrambled to capture the co-ed's weight before she met the floor. When he succeeded, Law made a clicking sound with his mouth. "I knew you were fast.

"As far as a shot at Weaver goes, you're S.O.L. That bastard tried to kill the woman I love. And me, not that I get bent out of shape over that. Plenty have tried and I'm still here.

"Wipe that damn smirk off your face and get lost."

"It's too dark to see my smirk," Street said.

"But I know it's there."

"I'll make sure she gets home safely, but I'm coming back. Director's orders." Street scooped the light haired woman into his arms and tucked her face in the crook of his neck. "The door?" Law opened the door and watched as they headed toward the stairs. To anyone passing, they'd look like entangled lovebirds. When he could no longer see the kid's broad back or the pale legs and sandal covered feet swaying with each long stride he closed the door and smiled at Weaver's listless body.

"Get ready for one hell of a wake-up call, buddy."

About ten minutes after having his nose broken in a knock-out, Haltman Weaver came-to in stages. The pants of his narrow chest increased. White skin stretching taut over each thin rib gave him a skeletal quality. He moaned, the sound muffled by silver duct tape fastened over his lips. Noise escaped from the small slit Law cut in the center of the adhesive to keep the fuckwad alive. The bastard's head lobbed up then swung back down, until dark, demented eyes popped wide in horror.

"Feels a little different when you're the one tied up, doesn't it?"

Law lounged on the sofa, legs sprawled on either side of the dining chair where the weasel, as Magdalena called him, wiggled and jerked against the man's own leather restraints.

"I found your nice bracelets in the closet. If you'd only used them with consenting women, we wouldn't have a problem. But you went and ruined something that could have been a beautiful experience with violence and blackmail.

"If that wasn't bad enough, and it was, you royally fucked yourself by threatening someone I care deeply for."

Law sat forward, pulling in his knees and resting his elbows atop them. He scratched at the scruff of his out of control beard and huffed in Weaver's face. Law should have never questioned Baine's judgment in Mexico. Sure he smeared some lines to grey, but that's what you do for the people you love. As long as when it's all said and done you're still standing on the right side of the smug.

"I bet you're wondering where your men are, who I am, what I'm going to do to you. Let me settle your mind right now. Your security force is alive, but their first priority upon consciousness will be the hospital. Not you.

"I'm your conscience come-a-callin', and I'm going to do whatever it takes to get through to you. I'm going to do whatever it takes to get answers to questions." Law pointed his index finger at his own chest. "Demand." Then he stabbed it toward Weaver. "Supply." He stood and dragged the chair to the center of the room, the metal chair legs whining against the lacquered floor. The weasel tried to fight, but had already spent himself. "The sooner you understand our arrangement, the better your chances of survival." Muted hollers siphoned from Weaver's throat, filling the room with the dull burble of promising music.

"To make myself clear, we'll start with a little incentive. My ribs are really killing me right now. Your men did that. Would have done worse, if I hadn't severed their spinal cords and brain stems with a bullet each.

"If you don't wish to feel my pain, Halt, I suggest you start by telling me how you get these college-educated women to turn tricks for you and half the government's elite. Oh, before we begin, let me explain further that a broken rib can quite easily puncture a man's lung and cause him to suffocate on his own blood in agonizing minutes. Same goes for a broken nose, which you obviously have; it doesn't take as long though. I mean, look at all the blood. All it would take is a solid strip of tape right here."

Law slapped his hand over the man's mouth. The snap rippled through the air and Weaver's eyes filled with glistening moisture. His black-death eyes mapped with broken blood vessels and gaped as wide as a stripper's thong. "Bet that stung." With pinched fingers, Law gripped the edge of the tape and yanked. "Supply," he demanded.

"You'll never get away with this." Haltman sobbed. "They are powerful men you're— No! No!"

The slab of tape Law pulled from his neatly lined pre-cut row of four inch strips stuck to the edge of the coffee table ceased the watery refusal. It only took the man a second to realize the polyethylene, cotton, and adhesive lacked the convenient hole of his last gag. When his muscles strained it looked as if someone vacuum-sealed the skin at his neck. He thrashed, but could go nowhere.

Law jabbed his fist hard and hot into Weaver's low right ribs, mimicking his own injury with the crack of bones. The man sagged as far as the leather securing his chest would allow then convulsed in a battle for air. Law slowly unsheathed seven inches of black steel. "You might want to hold still." Weaver shivered, but stowed the wild antics while Law raked the tip of his KA-BAR across the center of the tape. While the weasel hauled rattling breaths, Law spoke.

"You don't follow direction very well and that's bad for you. The same demand, Haltman. If I don't get an accurate supply this time I'll have to give you one of these suckers." Law pointed to the jagged wound splitting his right brow. Weaver focused on the spot and shook his head as though he'd suddenly developed Parkinson's.

Law's phone vibrated against his thigh and he stepped back from the bound man. "Only a short reprieve, Weaver," he said, retrieving the phone from his pocket. He greeted Khani's encrypted number. "Pierce."

Magdalena's honeyed voice filled his ear. "Are you okay?"

"Of course." The desire to reach through the phone and hug her to him rankled. He couldn't even tell her how the sound of her sweet words warmed his heart. The fact that his tart spoke to him, instead of Khani, did crazy things to his insides. Turned them gooey. With Weaver watching he couldn't give anything away.

"Thank God," she huffed. "Law, they have Willow. I think Hues does."

"I'll find her," he vowed then discretely ended the call and continued talking. "If not, stay by the mail box and I'll ship you pieces of Weaver's sorry excuse for a dick, one pitiful piece at a time. How much do you want to bet he'll spill after I carve off half his tiny head? I mean, it'll hurt me, but not near as much as it'll hurt him."

He slid the phone into the pocket of his black fatigues and winked at Haltman Weaver. Joy exploded in Law's chest at the stark terror dilating the man's murky eyes.

"Since I'm a man of my word, we'll tackle the head wound first then the tiny piece between your legs. First demand is still in play. How do you get bright young women with promising futures to devalue themselves with you and other political puppets?"

Law ripped the adhesive from Weaver's mouth, ripping raw the skin around his quivering lips. The chav sucked in two shaky breaths and bit back a sob.

"We ferret secrets and use them as leverage."

"More."

"Sometimes it's their secret they don't want shared. Other times, it's their parents' secret or an old family one."

Crossing his arms, Law stepped back from the naked man and goaded him on with a raised brow.

"They'll do anything to maintain public pride. Their upbringing taught them it's the most important thing. Later we developed enough credit that we manufactured false truths or made tapes as insurance."

"Who is we?"

Weaver hesitated. Law shifted his weight to move, but words spewed from his throat along with spittle. "Livingston Hues. We started The Council for Higher Education and took on our first clients before we had any girls ready."

"How did you acquire your clients?"

"Oh, God." Weaver moaned. "Livingston and I were members of a high-end kink club, but were dismissed for misconduct. Our first four clients came from similar situations. Word spread."

"I'm a little disappointed you picked up so quickly on the inner workings of our arrangement, Halt. But I'm not finished demanding things from you. In fact, I'm just getting started. It would be in your best interest to continue cooperating, but don't do so on my account." Law tossed the man's clothes into his lap. "When I untie you, you're going to lead me to Willow Wren. And, Weaver, if I step into a trap, I'll use you as my shield."

Chapter Thirty-seven

Street arrived with a Taxi as Law and his hostage exited onto the rain-dampened sidewalk and arched a thick brow at him. Law ignored him, shoved Weaver in the car, and climbed in behind the chav. Street ground his teeth. Law guessed the guy was pissed over missing his shot at the man sandwiched between. He used what little room he had to text Magdalena and Khani the address and his list of directives for the take-down.

Khani replied, *"You know, I'm the one who's supposed to be giving the orders. But it's solid. We're in."*

His phone vibrated again, surprising him. *"I love you! -Magdalena"*

He wrote back. *"Stay up late tonight and I'll show you how much I love you."*

Law wiped at the perma-smile on his lips and stowed his phone. After a snail paced drive across town through evening traffic they reached Hues' residence, which was the first place he'd have looked for Willow, had Weaver been the type to hold back. They made the block and exited the cab three blocks down from the building housing Willow and the sexual deviant she'd spent far too many hours entertaining. For the sake of his sanity and the mission, Law didn't dwell on things he couldn't change. He waited until the black cab pulled away then shoved Weaver into a brick alcove.

"Weapons check," he ordered Street.

The man jutted his ample jaw and set to work on his Wilson Combat Supergrade nine elevens, inspecting the magazines and wracking a bullet into the slide of each.

"I think I have gun envy." Law sighed.

"I wouldn't say that too loud. Your Sigs'll get jealous. Bad luck to question your weapons before a mission."

"Well, here comes my good luck and your tough luck."

To his credit, Street didn't blanch as the grey Benz paralleled into a dime sized spot between a white Mercedes and royal blue BMW. Magdalena's small feet hit the pavement a second later clad in sleek cream heals. Her legs tapered into perfect curves and his cock saluted. When she stood she knocked him clean out. Law grabbed his heart and staggered as she dazzled him in a like-colored skirt suit, adoringly tailored to the sway of her luscious body. The faint lines of worry fell from her face and it lit with the curl of her lips and brow in playful joy, which he'd come to depend on in such a short time.

She walked into him, banding her arms under the leather of his holster and holding tight. Law gripped her nape, careful not to muss her neatly styled hair, but held her as securely as he could without compromising her breath. Street stepped toward Weaver, giving them some time, and he didn't rush it away. He treasured the feel of her warm body pressed to his, the smell of her airy floral perfume, and the earthiness of her exhalations, the strum of her heart over his middle.

Far too soon Magdalena loosened her death grip and stepped back. Moisture glistened in the well of her pale green eyes and it pinched his heart. "Don't cry, tart. It'll ruin your make-up. I've never seen you in make-up. It's nice." He lowered his head to her ear. "Though, I'll enjoy melting it off your pretty skin even more. I want to see those freckles."

"You are too much," she whispered.

"Nope. I'm not enough, but I'll try to be." He kissed her red lips.

"All right, you two need to get going," Khani barked. "Are you sure you don't need the ass-hat?"

"He already spilled his guts. It'll be an in-and-out. Don't worry. Either of you." Law narrowed his gaze at Magdalena. "Are you sure about spending quality time with him?"

"Yeah." Magdalena nodded and let her voice carry. "You taught me how to shoot a gun. If Weaver screws with me, I'll just show him my newfound skill."

Law gave Magdalena his signature wink and turned toward Weaver. "Last chance to confess. If I live through an ambush, and the odds are very likely I will, I'll make sure you live the rest of your life dickless. Not that you're far from it now."

The bloke had the mind not to glare when he replied. "I've told you everything, enough to get me killed by a thousand different men."

Law turned his gaze on Street and gestured toward Khani. "Hand him over." The big chap frog-marched Weaver across the concrete to stand next to his tall, leanly muscled friend. Standing side-by-side, Street and Slaughter looked ready to rip each other apart. Law just couldn't tell if it was in a good or bad way. He doubted they knew which side the arching tension favored.

Street released Weaver and got in his face. "You fuck with either of them, I won't stop at your dick. You'd be truly amazed what a man can live without." He straightened and the snarling beast receded as a smile spread across his face and he chucked the chav's shoulder. "Eyes. Nose. Ears. They're all nonessential. Can you believe that?"

Law finished his weapons check and turned to Magdalena. "Not too early, okay?"

"You be safe and I will too." She pulled him down for a quick brush of her lips then shoved him toward the alley. "Now go. I can't stand imagining what he's done to Willow. Waiting is eating me alive."

He turned and hustled down the sidewalk to the narrow alley with Street at his heels. Their boots clopped softly against the damp pavement. At the next building they climbed the fire escape in complete silence as they'd done once before earlier in the evening. Law stilled at the top, listening for any sound. He heard the splashes of cars driving through large puddles on the main road, the bustle of the city, but nothing beyond.

Law eased his gaze over the edge, but found a guard in his line of sight. He climbed over the metal ornamentation at the roofline and jumped to the tar top with a whisper. Street followed and they split, crouching low and circling an ornate greenhouse overrun with twisting vines from either side. The guard kicked back on his ass, fingers clasped behind his head. Street reached the man first and Law felt a little sorry for the guy. The kid's meaty fist caught his attention too late and put him to sleep for the next hour or so. After securing him with a series of zip ties they left to scout the other rooftops.

The second roof went similarly, but he and Street both had some fun at the rear entrance of the swanky building. Both guards covering it fancied themselves ninja, but they needed more practice.

 With a regular doorman at the front they opted to go in through the back. It took Street less than ten seconds to pick the lock on the thick metal door, and again Law hated being impressed. Law picked Livingston's front door in eighteen seconds and those three extra seconds raked the bloody hell out of his nerves, until he heard a woman scream.

"No! No! You son of a bitch. I hope you die of a heart attack."

Shit got real in a flash. He and Street moved through the high-dollar hell. Guns drawn and ready, they cleared the area with economic sweeps. The gilded den and state of the art kitchen held nothing of interest, but Law's stomach roiled in the dining room.

A twelve-foot long, carved cherry wood table held two place settings. One plate held only a charger, but no plate of food, while the other was littered with throwaways of a rack of lamb, potatoes, and green beans. The chair at the head of the table with the used plate was kicked at an angle toward the one to its left, which hosted leather restraints at the polished arms and legs. Just like he'd used on Weaver.

Law gave a hand signal and they moved like silent death through an office and a guest room with restraints and rumpled bedding. The final room sat at the end of the hall, its door opened wide, inviting them in to a show they didn't care to watch. Street's body was loose, but his jaw worked and nostrils flared, as Law knew his did.

Law holstered his gun, waited a count of
three, and they moved in tandem. Street went low,
scanning the area with the black barrel of his 1911
while Law went high. High speed, collecting more as
he steamed across the room, and plowed into
Livingston Hues. Law's force ripped the pig's
potbellied nakedness from the back of Willow's
bruised body. The man screamed as he tumbled
onto the floor. When Law landed atop him the cries
muffled. Law looped his left arm under Livingston's
soft jowl and constricted like an anaconda, sinking
his biceps into the man's windpipe.

The old man wiggled, imitating a fish caught
in the jaws of a shark. Law's right fist balled,
shaking with fury and the relentless urge to
pummel the piece of shit into a pile of slushy bio-
waste. He settled for one bone-shattering blow to
the kidney. With any luck, Hues would piss blood
for weeks and breathe with a hitch for far longer.

Livingston's trembling body slackened as he
faded into unconsciousness. Law released his hold
and stood before the chav moved past oblivion and
slipped into death. He didn't deserve to die so
painlessly. Law would let one of the hundreds of
warlords and disgraced government officials Weaver
and Hues entertained with blackmailed young
women hire a prison yard hit. First, he'd watch
them stripped of every luxury their twisted scheme
earned them. Then he'd see them crucified in the
media spotlight and public eye.

Law turned to see Street hustling through the
door with the comforter from the guest room bed
tossed over his arm. Willow lay belly-down in an X
across the crisply made bed, the deep red paisleys
contrasting her pale skin with a gruesome pop. Her
leather-cuffed wrists and ankles were secured with
a length of braided rope to each of the four

intricately carved posts. The angle of her neck craned toward him and Willow's muddy eyes challenged him. Streams of coal-watered mascara didn't diminish their defiance.

His knees met the hardwood where he stood a good ten feet from the bed and offered Willow his palms. He raised his chin to Street who took the cue and hung back. Law held her gaze. "Willow, we're friends of Magdalena. I'm Law Pierce, Baine's housemate." Her lips parted on a gasp. "The man behind you is Street." She stiffened. "He's a friend too. We're going to get you out of here."

When the tension on the ropes and in her body slackened, he continued. "Street has a blanket to cover you with then we'll cut your binds. Do you give us permission to help?"

"Yes," she croaked.

The rasp of her voice brought Law back to a dank hut in the middle of the misty jungle. Back to the ruined sound of his own pitiful cries. His hands gripped the fabric stretched over his thighs and bit down. *The fucking bastards. Then and now.* No matter how strong he'd been mentally, his body betrayed him, cowing in vicious growls then wrenching screams that clung to his brain like starving leeches.

How dare they do that to her?

Siren trills whispered in the distance. Law collected his past, shoved it into the dim recesses of his mind then trained it on the present. He looked to Street and the bloke stepped forward, covering Willow's bareness with an inscrutable expression. Law unsheathed his KABAR. A tear slid over the curve of her chin and fell to the pillow.

"For the bonds," he reminded in yoga calm.

She gave a wobbling, lopsided grin, and he lunged at the leather straps. After the hide separated he pushed toward the band at the head of the bed while Street mirrored his movements on the opposite side of Willow. She flailed beneath the garish gold coverlet, trying to reclaim her body.

Street's rage flashed white-hot on his face as the behemoth stalked toward Livingston's unconscious heap. His brows slanted toward the floor and his head dropped low like a dog ready to attack. Law held his tongue, anxious to see what the rookie would do. Angered or not the kid stuck to the plan, pulling a chair from the corner desk and shackling the rat bastard to it. Law turned his attention back to Willow.

"The feeling will come back to your extremities slowly. You'll feel the pressure at your wrists and ankles for the next couple of days. Just breathe through the panic when it comes." He stepped toward the bed. "I'm going to adjust the blanket and pick you up. We've got to move."

"The police," Willow whispered. She collapsed onto her side, gasping. "He has to pay. They have to pay for what they've done. I have to tell, no matter the cost. I have to believe my dad would agree that what they're doing isn't worth his secret or now mine."

"You're one brave lady, Willow. You can talk to the police after I get you to a hospital, but Hues and Weaver are going to be buried deep whether you come forward or not."

"No." Her voice quavered and her body trembled so profusely the tassels on the mounded pillows undulated. "I almost got Magdalena killed because I didn't tell the police. I will, but I should have sooner. I'm not brave. I'm broken. The thought of being examined, of going to the sterile confines of a brightly lit hospital, makes me want to curl into a ball and die. Just end it all."

"Broken doesn't fight back." He pointed to her raw and blistered wrist. "Broken doesn't speak its mind. Broken doesn't recognize the ease of death. It submits to death without a thought, without a word."

Law slid his arms under Willow's head and thighs and held his breath as he lifted her. The grimace on her face screwed tight, but when she didn't cry out in pain he let out the imprisoned air. "You're not broken. Chipped around the edges, but take it from someone who knows. The jagged points dull over time."

Willow relaxed into his hold and whispered, "Thank you. But still, no hospital."

"I know a clinic doc, but he'll probably scare you more than a hospital." He turned to Street who scattered the printed proof of Hues' and Weaver's crimes around the naked man's feet. "Let's get out of here before one of us kills the piece of shit."

"Finally we agree on something," Street said.

Chapter Thirty-eight

"That's your cue," Khani said with an elbow to Magdalena's upper arm. The nudge caused a major collision of the stacks of paper she held in each hand. Pages curved and bent at odd angles, voicing their protest with pops and snaps. Her white knuckled grip on the facts of Hues' and Weaver's terrorism held firm as her heart skipped at Khani's words. She tore her gaze from the black ink, and then pasted it to a white van with BBC block letters parked a few feet away on the main street.

"I'm going to throw up on my fancy shoes."

"Just do it after you get out of my car. I already have to get the trunk detailed from Weaver's rancid ass."

Thinking about the weasel, who had hurt her best friend and tried to have her and Law killed, trussed like the pig that he was eased Magdalena's nausea. Thinking about him and his sleazy partner getting their comeuppance steeled her backbone. She straightened her stacks of proof into a neat pile and turned to Khani.

"How do I look?"

"Like a budding journalist." The last of the tension Mags had sensed in her new friend finally ebbed as Khani smiled, a nearly imperceptible curve of her vivid lips. The grin she'd given after slamming the trunk on Weaver had been bigger, but this one was honest. "Now, get out of here. So I can hand deliver this trash to the Met and you can tell the world what they did."

Magdalena spent the next hour reporting the biggest news story since the queen's trip to Ireland or the proposal of the Scottish Independence Referendum. After tonight, she guessed Law could call her a reporter. As long as he tacked on *and journalist* to the end. Her favorite shot of the night was detailing the two men's scheme while the police escorted Livingston Hues from his posh flat in boxer shorts and handcuffs. If there was any liberation for the women they'd hurt, this was the first step in the winding staircase.

Minutes after Hues had been hauled away, news vans, police cars, and onlookers littered the tight one-way street, choking off any hope of escape. Magdalena exhausted every angle the directors could possibly want on the scarcely believable drama. She handed the clip-on microphone to the cameraman, a sweet old pro, and wiped her damp palms on the waist of her jacket as though smoothing it out.

"Thank you so much, Arthur. I couldn't have done it without you."

"Call me Art, Ms. Wells. You're a natural with the story punches. We'll get your camera fright under control in no time, not that anyone watching would notice. I've never seen anyone who can fidget so much below the waist and keep stock still on frame."

"I'll take that as a compliment and would love to work with you again, but I think this was a one shot deal."

The salt and pepper bloke snapped his fingers and tapped an index to his forehead. "I'd forget my blood pressure meds, if Irene didn't shove them down my throat every morning. Don't know what I'd do without that woman. Take a breath and I'll be back in a sec."

"All right." Mags shrugged and tried not to tap the sole of her shoe on the hard concrete. Art disappeared into the back of the van in a spry hop for a man with close to thirty pounds of steady cam rigging and recorder strapped to his chest. She released the air she'd fortified herself with in Khani's car, oh so long ago, and nearly collapsed on the sidewalk. The weight of everything suddenly seemed more than she could endure.

The rumble of a far-off engine pricked her ears. Magdalena snapped her head up so fast she stumbled on the towering heels. She righted her stance and scanned the crowd and gridlock of cars, but didn't see the smooth looking ride she sought, nor the man she wanted so desperately. She hugged her arms around her middle.

People hollered as the motor roared and the crowd on the sidewalk parted. Law maneuvered the Hog through the angered mass and up to the police blockade where a small officer with an even smaller hand told him to S.T.O.P. At least that's what she gathered from the gesture.

Magdalena's hands fell to her sides. She took a step toward him then another. The instinct to run to him took over.

"Hold up a minute, Ms. Wells. Opportunities like this don't come along everyday. I don't think you want to pass it up."

She didn't want to pass Law up. Not ever. Not for anything. She smiled back at Arthur. "I have someone to meet."

"Is he more important than a job with the BBC?" He held up a thick packet of papers and shook them at her with *are you crazy* eyes.

Shock stole her tongue, but only for a moment. "Yes, he is."

"Good, then he'll wait thirty seconds while you shove the contract in that briefcase of yours." Art came forward and shoved the stack into the guts of her teal tote, along-side the other sheets she had stowed. "Enjoy tonight, but review it and get it back to the boss as soon as you can. He's ready to put you to work."

Magdalena grabbed Art's hand and squeezed. "Thank you. Get on home to Irene."

"I've got some b-roll to collect, but she'll wake up when I get home." The sly dog winked.

Mags blushed to her toes, turned, and ran on three inch heels toward Law. He sat like an immovable wall of black from helmet, to leather jacket, to pants and boots. Her heartbeat kicked up a notch. She weaved around the barricades and eagerly accepted the helmet he held out to her. With a hike of skirt and swing of her leg Magdalena slid behind him, not caring one bit how indecent she appeared to the throng. She held tight to her bag and banded Law's torso with her other arm.

For a long while neither said anything. They weaved through dense city traffic, exchanging scorching body heat and sharing the freedom of the ride. How far she'd come in such a short time. From fearing the pulse of need and love, of abandon, Law stirred inside her, to craving it like the air she breathed. She hugged him as hard as her muscles would allow then decided she needed to lift weights because her grip wasn't nearly strong enough to convey her love.

"How is Willow?"

"She is strong and in good hands. It'll be a long road, but she'll work through it because she has people who care about her."

"Can I see her?"

"I'll take you as soon as she gets to her father's house."

"Where is she now?"

"At Dr. Dylan Cole's clinic. He's keeping her for observation tonight. When I left she was sleeping with the help of a few drugs. Her dad sat beside her bed with his boyfriend, Roark, holding his hand. And doc is staying the night."

"You are too good to me."

"Not even close."

"How did you get me a crew, special anchor spot, and a job with the freaking BBC?"

"On your merit, with a little records help from Mrs. Fry. But they'd flagged your stories for the UN. You were already on their radar.

"Magdalena, can I take you home?"

"Only if by home you mean your home."

Chapter Thirty-nine

Magdalena's eyes opened then blinked into uncomfortable clarity the rays of daylight filtering through the windows. The room greeted her with the familiar scent of her man and she slumped back into the fluffy down. Tiny bits of fabric and feathers launched into the air and wafted through the streaks of day in casual eddies. Remembering waking in this house similarly two-and-a-half weeks earlier, she smiled so wide her cheeks hurt.

So much had changed since then. Not the least of which was the fact that she was about to propose. Screw waiting. Boink tradition. Mags knew what she wanted and who she wanted it with. Forever was a long damn time. If Law didn't turn tush and run, she'd cherish every day she was given.

Since Hues' and Weaver's arrests he'd been whatever she needed him to be. A sounding board for career decisions. Firm arms to hold her up when she'd taken care of Willow and bore witness to the effects of the atrocities she'd endured. A shoulder to cry on when it all became too much. An ardent lover, kissing away the pain. Quick hands to catch her when she met Baine's love, Sloan, and found out he was getting married in a week. Which happened to be today.

Mags rolled toward the center of the bed, but, as she'd expected, found it empty. Well, not empty. Just void of the person she wanted most. In his place as it had been for the past few mornings was a handwritten breakfast menu.

Lordy, if he doesn't know the way to my heart.

Two minutes later Law strolled through the door, his chest resplendently bare save for the breakfast tray and its accouterments blocking the carved ridges of his abdomen. Over the last two weeks she'd mapped the topography of his body with her tongue and knew every hard inch of him intimately. Enthusiastically. Even the parts hidden beneath his flannel pajama pants.

"Strawberry waffles? I'm so spoiled, I may never leave."

Law set the tray on the side table and bit at the hand she used to steal a crinkled bite of bacon. Mags squealed, shoved the *burn her tongue* hot morsel inside her mouth and huddled back in the bed, carefully holding the near sizzling piece of meat between her teeth until it cooled.

"You don't have a flat to go back to, not that you couldn't buy a nice one with your new job." Law's muscles flexed as he arranged things about the tray, blocking her view.

Mags chewed the warm, salty tidbit and swallowed. "The flat held bad memories for Willow and me. Selling the place was a healing step. She's looking so much better in just a short time. Cole is good for her. He pushes her, but no more than she can handle. I really can't thank you enough for what you've done for her. And me."

"You don't have to thank me, tart. But I thoroughly enjoy the effort you put forth in that department." Mags thought she heard a smile in his voice, but he turned with a slanted grin and a predatory gleam in his eyes. His stalk toward the bed curled her toes.

"I don't have time to thank you much more or buy a flat with my dissertation and job. I can't believe I'm a BBC journalist *and* reporter." She giggled, trying to ignore Law as he gripped the covers at her feet and flipped them over his head. "I don't even have time to enjoy you nibbling my toes..."

He bit the arch of her foot. She yelped and instinctively jerked, but his firm hands held her to the bed at her thighs. Law spread them wide, nestling his wide shoulders between them.

"My calves..." His lips molded adoringly to the gentle curve of her lower leg then higher. "My thighs..."

"My...oh my God." She moaned as his tongue slid devilishly from her cheeks to her clit. Her body opened to him, quickening at his touch. But far sooner than she'd been conditioned to expect, Law glided his magic mouth over her belly and up between the valley of her breasts.

He tongued her right nipple then kissed the left before sealing one over her heart and surfacing from beneath the covers. The brilliance of his face stole her breath for the thousandth time. His full brows and green eyes, firm jaw and full lips, his stubble and sweet smile swelled her heart.

"It's your day off, remember? Wedding day."

"Yes, I do. We just disbanded a sex slave ring, but you've kept me imprisoned in this bed every moment you could for the past couple of weeks. How could I forget?"

"You're free to go at any time." His lips thinned.

"Really?" Her brow quirked.

"No." The smirk playing around his lips fell. Law bracketed his weight on either side of her body, snuggling his hot skin to her thighs and arms. He grabbed her left hand and held it in his own.

Magdalena took a breath, knowing this was the perfect moment. "Law, will you…"   His words overtook hers. "Remember when…"

Noting the set of his jaw and the vulnerability in his wide gaze, she let him have the moment. There would be others.

"Remember when I asked if I could bring you home and you said, 'If you mean your home.' I want us to make our home. Here or wherever you'd like. Whether we have twenty more days or eighty years on this rock, I want us to live them together."

Tears blurred her view of his face and Mags blinked them away.

Law rubbed the wet trail down her face. "Magdalena, will you marry me?"

"Yes!"

Her morning breath probably kicked him in the face, but it couldn't stifle the toothy grin she sported. Neither did it repress Law's affection. He grazed his lips over her tear-stained cheek to her open mouth and attacked with precision and strength. When they both panted he broke the kiss and levered over her. He kissed the ring finger of her left hand, the one he straightened for her, then slid a ring that froze the synapses in her brain over her first knuckle.

"Holy shit. It is… You get me," she stuttered.

A rectangular emerald hid the width of her finger, but it was far from humdrum. Carved like a starburst, the face of the gem exploded with character while below the surface, grass and sea green battled, claiming equally dazzling property. Diamond baguettes fanned the longest sides of the stone, anchoring it in place and snaking around the platinum band.

"It's not a diamond."

"No," she agreed. "It's better." Law flashed her his one shallow dimple and she could have burst into song, but she spared them both. "I love you," she laughed.

"I love you, Magdalena."

A firm double knock sounded on the bedroom door. "Mags, thirty minutes till torture time. You love birds better get in one last quickie before we leave," Sloan hollered.

"You bet," Mags called back. She poked her bottom lip out at Law. She looked at her engagement ring then back at Law. "We can't tell anyone until after their honeymoon. I'm not stealing anybody's thunder."

Law kissed her nose and reached for the breakfast tray. He pulled a long thin chain over her shoulder. It tickled and chilled its way across her neck and pooled over her heart. "It won't fit on your finger for another couple of weeks anyway."

"What?"

He unlatched the clasp then grabbed her hand and pulled it to his mouth. His lips warmed her top knuckle. "Swelling from the dislocation. So, I guess we can wait to tell people, but do not let my mom find out I asked before she or my sisters found out." He pulled the ring from her finger and looped the beauty around the chain and fastened it behind her neck.

"Until you can wear it on your finger, it can hide out in my favorite spot." He adjusted the clasp and tugged the length, which settled in the valley of her breasts.

"I'm not putting this gem in my pussy," she quipped.

"My second favorite spot," he countered.

"Not in my mouth either."

"Fine, my third favorite spot."

"I've never titty fucked an emerald or diamonds before."

"Can't believe Tony Hall lets you on the air with that foul thing." Law scrubbed his thumb over her bottom lip.

"You love it."

"More than my life. Now, about that quickie…"

Epilogue

"Are you all right?" Mags asked. "You look a little pale, and coming from me, that's saying something."

Sloan closed the partition she'd peeked through, clasped her hands at the trim fitting ivory lace and silver beads covering her waist, and sucked a deep breath through her nose. She let it loose in an open-mouthed gush. "I think I'm going to be sick."

"Are you pregnant?"

"Not helping." Sloan's amber eyes flashed on Mags then rolled heavenward.

Magdalena grabbed a book from the well-ordered shelf and fanned Sloan. "Are you having second thoughts about—"

"No. Not at all. It's just, when Baine said, 'Army & Navy Club with a few of our closest friends,' I was thinking more guns and less people. There are at least thirty people in the room already."

"And you could kill every one of them with your bare hands. I don't really understand the problem."

"It was supposed to be me and Baine, Easton and Ruth, Ryan and Commander Tucker, Mrs. Pierce, you and Law at the registry office. But your dad, Ruth, and Law's mom found out the place was being renovated and took over.

"Congratulations, by the way." Sloan smiled at the last and a bit of the color returned to her cheeks.

"Congratulations?"

"Please, I don't need to be a professional observer to see you're so giddy you're about to float away. And you've been toying with that sweet ring all morning."

Magdalena gasped and looked down at her non-fanning hand. The emerald twirled around her pointer finger in a slow loopty-loop. Sloan bit her lower lip in a wicked smile. "It's a good thing I came to get you. Otherwise you two would still be trying to bang the bed through the wall."

Their cackles were cut off by the director's appearance. "Ladies, we're ready for you. Ms. Wells first. Wait a twelve count, Ms. Harris, then you follow."

Mags shoved the ring behind the sweetheart neckline of the soft pink knee length dress they'd chosen the week before and nestled it between her boobs. She reshelved the book and turned to go as instructed, but Sloan grabbed her arm and whispered, "I'm not a ballerina. What is he talking about?"

"Just count to twelve slowly. You're about to be a part of my family. The only thing you have to worry about is not getting fat around my father's, and apparently Law's, cooking." Magdalena kissed Sloan's cheek, picked the orange, pink, and cream bridal bouquet of peonies, ranunculus, and tulips from the table, and handed them to the lady of the day. "I'm so happy for you and Baine."

The doors opened and Mags plucked up her smaller clutch of the same and walked on cream sling-backs down the isle. Strangers and familiar faces lined each side on white cloth covered chairs with wide bands of whisper pink. But not even her father and Ruth could hold her gaze from searching out the men at the front of the room.

Her smile grew genuine when she spotted Baine's wide set shoulders, slightly wavy dark hair, and rare grin, which had become more frequent over the last few weeks. The man didn't grin. He laughed on occasion, but the beam radiating from his bearded face was crafted for this very special occasion.

Mags knew the moment Sloan walked into the room because her brother's gaze left her and widened at a spot behind her head. Just as well, because her gaze moved from his dark to Law's bright. They welded together as she stepped to her mark at the front of the room. He winked. By force of will she silenced a moan and winked back instead. Then they turned toward the union of a dear old friend and a lovely new one.

In no time at all, Baine and Sloan were hitched and in a lip lock ferocious enough to make Law blush. They exited into a small banquet hall assembled with round tables and all the finery of a meal, a modest wooden dance floor, and jazz quartet. The happy couple were overtaken by guests in a blink with congratulations and well-wishes.

Law grabbed Magdalena's arm and pulled her close. "You look good enough to eat." The breath from his words caressed her ear.

"You've already done that today," she said, banding her arms around his torso and tilting her head up for a kiss.

He nipped her lip. "Haven't had my fill."

"Lucky me." Her entire body quivered.

"Now, son. You have some introductions to make." Mags turned at Poppy Pierce's voice and pulled one arm from Law to scoop his mom into a group hug. Magdalena's head could have nestled nicely in her full rack. Law obviously got his height from every branch of his family tree. But Mags arched her chin and hugged the woman tightly, thankful for the love she readily dispensed.

"You two have seen each other about a hundred times in the last two weeks, Mum, and if I'm not mistaken, you met her before I did." Law shook his head and hugged his mother close.

"Yes," she agreed. "But, you haven't introduced me to your fiancée." The woman's elegant face curled into a smile only a mother could give, mixed with familial pride and *I told you so*.

Magdalena bit her lips together and cut her gaze at Law who bobbed his head, his mouth narrow as her own.

"Well," a deep voice said from behind Law's mother. "You shouldn't look so shocked, son."

"Pop." Law smiled and extended a hand to his older mirror image.

Mags found her hand tightening on Law's suit coat because the man she loved was going to age like a fine wine. A fit, smooth, and sexy cabernet.

"You only got part of your skill set from me. The other, you got from my Poppy." Law's father extended his hand to his wife with a lopsided grin. "Shall we give these two a minute to process the fact that they're not as sly as they'd like to imagine?"

"Only if you promise me four dances this evening," she countered.

"Four? Greedy woman," Pop shot back.

Poppy kissed their cheeks and sashayed away with Pop in a stunning display of love and middle-aged hotness.

"Law." Her lover's name came in stereo from two gorgeous blondes half way across the room. They'd never been out in public together and suddenly Mags found her back up over two women calling to her man with open adoration and familiarity. Law scooted from her hold and held his arms wide.

The abandonment stung, but Mags didn't reveal it. Law loved her and she loved him. Sure they had some social awkwardness to work through. What new couple didn't? She consoled herself as two leggy women wrapped their arms around Law in turn then stood back and folded their arms in disgust.

"I can't believe you didn't tell us," the shorter of the two, which still made her a head taller than Mags, said.

"Fuck," the second whispered. "We had to learn about it from Laird."

About the time Mags worked everything out in her mind, Law draped an arm over her shoulders. "Does no one in this family know how to keep their mouth shut?"

"You already know the answer to that," a slightly older and taller version of Law said from behind the two women.

"Magdalena, I'd like you to meet my sister, Lilliana." The pixie-faced shorter blonde gave a strummed finger wave then leaned forward and kissed her cheeks. "Where are Tony and the little guy?" he asked, referring to her husband and baby.

"Helping Luca park the car, and taking their time about it. None of them are too fond of weddings," she answered with a shrug. "Why do you think we're late?"

"Because when we're together we're always late," Law answered.

"True." His other sister stepped forward and extended her hand. "I'm Lovella."

"And you have a foul mouth," Mags said. Law's siblings' eyes widened for a second until she added, "I think we're going to be fast fucking friends."

With a boisterous laugh and crushing grip, Laird mimicked his sister and introduced himself. "I think we'll all get along just fine."

"I don't know," Khani said, stepping into the mix. "She curses more than Larkin."

Laird laughed. "More entertainment for the rest of us."

"Yeah, someone else for Poppy to chase around with the fly swatter," Lovella agreed.

"What's the fuss? I hate missing the good stuff." Magdalena turned to the shockingly, intimately familiar voice. Though she'd never heard it take that tone, she'd heard it every day for the past two weeks and planned to hear it every one for the rest of her life. But not from anyone other than Lawrence Pierce. The world ground to a halt in an instant as she held tight to the man she loved and stared into the face, behind Laird's shoulder, of the man she loved. "Bloody hell, Law. You didn't tell her? You might want to firm your grip. Your girl's listing to the side."

An orchestra of indignant voices piped all around her, but Magdalena zeroed in on Law. "You have a twin and didn't think to tell me?"

He smoothed a hand over her cheek and kissed her firm on the mouth. "We've been a little busy and I honestly forgot myself. I mean, I've grown accustomed to them over the years, even though these days I never see them."

"And whose fault is that?" Law number two shot back.

"Them?" Mags asked.

Law pursed his lips then blew out an exacerbated breath. "Triplets. I'm the smart and brave one. He's Luca, wildly talented with a microphone and a guitar. Larkin is the unpredictable one."

"And I'm the handsome son. Thank goodness my mom had me before the ugly ducklings came along," Laird added.

"And you're all so humble," Lovella huffed.

The band's upbeat tinny faded away. "Oops, that's our cue." Lilliana waved a *come the hell on* hand at Luca and turned in time to meet a handsome man with his arms open, and receive a smacking kiss on the mouth. "Well, hello to you. Where's Milo?"

The bloke planted a palm to his forehead. "Oh, I knew I was forgetting something." He turned back toward the door and Lilliana slapped his ass. "Ow, babe. Poppy has him, of course. Can't get in a ten mile radius without that woman thieving him."

Law tapped Khani on the shoulder and jerked his head in a *come closer* nod. "Speaking of where's who...where's Street?"

"Why the hell should I know?" Her whisper had teeth. Law didn't say a word, just waited. "Screw you. He's at the bar getting legless with Grizz."

"He likes to have a good time," Law said. "He's got some maturing to do."

"I don't even care enough to be talking about him." Khani's fire-engine red lips, which matched her stunning one-shoulder dress, thinned to a line.

"Oh, are we talking about a chap?" Lilliana leaned into their clutch.

"What chap?" Lovella crowded over Lilliana's shoulder.

"We're not talking about any bloody man, you nosey Pierces," Khani near shrieked.

"I'm a Landing now," Lilliana offered.

Khani growled. "I'm going to get a drink."

"But you don't drink," Law reminded.

"Fuck it all, I'm going to get some air." Khani poked her tongue at all of them.

Magdalena's cheeks cramped she smiled so big. The music changed and the two hurried over to the band and grabbed microphones. Her attention shifted to the small dance floor and through a part in the crowd saw Baine pull Sloan away from a cluster of old people and onto the dance floor.

Sloan's gown, while modest in the front, plunged at the back in a V of scalloped lace and stunned the eye against her smooth mocha skin. Baine's right hand cupped the bare skin just below her shoulder blade and reeled her close. He brought her left hand to his lips. From the distance, Mags saw the light catch tiny inset diamonds on the bands of platinum embracing the much larger rough cut diamond in an off kilter X.

The violinist pulled a few magical cords from the instrument with artistic sways of her lean body while the pianist's fingers ticked off a low melody. When the first word left Luca Pierce's mouth, the air stilled for all except the oblivious couple on the dance floor, breathless from their own building passion. Soulful notes danced through the static room whirling around the dumbstruck audience.

John Legend's *All of Me*. Magdalena recognized it from the first notes, but her throat constricted on any words she tried to form. Then Lilliana's silky-sweet resonance joined in the chorus. "'Cause all of me loves all of you. All your perfect imperfections. Give your all to me. I'll give my all to you. You're my end and my beginning.

Even when I lose I'm winning. 'Cause I give you all of me, and you give me all of you. Oh..."

As Baine led Sloan in an easy foxtrot and the lyrics and melody coalesced, Mags and all the other women in the room lost it. Hankies flew from pockets left and right and make-up ran in tiny rivulets with happy tears. Law's arm cinched around her shoulders and she leaned against his firm body, avoiding rubbing her cosmetics on his tan tux.

"It'll wash," he whispered.

He held her through the song and into the next, swaying them to the music. At the beginning of the traditional father-daughter dance, a dapper man in a striking grey suit tapped Baine to cut-in. Magdalena's brother kissed his bride and shook the man's hand. The hot silver fox bowed his head to Baine then swung Sloan into a waltz, eating up the floor as they went. The dance seemed incongruous for the icy expression on the bloke's face, but Sloan's shoulders were relaxed and she appeared unfazed by it.

"Who's that?" Mags wondered.

"Sloan's old boss, Commander Tucker," Law said.

Whew. She wouldn't use the word old to describe the man. Former boss and dashing rogue would be more accurate.

Baine maneuvered through a clump of people, heading for her and Law, when Easton Wells railroaded him in an embrace. Magdalena's heart squeezed in her chest. Given the sudden moisture in Baine's dark eyes, he was as surprised as she at her father's show of affection. Her dad was a man of many words and caring actions, but he reserved the touchy feely stuff, as was a butler's way she supposed. Sure he hugged her, but never anyone else.

"I don't think I've ever seen Easton hug anybody," Law mused.

"I know."

The two men straightened themselves and parted ways. Her dad returned to Ruth's side and Baine sidled up to them, watching Sloan. "Wasn't really prepared for that."

"You should've known," Mags said. "He gets sentimental at weddings and funerals. He'd be uncontainable at a baptism." Both men stared down at her as if she'd grown a baby bump in the span of a second. "I'm just saying. There are no baby bumps here. Or there." She pointed to Sloan. "I don't think. Then again she was nauseous this morning."

Baine shoved her shoulder. "Shut up. Would you?"

"Hey." Law secured her to his side and shoved Baine back.

Magdalena's sides ached she laughed so hard, but no sound came from her lips. Silent laughs. The best.

"Shit, boys." Lovella chimed. "Baine, if you keep hanging around these two, you're going to get thrown out of your own wedding."

"I'd go get my wife, officer, but she's tied up with another man right now." Baine shrugged and his laugh joined the quiet concert of snorts and giggles.

"God save me from these apes," Lovella complained while laughing along.

"Mind if I occupy a moment of your time?"

Behind her Law went on alert, his stance moving from casual to rigid in a blink. Baine folded his arms over his chest, straightening to his full

height, which was a good two to three inches over
the newcomer's sandy blond mop. Mags had no
idea who the bloke was, but it seemed he was
unwelcome to say the least.

"A bloke who tries to steal a man's girl has
some set of brass balls showing up at his wedding
to that very girl," Baine said, his voice low and firm.

To his credit the man stood his ground, not
blinking or shifting in the slightest. Though Mags
thought he might have been wise to shift right the
hell out the door. Beside her Lovella even shuffled.
Probably preparing for the coming blows.

While Magdalena's brain calibrated to the
situation, she took in the smokin' hot specimen
willing to go toe to toe with Baine McCord, and
quite possibly, Law. The guy filled out his dark tan
tweed but good and held himself like a warrior. Just
like Baine, Law, Lovella, and even Sloan. She'd seen
her go warrior-woman the other day when an
overzealous reporter had tried to maneuver his way
into her and Magdalena's cab for a scoop on the
Hues and Weaver story. The guy trying to get his
ass kicked was Ryan Noble. She'd heard a story or
two about how Baine and Law met Sloan, and his
name had come up a time or two. But a kiss? She
hadn't heard about that.

"Take a shot. I earned it. And it was worth a
broken jaw to know we weren't meant to be." Ryan
added, "I'd have always wondered otherwise."

Baine shot out his hand. Not in a fist, but in
an open offer of peace. "I'd have called you a
fucking fool for not going after her and taking your
chance."

The men exchanged a firm shake and the
collective sighed in relief. Ryan smiled and Mags
swore someone turned up the wattage on the bulbs.
"All right. Now that I'm not being carried out of here

on a stretcher, I'd say it's time to celebrate. Who wants a drink?"

Lilliana's husband spoke up for a club soda. Lovella said, "After that exchange, I need a shot of whiskey. Make it a double."

Mags declined the offer as did Law, but her man presented his hand to Ryan. The men exchanged a hardy shake and he presented her. "Noble, I'd like you to meet my fiancée, Magdalena Wells."

Ryan collected her hand in both of his for a moment before releasing it. "It's wonderful to meet you. Congratulations to you both."

Baine's grin widened and Mags placed both hands on her hips. "You knew too?"

"Of course." Baine leaned in and kissed her on the cheek. "Congrats, Mags. You couldn't have found a better man." His gaze shifted to Law. "And you are one lucky bastard."

"I know." Law agreed with a smile.

Baine tossed his arm over Ryan's shoulder. "Let's go get those drinks."

The dance floor opened to all and Lovella shoved at Lilliana's husband. "Come on, Rich. Dance with an old maid."

"Lord. An almost fight. Willow's on the road to recovery. Baine and Sloan married. My dad head over heels. Your wildly amazing family. You're a damned triplet! We're engaged. I'm spinning from it all."

"Not yet you aren't." Law extended his hand, ushered her onto the dance floor, and twirled her into his embrace.

Mags laid her head on Law's chest as they swayed to Luca's and Lilliana's voices. She angled her head at him. "Can you sing?"

"Not like that." His white teeth appeared behind his sensuous lips. He lowered his head to her ear. "There are other things I can do that he can't."

"Like love me forever?"

"And so much more."

STRANGER MINE
A BASE BRANCH NOVEL

One takes control. One finds balance in letting go.

Base Branch operative Ryan Noble is accustomed to taking orders whether from his commander or his overbearing mother. His best friend urged him to take control of his life, but the only thing worse than an angry woman is a teary one. He has no desire to upset his mother's fragile emotions. Losing his sister was hard enough; his mom couldn't bear losing another child. Even if it is to the other side of D.C. It's a damn good thing she doesn't know what he does for a living.

On a routine mission to destroy a cargo-free human-trafficking facility and exterminate its operators, Ryan blows his extraction to rescue a woman he finds chained inside.

Piper Vega is caught between metal and a hard place. She needs information and it has taken far too long to cull it from her leads—also known as her captors. She finally has the facts she needs to complete her task, but it'll take a miracle to set her free and see it achieved. Santo Padre knows she never expected her good favor to come in the form of a man.

Through intense battles of will, Ryan takes the reins of life in his sturdy grip while Piper discovers balance in loosening hers.

WARRIOR MINE
A BASE BRANCH NOVEL

A silver fox learns new tricks.

The Base Branch office in Washington D.C. is so heavily fortified it makes Fort Knox look like a 7-11. After twenty years in covert ops, nothing fazes Commander Vail Tucker. When a lighting bolt of feminine fury crashes into the interrogation room, holds him at gunpoint, and takes over the task with his prisoner, he's more than surprised. Even his elite operatives would have one hell of a bad day breaking into the fortress and a harder time leaving.

She escapes without a trace, but Vail is unable to remain dispassionate. He must know what is so important the beguiling woman would risk her life to find. Following instinct, he'll stop at nothing to find the answer.

Carmen Ruez is deadly and desperate—a combustible combination. Born into the remnants Arellano Felix Organization, drugs and violence kept her in a gilded cage. Until a turn of fates showed her the roots of their riches, making her yearn for freedom. She works for it. Fights for it. But her brother crosses the line to keep her loyal to the treacherous family she is determined to leave behind.

Vail struggles as a bond he never expected forms. It's not with the woman who stirs his every desire. But with one, young and vulnerable, who galvanizes a protective instinct he hadn't known he possessed. Now, he just has to get the other one to come around. Though none of it will matter, if they can't work together to take down those loyal to Carlos Ruez and the AFO.

Megan Mitcham was born and raised among the live oaks and shrimp boats of the Mississippi Gulf Coast, where her enormous family still calls home. She attended college at the University of Southern Mississippi where she received a bachelor's degree in curriculum, instruction, and special education. For several years Megan worked as a teacher in Mississippi. She married and moved to South Carolina and began working for an international non-profit organization as an instructor and co-director.

In 2009 Megan fell in love with books. Until then, books had been a source for research or the topic of tests. But one day she read *Mercy* by Julie Garwood. And oh, Mercy, she was hooked!

Megan lives in Southern Arkansas where she pens heart pounding romantic thriller novels and window-steaming erotic romance. For information on releases and giveaways subscribe at meganmitcham.com!

Facebook: @MeganMMMitcham
Twitter: MeganMitchamAuthor
Pinterest: MeganMitcham5
Goodreads: Megan_Mitcham
Website: www.meganmitcham.com

FOR INFORMATION ON NEW RELEASES & GIVEAWAYS, SIGN UP FOR MEGAN'S NEWSLETTER AT WWW.MEGANMITCHAM.COM.

www.ingramcontent.com/pod-product-compliance
Lightning Source LLC
Chambersburg PA
CBHW061542170626
46811CB00001B/61